I0702062

You know the expression, "the second book is harder?" They weren't exaggerating. This was far more difficult than I ever would have imagined.

To my ride or die: Elissa. I am both stunned and grateful you are still the first person in my dedications. I don't know how I would function without you in my life.

To Kriszta: this story was always meant for you. "I hope by the end of your time, you find a way to love yourself" the way I love you.

To CJ Smith: you read this in such a brutish form and still found a way to fall in love with the story. Raj deserves someone like you.

To Beth: for always being there to pick me up when I'd rather stay curled up on the floor.

To Rachel Schade: you will always be inspirational. For some reason you were still up for the task to come through each word for all those pesky scones on walls and lemons. And your willingness to read this second book, knowing perfectly well how it would end.

To EK: your appreciation for this story gives me the strength to continue forward. Any time I lose myself in my self-doubt, I know you'll be there by my side.

To Hailey: for believing in me long before I did.

To Matt: for always pushing me to perfection through all my 'dances,' 'towards,' and all my other turns of phrases.

Thank you, Rachel George (again), for a stunning cover illustration I can't get over.

Thank you, @chicklen.doodle, for making trading card character art, bringing even more and more characters into reality.

Thank you to my beta readers who jumped in to provide their incredible feedback.

Thank you to everyone who fell in love with *Lume* and wanted to find out what would happen next. If it wasn't for you, this story never would have been completed.

And, again, I owe the world to YOU, the reader, most of all, for picking up this book.

To <u>my</u> GAMERS: don't forget you can save, taunt, or abandon those little animals during your escape. Through everything, I love you.

Book Cover Illustrated by Rachel George Illustration
Title Page Illustrated by Rachel George Illustration
www.rachelgeorgeillustration.com

AISN (ebook) B0BP87L66Q • ISBN (paperback) 979-8-9867457-1-8

PETRAM

TM Ghent

*for my husband
and for the ones who stare challenge
in the eye and refuse to blink first –*

*"Most of life is grey,
with a little tiny bit of
black and white."*
- Bill Henson

Before

The Umberto daughter despised her father after her promised future had been stolen away and given to her brother instead. In light of her father's brash decision, she made it her life's goal to defy him at every point possible. After she'd been given the singular backup tempat to 'only be used in extremely urgent circumstances,' the opportunity presented itself to break that rule too.

The daughter remembered the first time she'd used it; they'd shown her the proper dial turns for a portal to open and let her access the old world of Lume. Of course, she would've eventually figured it out, but being taught sometimes lent its own advantages. At first, she'd merely done it to go against the parameters given to her, but she didn't expect how quickly she'd become fascinated by the old world.

The stories of what life was like before when their long-since dead ancestors escaped that cruel and hard world to find this one where they could create a place of peace. The Umberto daughter became fascinated by their chaos and lack of rigid structure, how they clung to life and love—so at odds to the world she'd been raised in.

She grew up watching them from afar, sometimes sitting in their market squares or in one of the restaurants, listening and learning. On Petram, knowledge and information were free, but on Lume, you had to heed the stories woven into gossip, dissect it for truths disguised as lies.

It had felt like a lifetime, but the Umberto daughter settled into this new way she spent her day.

It wasn't until she heard of the soon-to-be-princess running away the night of her wedding that she really took interest in the politics of Lume. Upon returning home that evening, she began attending the Council meetings, eager to learn what would cause someone to run away. She watched those Lumens for so long, grew attached to them, and knew they didn't abandon each other on wedding nights. They didn't run out on family—they stood together, solid and unwavering, against the passage of time.

The daughter swiftly returned to Lume, eager to seek the lost princess. Luckily the rumors told her the runaway bride traveled south, leaving two options: the windy, forest route to the seaport of Freta, or the treacherous mountain pass to Conlis. Freta seemed the likely choice.

It wasn't until almost a petrik later, the Umberto daughter sat inside one of Freta's most popular taverns, The Last Stop. It was dark and worn, opting for hanging candles and sconces along the wall instead of the lampposts she'd come to see in the other Lumen cities—and clearly more rustic than anything compared to home.

A steaming bowl of creamy lobster soup sat before the daughter, a dish that became a habit for when she traveled here—it warmed her bones, and the spices made her crave more. She'd dug the spoon in for another bite when a cloaked figure entered the tavern. Shadows were cast over most of her face, both from the dim lighting and the hood. But the figure carried herself with grace and confidence only someone raised as royalty could. It wasn't until the figure moved to walk past, when she caught the feminine features of her face, that she knew it was the princess.

And maybe it was because the princess had her future stripped away from her too, but the Umberto daughter was too intrigued to pass up the opportunity to befriend her.

Lume

Flashes of the past blinked through his mind's eyes, the chaos and destruction they'd dragged Lume into. And wasn't it by their own hand? Rajveer wasn't sure anymore…

He remembered being in the dining room. How Cora strode in a blaze of fury accusing him of being a traitor. With being a loyalist to Lume herself, could he still be a conspirator to the crown?

He tried to move his arms, to rub his face, but he couldn't feel his right arm and the one partially made of metal weighed him down, almost as much as the unseen emotions on his shoulders.

He focused on what happened next, fighting through the haziness, which was successfully blurring his vision. He knew Theodora had abandoned them, but did she succeed in killing his father? The thought felt like a punch of regret in his gut. He swam through the swaying in his head, afraid he might drown in his own subconscious.

With forced breaths, he sucked in air, trying to get his brain to focus on the last thing he could recall, the last image before everything succumbed to this utter darkness. And it finally broke free, the scene playing in his head, blurry on the edges at first and sharpening with each recalled detail.

Amicus had a shinegun and killed one of the Lawless. And then his shoulder flamed in pain, and then…. nothing.

∴ ∵ ∴

Pain. It was all pain.

Theodora felt the world crack open as her heart broke. Then a part of her was flying out of her body, a floating experience completely indescribable with words…

And then there was nothing.

She felt no pain. No grief. No sadness. No rage.

But also, no happiness. There was no ecstasy or hope.

Merely a thought, a small thought that expanded into fact. A complete and solid fact that she was dying.

Valix had stolen her life away.

∴ ∵ ∴

He'd been King Regent for all but a few minutes before Maddox was excusing himself from the collection of Satelle guards and nosy Lumens to let Valix supervise the control over the castle so Maddox could have a moment to regroup.

He slipped up the stairs to the late king's bedroom; one Lumens would expect to become his in the near future. Almost as quickly as the silence fell around him, the closed bedroom door shutting out the drone of murmurs, thoughts of Theodora floated into the forefront of his mind. His fingers twitched to grasp the pocket watch in his hand so he could feel he had some semblance of control again.

Forcing her from his thoughts, he demanded his focus to shift in order to prioritize his obligations once more. Theodora was never meant to be on his list, and she shouldn't be, however briefly now.

Secure the throne, report home, and ensure the prince was in fact dead. That's what they needed to do—what *he* needed to do. His time had come and regardless of any unlikely dreams he had for Theodora, he wouldn't crumble over mere memories of her.

Collision

King Rajveer Klauduisz had been stabbed in the back. Figuratively, but the severe pain in his shoulder told him literally as well. Using all the energy he could muster, he attempted to lift his head from the stone floor, in hopes to figure out where he was.

"Stay still," someone hissed at him as they pushed his face back into the dirt and dust covering the floor.

Miles.

"Fuck, it hurts," Rajveer responded.

"I'll bet it does, sir. You're bleeding everywhere, but I need to get you patched up so we can leave."

"Leave? Miles?" Each of Rajveer's breaths was a large feat, quick and encumbered. "I can barely hold on as it is. I'm not sure moving is a good idea."

Miles, as if to ignore him, dug his hands into Rajveer's shoulder. "Alright, sir, this is going to hurt."

Rajveer wasn't sure he knew what Miles was talking about; his shoulder was already in pain, then a sudden surge jolted into his shoulder blade, radiating deep into his body. He heard Miles gag next to him, and Rajveer's own stomach turned at the sound. Rajveer forced the bile down, the taste coating the back of his throat. "Can't I get wine or something?" He coughed down another gag at the sound of Miles retching.

"Hold on, sir. Help is almost here."

He barely held onto his consciousness, but the sound of shoes tapping on the floor distracted him enough to stay awake. He gathered enough energy to attempt once more to lift his head in the direction of the hurried gait.

The heeled shoes shuffled to a stop nearby, yet Rajveer couldn't place where they were in relation to himself, the waves of dizziness clouding his senses. Usually when he felt this way, he was piss-poor drunk and didn't *feel* anything else. A clatter of movement made his head hurt and then a woman's voice broke through Rajveer's mental haze. "We need to get her back up to the throne room soon."

Miles responded to the person. "Sure, sure. I'm finishing up the king now. Can you come over—"

"King?" Rajveer's words came out flimsy. "My father's here?"

"No, sir." Rajveer felt Miles place pressure on his other shoulder and imagined Miles was attempting to comfort him. "Theodora succeeded. Your father is dead."

His father was dead. It should be a joyous occasion. One to celebrate but instead rewarded with agony, and not entirely physical either. Rajveer felt softer hands against his naked back, pulling him from his darkened thoughts. Rajveer blinked against the soothing touch and forced his eyes open.

She knelt next to him, and he focused on her face. Her deep brown eyes highlighted by long lashes, accenting her sculpted brows. Rajveer couldn't see the pout she wore through the fog of his brain, but he could remember what it must've looked like, just as he remembered the gold ring tucked around her left nostril. He couldn't see her hair, noting a headscarf wrapped around her head, framing her face in a soft glow from the dimmed lighting.

Rajveer's eyes closed involuntarily, and he forced them slowly open once more. Recognition finally caught up in his brain; he *had* to be dreaming. A collision of truths and lies swirled before him, because Alouette shouldn't be here.

Betrayal

A sharp tug and Theodora felt as if she'd been ripped from a deep sleep and startled awake, but she wasn't entirely sure she'd been dreaming, or even asleep. She tried to recall back to what the feeling was, but almost instantly the searing pain in her gut removed every other thought in her brain. Theodora took a shuddering breath, a shot of roaring flame rupturing deep in her belly, and she tried to twist her body, to curl inward, but hands on her shoulders kept her pressed against the hard slabs of stone beneath her.

"You're okay," Miles whispered. Another pain shot up through her core and Theodora bit back a strangled noise in her throat. "Don't move. It's going to heal, don't worry, but you need to stay still a little bit longer."

Theodora opened her eyes, seeing Miles' face above hers, his hair falling forward over his eyes. He lifted his gaze away from hers and looked at someone else.

It was a rush of memories. Miles and Rajveer, her task to kill the king, Maddox's betrayal, and Valix.

Valix. He'd killed her and somehow, she was here; although writhing in pain, she still found air in her lungs once more.

Miles spoke to a shadowed figure nearby and Theodora almost chastised herself for not realizing another person was nearby, except the burning in her gut didn't allow her to get that far in her thoughts. "Can we get something to make her sleep a little longer until this has fully healed?" Miles asked.

The shadow moved closer, but Theodora's gaze couldn't focus on their face long enough to figure out who it was. "I can't give her much because we'll need her on her feet moving again, soon." The voice was lilting, reminding Theodora briefly of her mother.

"It's okay, little dove." The voice spoke to her, closer than it was initially, but Theodora's vision darkened as she felt a pinch in her arm. She tried to force her eyes open, to locate the source of the graceful tones, but sleep begged her, and Theodora happily obliged.

∴ ∵ ∴

A scuff of a boot along stone alerted her brain, waking Theodora. She jolted forward, grabbing at the searing rip she felt in her stomach. The wound was angry-looking and red, but the pain wasn't nearly as severe as before and it was healing. She didn't know how it was possible. In search of answers, she looked around to realize she was in an alcove. Stone walls rose on three sides of her and the musty smell around her threatened to make her sick, but she swallowed down the bile, glancing in the direction of the noise.

Alouette walked over, a mug in hand and fabric tugged under her arm. Theodora never was personally introduced to Rajveer's betrothed, but following the announcement to Lume, the prince and future princess were displayed across the continent quite regularly. "It's a brew of willow bark and gelsemium. It won't do wonders like the last drink, but should taste significantly better."

Theodora tentatively took the mug, sniffing it briefly. She didn't know if she could trust either Miles or Alouette; fates, she wasn't sure if Rajveer was even trustworthy at this point, yet she drank the brew anyway, the alternative seeming much worse.

"What happened?" Theodora's voice was hoarse. But she couldn't wait for the answer to that either. "Where am I? How long has it been?" She had so many more questions bubbling to escape, but Alouette squatted beside her, placing a hand on her shoulder, quieting her.

"You're alive. You're alive and safe, for now."

"What—" Theodora went to speak again, but Alouette shook her head, interrupting her once more. Tears threatened, burning along the edges of her eyes, the knot solidifying quickly in her throat.

"We don't have a lot of time." Alouette shifted, holding out the swarm of fabric, which Theodora saw were clothes. "It's not much, but they're clean. Rajveer isn't coping as well to the healing process as you did. He keeps slipping in and out of consciousness, but I think we'd agree we need you back in the castle and investigating what's happening."

"Who else is down here?" Theodora took another sip from the mug before placing it down on the ground next to her. "I'm not just going to do what you ask without you telling me what's going on."

"Alright," Alouette said, rising quickly as she swiped a hand across her brow, dropping her gaze to look back at Theodora with indifference. "You get dressed and I'll talk. If you want your chance at revenge, you need to move."

Alouette shifted slightly, showing Theodora more of her back, and when Theodora still didn't make to get dressed, Alouette turned her face over her shoulder, letting the silence stretch further between them.

Theodora let out a frustrated sound, a mixture of a sigh and a groan, as she started to move her body to change. She moved slowly, still not accepting the mostly healed skin along her stomach. She had scars that looked worse. When she shucked off her tunic, Alouette spoke.

"I don't know all the details that happened here because I was still in Freta when I got word of the possible assassination. Miles had sent me a note, telling me what Rajveer planned and asking me to come home. I'm not sure if he hoped I'd stop him, but if he did, I never would've gotten here fast enough. In any event, I've been in touch with someone." The last part of the sentence came out forced. Alouette looked like frightened prey, and Theodora stopped moving entirely, fearful she might scare her away from continuing. "We became friends shortly after I escaped from the capital fiedations ago. She must have some connection with Seclus because for as long as I've known her, she always has these odd gadgets and knickknacks and things." Theodora watched as Alouette fidgeted with her golden bracelets along her wrist. She didn't know Alouette well enough, but she could tell the woman wasn't expressing the entire truth—was hiding something. The question was whether it was important enough for Theodora to dig deeper for it.

Alouette continued. "Anyway, look at me rambling about the unimportant." She waved a hand dismissively and Theodora shifted to slip her trousers on. "So, she was able to help heal you. From what she told me, it seems you were near death and with whatever medicine and equipment she had, she got your heart started again and the important pieces stitched back together."

"Is that the other person I heard talking?" Theodora asked. Alouette turned around more fully this time, her brows scrunched forward in silent question. "I guess I came back into consciousness," Theodora continued, "and Miles was talking, telling me to be still. He asked someone whether they could give me something, and I must've fell back asleep."

"Yeah, that was her."

"What's her name?" Theodora finished buckling her belt and looked around for her boots or any shoes.

"Don't worry about things that don't matter now." Theodora's face must've had an incredulous look, because Alouette raised her hands in mock surrender. "I know you're smart and I know this is a lot of new information being thrown at you right now. Unfortunately, there isn't a lot of time. You'll just have to keep your wits and figure it out along the way."

"Enough time for what?" Theodora demanded again.

"Come on." Alouette waved a hand. "There are others who can give you a little bit more information before you head back out."

Theodora opened her mouth to question 'out where,' because she didn't even know where they were, and 'what about shoes,' but Alouette had already turned from her, briskly moving out of sight. Afraid to raise her voice and alert *whoever* was *wherever* they were, Theodora stepped out of the hiding place. It was only a handful of steps, but the movement made Theodora's stomach lurch and she quickly worked at the strings of her corset to tighten it as she noticed Miles further down the hall. Her face must've contorted into some sort of pain because Miles' voice was gentle when he spoke.

"They said it might take a couple days to feel normal again, but the wound should heal up fully by the end of the day. Here's your boots and your guns." Miles strode forward with them.

She had no other gear, all her pouches still at home, and her dagger had been left with the king. Or at least, that's the last time she'd seen it. She bent down to begin putting on her boots.

Miles ruffled his hair with his hands, exhaustion clear on his face. "What happened with you?"

"What do you mean '*with me*?' I left to fulfill my obligation of killing the king at your *prince's* request." She spat the words out. "I don't know what other plans you made, but when the Satelles rushed in claiming Rajveer as a traitor, I knew we'd been sold out."

"Who got you?"

Theodora glanced down at herself, as if the answer would be marred in her skin like the wound. "Valix."

"I thought they were working with us." Miles let out an irritated breath.

"Clearly not, Satelle. It seems not everyone is as they appear. So, forgive me if I don't entirely trust either of you at the moment." Theodora fixed her guns into their appropriate mechanisms inside her boots. "How long has it been?"

"Only a couple hours. I'd already sent correspondence for Alouette and by grace of the fates, she brought someone to help. They're the one who healed you." Theodora only looked up briefly for him to continue as she kept working the laces of her boots. "After you ran out of the dining room, the Satelles and Seclusians ambushed us. We didn't know who our allies were, and which were our enemies. I worked trying to keep the prince safe, but a Seclusian somehow got a stelgladio blade into his shoulder. I was able to catch the blade before it did too much damage, but we knew running away was our best bet. I worked with Cora to get the prince down here, and Amicus went searching for other Satelles who we could trust. When he returned, he was carrying you and saying we needed to try to heal you. I wasn't entirely sure why, but it wasn't my place to question it. Amicus was here checking on you again a few minutes ago, but he's back out in the castle trying to figure out our next move. He said Maddox and Valix are still in the castle. We think—"

It must have been a nervous tick for Miles, because he'd rambled about everything that *didn't* answer her question. Yet any thought of figuring out who the mysterious healer was vanished once Miles spoke Valix's name. She didn't want to know about any elaborate plans these Satelles might concoct without their prince—or king, or whatever other damn royal name they so decreed.

"We're still in the castle?" she seethed.

"Yeah." The word was dragged out. "We're currently in the tombs underneath it."

"Where are they?" To clarify, she asked, "Where is Maddox and Valix?"

"Up in the castle." Miles pointed, as if he didn't just state the direction out loud. She immediately turned to where she imagined the stairs to be, opposite the tomb.

"Theodora," Miles shout-whispered, and she stopped to face him, crossing her arms over her chest in irritation. She had to willingly tell herself not to tap her foot in the same annoyance. "I don't know what's about to happen, but we're going to try to make it to Amabel's house. When it's safe for you, meet us there. We'll regroup and figure this out. Hopefully, the king will be awake by then, too."

A sad chuckle escaped against Theodora's wishes. She was certain she wouldn't be returning. She'd find Valix, kill him, and run off to her cottage with Down River. The assassination of the king was the end of her tale in Lume. He didn't need to know any of that, so she offered him a brief nod before following the long hallway to the stairs once more. Keeping to the shadows, Theodora crept upward into the castle.

Worries

Rajveer forced his eyes open, which his body immediately regretted. He blinked, slight tears involuntarily forming from their lack of use. He felt groggy and wanted nothing more than sleep.

"He's awake, Miles." The voice he thought he'd imagined wasn't a dream—it floated to him on memories, her ethereal articulation as she spoke fat vowels and rounded consonants.

Rajveer shifted his body, his limbs feeling slow to respond and his muscles shaking beneath his weight. Strong hands steadied him about the shoulders until he finally found himself seated. The burn of his shoulder didn't lessen with the new position, but at least he felt less idiotic than he did having his face plastered to the floor. He blinked slowly, his eyes still adjusting as he finally recognized where they were, in one of the recesses of the catacombs. His father's would-be resting place. It was almost ironic given the situation, and highly foreboding.

As much as he wanted to focus on his father, the assassination, the betrayal of Theodora, or Lume being in absolute chaos, his mind couldn't abandon the thought that Alouette was with him. Endless questions surrounding her sprouted in his mind: their would-have-been future, those stripped possibilities. Of course, it was then Rajveer reminded himself that Alouette had left him, gone on the wings of night.

Rajveer forced himself to turn his head away from her, choosing to direct his attention to Miles instead. He could feel her gaze on him, his skin hot beneath her stare, a fire burning as he attempted to focus on other pressing matters.

With a sigh, he let his head fall onto the wall behind him when Miles started rambling and Rajveer registered none of the words. He held up a hand, stopping his chatter.

"Before we get into any of this, I need a drink." Rajveer glanced down at the bandage across his chest and over his shoulder. "And a shirt." Rajveer's voice was hoarse, and his throat burned from the dryness. Miles shuffled nearby before dropping next to him, handing over a skein and what appeared to be an old Satelle training tunic. Rajveer took the fabric and a tentative sip from the skein, with wishful thinking of what the liquid inside would be. His mouth twisted at the taste of water. "Do we have a plan?"

"Right now? No, except to get you healed and to get away from the castle."

"And what of Maddox? And Lume?"

"Maddox framed the assassination entirely on Theodora, which is partially true, I guess. But we don't have to worry about Lumens finding out you hired her. At least, not yet. But in the confusion, Maddox has taken control of the unoccupied throne."

"How'd you figure all this out? Wait, how many days has it been?" Rajveer thrusted his metallic palm onto his brow.

"Not even a day yet. It's about mid-morning now."

"It's been that short?" Rajveer's gaze snapped in Miles' direction.

"Yeah. When I saw you get injured, I worked with Cora and a few other Satelles to get you down here undetected. Amicus was still in the castle trying to secure control when he came down carrying Theodora. She'd been shot and we were trying to figure out what to do next when Alouette and Helena arrived."

Rajveer ignored the last statement; he'd have time to dissect Alouette being here later. Rajveer rubbed his metallic hand along his forehead. But he didn't know where to start—the crux of the issue. He felt helpless. His father never allowed him in any sort of position of power, rarely allowed him the opportunity to make decisions, and when he did, they were quickly dismissed or rejected.

After a few moments of silence, Miles spoke up again. "What do you need to know from us? How can we help?"

"How many Satelles do we have? Where are they? Regrouping and revaluating needs to be our first priority."

Miles shook his head. "I know little at the moment, but Amicus is putting out a report to Satelles willing and able to meet at Amabel's after Fiedel sets."

"Amabel's is a risk."

"Everywhere is. But we figured Hakon's was the worst of our choices and until we know who we can trust, Amabel's a safe bet." Miles paused and Rajveer noted how he looked around the tomb. It must've been the first moment Miles truly had to absorb the calamity of the situation, where they'd ended up.

"Do you know if it's secure?" Rajveer joined the unappreciation of their surroundings.

"For right now, I think so. Some Lawless came snooping around initially, but it seems once they realized it was only tombs, they haven't returned."

"Yet," Rajveer said before he took another disgusted sip of water.

"Yet," Miles parroted before he asked, "Do you think it's safe to stay down here until night?"

"We'll be fine. Is Theodora okay now?"

"As much as she can be. She was on the brink of death, but with a miracle from Alouette, we've been able to get her back on her feet. She's extremely eager that she returned back up to the castle to track down Maddox for us, which will keep him busy enough so we can get you out of here safely."

"Wait, what does Maddox have to do with this?" Rajveer's mind slow to catch up, and it felt as if everyone else knew what was going on besides him.

"After we saw you stabbed with the Lawless' dagger—" Miles began, "a little unconventional but clearly effective—Amicus ordered for a group of us to get you down here. We waited until he showed up again with Cora, but this time he was carrying Theodora in his arms. He said he saw her get shot by those four who were *working* with us."

"Can we trust her?"

"I don't think we have much choice at the moment."

Rajveer thought back to the final moments of their dinner before. *Could they trust Amicus?* "Did you know Amicus had a shinegun?"

"He did?"

"Yeah, I saw him use it to kill a Lawless before I was attacked." Miles' only response was to continue to stare. "Fuck," Rajveer let out in a grunt. He had no other words to convey his feelings. Miles was Satelle, yes, but he had limited experience, especially when it came to strategy. Even worse, with the few fiedations they had worked together, Rajveer knew Miles was more peacemaker than fighter. He could wield a stelgladio if necessary but chose to disable Lawless first and foremost instead of killing them.

Rajveer felt trapped. Alone. It was unclear who he could trust and how they would handle everything. Rajveer looked around the room again, a possibility alighting itself. He went to speak, swallowing down the lump that had formed in his dried throat. The few words he had spoken stripped him of what little hydration he had, the endless issues he faced wrapped around his neck, ringing him arid.

He put the possible solution on hold, glancing down at the skein of water that lay waiting on the floor. But water would never quench his thirst, not like the sweetness of Lumen wine, the way it ignited him from within and warmed his chest, destroying what emotions sought to surface.

Rajveer slowly rose to his feet, and Miles was immediately there to help him up. "What do you need, sir?"

Pushing him aside, Rajveer shuffled to the entrance of the tomb. He'd hidden away his own hoard in these future burial sites, knowing any reason he was down here would require it. He gripped a loosened stone, gray and dusty with time, and jerked it free before shoving his metal hand into the darkened space. No sense in getting bitten by some rat or snake that had begun calling this hole home, he told himself, as he pulled the unopened bottle free. In the muted light, the blue liquid almost seemed to glow.

"Rajveer, I don't think this is a good idea." Alouette finally broke her long silence to berate him.

"Sir, you still have high amounts of medicine in your body." Miles jumped in, probably attempting to lessen the blow. "Plus, we will be leaving shortly to meet up with everyone else. Let your body rest."

Rajveer didn't look away from Alouette though, her past abandonment clashing against the feelings within his heart. "Seeing as I'm down here with a woman who ran away the night before our wedding and an inexperienced Satelle, all after a friend betrayed me before killing my father, and a Lawless sits on the throne…" The words left his mouth rushed like poison. "I think a drink is exactly what I need!"

Not even bothering to remove the cork, he shifted the neck of the bottle into his metal hand, squeezing down on the glass to let it shatter. The bubbles immediately raced to the top in a stream of cyan, wildly escaping free.

Alouette's warm eyes enveloped him in memories as if to plead with him not to give into the temptation. He glanced down to her full lips and the thought of whether she still tasted the same entered his mind unwanted. He tugged his gaze away from her, reminding himself that *she* had left *him*. He lifted the bottle into the air, tilting his head back to drain it as quickly as possible, engulfing his regret and worries in Lumen wine.

Reason

Theodora followed the walls of the hall away from the throne room and deeper into the living spaces. A voice rumbled, stopping Theodora in her tracks. It took her a moment to fully register whose voice it belonged to. Valix was talking about hangings, the words slightly muffled by the castle walls. She took a couple quiet paces forward and stopped to lean around the corner in the direction of his voice. It remained empty until Maddox appeared from a room and headed in the opposite direction, Valix close on his heels.

Her heart immediately lodged in her throat.

Footsteps sounded behind her, and Theodora shifted quickly into the archway of a darkened room as she waited for whomever it was to pass. They were unhurried, yet purposeful. She assumed they had to be more Seclusians, or if what Miles told her was true, it could also be Satelles, or even Lumens.

She couldn't reconcile the hatred bubbling internally from the betrayal and lies. So many lies… She didn't want to think about what happened between her and Rajveer. She didn't have time to wallow in her uncertainties about Maddox either.

Theodora forced her emotions away as the footsteps faded from her hiding place. She followed silently behind and peeked into the hall again, ensuring it remained clear before following the direction Maddox and Valix had gone.

A set of doors appeared before her, sheer fabrics framing where they opened unceremoniously onto a covered terrace. Theodora pulled the curtain aside slightly, allowing for a small crack of an unhindered view where four shadows were revealed as Maddox and his own entourage.

She held her breath, careful to not have the curtains move any more than necessary, as she watched Maddox fiddle with his pocket watch, the fiedelight reflecting off it at certain angles, when abruptly, a large oval formed in the center of the terrace. It was like looking into a mirror except she couldn't see Maddox's reflection within it, or the twins on the other side. Instead, it showed somewhere completely different. Gone was the covered terrace of white pillars and plants succumbing to astrum. What filled the oval now was something far grander. She didn't know *where* or *when* stood within the sphere enveloped in yellowish gold. Whatever it was, it wasn't the castle. She watched as all four stepped through and into its beyond.

Theodora hesitantly watched for a moment, before following them, afraid of when the mirage in front of her would disappear entirely. As she passed under, an electric current rippled across her skin, like the shift in the air with a coming storm. She saw Valix and the twins break off into a run in the direction of what appeared to be buildings unlike anything she'd seen before.

She stopped suddenly when Maddox didn't follow suit but instead slowed his progress. As Theodora debated whether to turn back to the safety of the terrace, the current pulsed behind her before swooshing closed. She'd nowhere to hide. She didn't even know where she was, except in a field of green, a warm breeze snaking around her and filling her nose with a dry scent of the flora around her.

Maddox turned to face her, the hard lines of the buildings behind him wrapped in brilliant greenery, framing his body. He was slow, hesitant; for once, moving like prey instead of predator.

Theodora stomped her foot on the ground, the dumgun rising to meet her hand. She wouldn't allow for mistakes this time; she wasn't going to stand idly by again. A gust of wind attempted to push her back yet only succeeded in whipping strands of her hair across her face. Theodora ignored them all, keeping her attention focused solely on him.

"Give me one good reason I shouldn't shoot you right now!" she yelled over the distance between them.

It was an empty request, and she knew it because there was no good reason he could give her, no half lie he could conjure that would be good enough. But the last words she'd heard Valix say to Maddox before she passed out in the throne room, not even a day ago, gave her the reason to pause: *you hesitated, sir.*

Petram

Maddox looked down the barrel of the dumgun Theodora held angrily in his direction. He didn't feel fear. He didn't feel anything, except maybe relief, relief that she was still alive, somehow.

The urge to close the distance was significant. He remembered the softness of her skin against his fingertips, the feeling of her emotions as they radiated beneath her skin, a spectrum of them which found ways to elude him.

All of which he could not give her in return.

"I can give lots of reasons why you shouldn't shoot, charm, but no matter what I tell you, you wouldn't believe me anyway, would you?"

Theodora's eyes ignited with bitterness, but Maddox noticed the slight reservation, doubt sown because of their surroundings. He used it, distracting her from her current aggression. "Where do you think we are, Theodora?"

Maddox watched as Theodora's eyes skimmed the horizon, her pupils alighting at different items or clues as she picked up on them.

"I haven't any idea. I rarely got to visit some of the farther cities of the continent. I've traveled to Freta once or twice and I know this isn't it."

"We aren't anywhere on your continent."

"What is that supposed to mean?"

"Your Lume, your capital…"

"Why do you keep calling it mine?"

"Because that's what it is. Your world is there." He pointed, not in any sort of navigational direction of north or south, nor east or west, nor any of the directions in between. Maddox pointed up, beyond Theodora, to where a planet hung in the sky. Lume. It hung similarly to how Petram did in the Lumen skies, but Lume's world was mostly blue with a blemish of green for their continent, peeking through smudges of white. Maddox wished he could've seen Theodora's face when she looked behind herself, to witness the shock and realization of where the portal had taken her.

"As you can see, charm, you're stuck on Petram with no way to escape." Maddox felt the edges of his mouth curl in satisfaction. "That's probably the best damn good reason not to shoot me."

∴ ∵ ∴

With a bit of reluctance, Maddox watched Theodora drop the dumgun. She didn't replace it in her boot though, instead tucking it into the waistband of her trousers before he gestured for her to follow. They strode in the direction of the high community. The buildings were stacked near each other, tall spears of metal that shot from soft soil, their hard lines softened by waves of green, entanglements of vines and leaves. A clash of glass and technology with that of nature, but it wasn't a war. It was a beautiful compromise.

It was the beauty of his home, which Seclus never hoped to equal.

Home. It felt odd to return to Petram, because he spent much of his time immersed in Lume and their own traditions of life. But having Theodora here with him, all barriers dropped. He realized how much he missed the unending green and sense of community Lumens seemed genuinely to lack.

They entered the middle of the high community, an open courtyard surrounded by a staggering of balconies and room units tucked away behind flora, like a collage. The courtyard was adorned with small bubbling pools of water and gardens of blooming shrubs. Gone was the chilled air of Lume's astrum.

"Where are you taking me?" Theodora's voice was but a whisper over the birds that sang throughout the scattering of tree branches.

"To a room. Unfortunately, we don't have dungeons or prisons or anything of that sort here. Everyone does what is expected of them. You either fall in line for the survival of Petram, or you sacrifice your life." Theodora's brows creased in question. Maddox continued. "Yes, Lume is crawling with rebels, Lawless, unfaithful, or whatever new term you want to call them. We don't have those here. We work as a community for the betterment of Petram. It's not uncommon for those in old age to request sacrifice, especially when they are unable to continue offering adequate contributions."

It was refreshing to speak so openly to Theodora about Petram now, no longer required to twist his words around her, and for her to know some truths.

"You love it here, don't you?"

Maddox didn't respond right away, giving himself time to fully appreciate the question. "Why wouldn't I? Doesn't every person love the home they came from?"

"I guess so," Theodora responded with a despondent shrug. Maybe being an entire world away, Theodora could learn to see Petram as her home.

"Has the portal always allowed you to transport between different worlds? How does it work?"

"Now that will remain a story for a different time," he stated as he gestured her forward to the building entrance. As they approached, there was a whoosh from the doors as they slid open. Maddox forced himself not to look at Theodora, to see the wonder he imagined on her face at the newness of this world.

As the door shushed back closed, Maddox did a double take at the individual striding toward them. It'd been a few fiedations since he last saw her, his brief visits home typically only before the Council, not allowing time for family.

"Helena." He addressed his sister with barely a nod.

"You should've stayed on Lume." Her words were like death and the smirk targeted at him like a promise. "The Chancellor would like to see you."

Patience

Time seemed to slow and drag as they waited for Fiedel to set. After draining the entire bottle of Lumen wine, Rajveer gratefully laid on the hard stone and slept, allowing his body the chance to heal and for his brain to push away any drunkenness which remained. Since he'd woken up, again, anxiousness flooded his brain with every ounce of soberness he gained. He paced the length of the room, the clicking of his fingertips an echo to his footsteps, his mother's sarcophagus grand in his peripheral.

Rajveer stepped out of the room and into the hallway, huffing out an air of annoyance when he noticed Miles and Alouette sitting pressed up against the wall. He felt trapped; one room with the memories of his late mother, the hallway with the woman who abandoned him.

Did he still love her? He did.

Was he meant to move on? He'd never done that.

Did she? Had she?

And with this tension continuing to build between them, it left Miles in an awkward middle ground. The apprehension on Miles' face before was apparent as he spoke. "I checked a few moments ago; it's about mid-day. We still have time until we start heading for Amabel's. Sir? Is there something I can help with?"

"Not unless you can help me find answers." Rajveer said.

"Answers to what, sir?"

"Anything. Everything!" Rajveer let out a frustrated growl from the back of his throat, a sound that startled even himself. He pushed his hands up over his face, scrunching them into his hair.

"Don't do that." Miles said. "Don't act as if we're against you."

"Isn't she?" Rajveer was quick to point a finger at Alouette. "She left me, Miles. Without a word, without warning. Abandoned me here, with not so much as a backward glance over the last few fiedations. For all I knew, she was dead."

"She's here now, isn't she?" Miles was quick to respond. "When it mattered, when she was asked, she showed."

Rajveer only scoffed, incredulous. "When *asked*?"

"Yes, when asked." Miles paused. "After we talked through the different alternatives for taking the throne instead of killing the king, I reached out to her. She showed up immediately."

Alouette had the audacity to look nervous, but Rajveer wasn't certain who he should focus his attention on. He wouldn't allow himself to meet her gaze.

"Rajveer," Alouette began, "this isn't the time. There are more pressing matters right now. Maybe after we get to a more secure location—"

"This isn't the time? Fuck, Ettie. You left me! I've spent every day thinking of no one other than you. I hired these Lawless, hoping against all else, you'd hear of it and maybe we'd still have our future together." The wine was clearly having some effect; he hadn't meant for so much to be unveiled in this moment.

"I didn't want to." Alouette's words were barely above a whisper. He glanced in her direction and uncontrollably flinched at the tears he noted filling her eyes. Although he was furious at the situation, he still loved her, and never wanted to see her hurt. "I didn't want to leave you, Rajveer." Alouette paused to wet her lips before she continued, even though Rajveer wasn't entirely sure if he wanted her to. "Your father took back his promises. He said we would have our chance at love but wanted to throw us at the same Lawless who destroyed this capital. I couldn't imagine you being forced to live a life like that."

"So, you just left? With no explanation? Abandoned me?"

"I had no choice, Raj."

"Of course you did. You left me alone, to deal with him. What did you expect would happen?"

"You never would've taken the throne with your father still alive," Alouette said. "He would've given you up to the Lawless and who knows where you'd be."

"So, he just let me live out the fiedations underfoot? If he wanted to give me up to them so easily, why'd he goad me instead?"

"I don't know. I don't have all the answers your father should have. He told me if I didn't leave, he'd have me murdered within a petrik. I was trying to give you a chance to live."

"Then why'd you return to Lume? When Miles contacted you, he told you I was going to kill him—so why show up?"

"I came so you wouldn't have to deal with this on your own." Alouette's said, her voice softer. "Grief can consume you. Whether you loved or merely dealt with your father, I didn't want you to have to face this alone."

"There is no grief, Alouette. I have no regrets."

"For now…" Alouette wrung her fingers together as if there was more to say. "I've been in contact with someone since I left." Her hesitation deepened, glancing nervously in

Miles' direction. "She visited me shortly after I arrived in Freta. She told me Lume was about to meet destruction. She would return every few petriks, explaining what was happening here in my absence." She swallowed, and Rajveer's chest tightened with anticipation. "Shortly after I received the correspondence from Miles, she appeared to warn me as well."

Miles interjected at the sound of his name, a mumbled excuse to leave the room.

"No," Rajveer ordered and pointed at him, "You'll stay here and listen to every word of this as well. Who was it?" He directed the question to Alouette.

Alouette gulped, and Rajveer had to quash the anger that threatened to boil over. "She told me if I wanted to save the throne, if I wanted to save *you*, I needed to get here before the Lawless took over."

"Who was it?!" Rajveer felt he was slipping, as if he were standing on the shores, the sand sliding between his toes with each crash of the waves, grappling for solid ground.

He watched as Alouette took in a deep breath and as she released it with an exhale, she said, "Maddox's sister."

Family

Maddox found his sister mildly irritating. With a smug look, Helena said, "You must've done something pretty extreme for him to call on you so soon after your, what do you call it, *mission* on Lume. And from a committer, too?" She tsked. "Such a shame."

"You're making assumptions. And seeing as you barely spare a moment to actively come to a meeting, I'm sure it's all smoke with you. Always show, no actual worth."

She either didn't have a retort or didn't find a comeback worth the time because she floated away, her smirk slipping into the scowl he was used to seeing when he was around. Here to stir up just enough shit before disappearing.

"Who was that?" Theodora's eyes followed Helena as she left before she followed Maddox into the main hallway. "I liked her."

Maddox let out a chuckle. "Of course you do. She's my sister."

"A sister? I didn't realize you had one." Although she continued the conversation, Maddox noted how her gaze tracked every piece of furniture, light, and small alcove in the hall. "Is she younger?"

"No."

"What's it like having a sibling?"

"Are you still trying to rationalize my behavior, charm? I don't know if any response I can give you will make you feel better. Siblings don't mean much here. My parents had a daughter first, but my father felt one was inadequate for their future, so they tried again. When I was born, the family name continued, meaning they felt no need to bear more. We were raised with the expectations of helping our world remain successful. Helena is nothing more than another person. She just so happens to have the same parents as me."

"You say you have the same parents, as in your parents are still alive." Maddox wasn't sure if she meant it as a statement or a question. "I didn't know you had a family."

"There are lots of things you don't know or could never begin to know about me."

Theodora flinched but remained silent, he assumed she continued to absorb everything around her. He stopped them before the transport doors. "There's no sense in trying to figure out an escape."

"Don't make assumptions," Theodora wagged a finger at him like a child, mimicking the tone he'd used with Helena a few moments earlier. "I'm waiting for you to explain what's going on."

"Why? So you can conjure up a plan to get away? You can't."

"Don't think so little of me," Theodora was quick to spit out when the transport pinged its arrival.

Maddox boarded quickly, with Theodora reluctant of the enclosed room. "I don't, charm. I just hold all the cards right now."

"As you always do."

The doors sealed shut and Theodora raised an eyebrow in intrigue. The transport accelerated upward, and she immediately grabbed the handrail along the wall behind her.

"What is this?" Theodora asked, her voice sounded partially curious but also wary.

"A transport. It lifts this car vertically to other floors instead of connecting with stairs or bridges by using a counterweight to pull it upward. There's a lot more to learn and be perplexed by here. You've seen bits of it as it's trickled into Seclus, but not to this intensity."

The transport slowed to a stop, the doors pulling open to reveal a long, sleek hallway. He led the way off the transport, with hers slow and reserved with each thump of her boots.

"Don't worry, the vertigo will only last a moment." Maddox said as he directed her down the deserted hall, gesturing to a closed door before them. "This is where you can stay for now. I have to attend to the Chancellor, but I'll be back shortly. Just stay here, trust no one, and don't do anything stupid."

"I thought we were heading there together?"

"You meeting the Chancellor wouldn't go well."

Maddox placed his hand on the scanner, the door unlocking, before he opened it for her to enter. He watched as her arms wrapped over her chest, as if physically trying to hold herself together.

"I'm supposed to just obey and hole myself in this room as if I'm some kind of prisoner?"

"Theodora..." He let out a sigh. He didn't know what to say, how to fix any of this. Maddox wasn't entirely sure if her being here was even the best solution.

"Where's Valix?" Theodora interrupted his thoughts.

"What?" Her question caught him off guard.

"I only came here for one reason, Maddox, and I'm here for my vengeance. You can lock me up here for now, but you can tell the Chancellor and your committees or groupies or whatever you want to call them that I'm here to kill him and then I'm returning home."

"They're called the Council. And you can try."

"You don't think I can?"

"I think you'll have far better luck with my help." He didn't wait for her reply before he pulled the door closed, locking her inside. He fixed his cufflinks and cravat and prepared himself to face the Chancellor.

Tempat

Seeing Theodora in front of her shouldn't have surprised Helena, but it still caught her slightly off guard. Maybe it was because she'd grabbed Theodora from the clutches of death and somehow the woman seemed almost eager to return.

She watched as Maddox led Theodora into the high community building before turning away, walking slowly as her heeled shoes clicked against the paved roadway, internally counting down the time she needed to let pass.

When she'd helped Alouette return to the capital after they'd both learned of the possible assassination of the *now* late king—using the tempat in hopes they would've arrived early enough to squash it—Helena hadn't thought of the possibility of her allegiances becoming more solidified.

Petram was home, sure, but she didn't love it like she'd somehow fallen in love with Lumens—their lives and freedom addictive.

Helena brought Alouette to the castle with the new Lumen King pathetically weakened and *the* Theodora with a fading pulse. As soon as the required time for the tempat passed, Helena opened another portal without a second thought and located the necessary equipment and drugs to give them both a second chance.

It wasn't until Theodora finally gulped down life again that Helena's actions caught up to her. She'd initially been willing to try to bring Theodora back from death's claims because Alouette and the other Satelle, she couldn't remember his name, had asked her, but also because she'd seen the way her brother talked about Theodora in the previous Council meetings.

Helena didn't usually attend the meetings—not that they were required, but someone of her *stature* had more expectations placed upon her and she preferred demolishing those—but eagerness to participate was sparking among Petrans with the growing opportunity of taking control of the old world and relocating their lost resources.

Belonging to the Twelfth Committee herself, Helena was involved with medicines and remediux, and attending Council meetings was all but enticing. The Council would listen to the various committee reports drone on. Her Committer was always present, offering updates on their remediux going through testing, but Helena learned it was best if she remained quiet and appeared complacent, especially when it wasn't long into having received her new assignment that she began forging documents.

Her ability to falsify the current stock levels gave her the opportunity to bring Lume lost herbs and attempt to reteach them forgotten remedies. It didn't help that Lume's lack of advancement meant they relied on books and stories for their history, both of which could be erased and manipulated.

The first time Helena smuggled tech through to Lume wasn't something she pondered on long. She'd settled on visiting Conlis to witness their all-consuming chill she'd heard about. At least she'd had her wits about her, getting a thicker jacket from Seclus, but that wasn't enough to fully prepare her for how the bone-chilling gusts slipped between the rocks. The vast mountains broke forth from the ground in a harsh terror.

The trek through the small town felt treacherous, especially compared to any other Lumen city. The buildings were smaller, like they huddled together in each other's warmth. Glowing lights angled from the windows provided a bare minimum to see through the snow that swirled from each blow of the wind.

When she finally made it to what appeared to be the only tavern, she settled at a table near the hearth and promised herself she'd leave as soon as the tempat recharged, never to return. But as she sat there sipping her ale, she saw how these people struggled.

Lumens always grappled to survive, fighting not only the typical woes of life but also their repugnant king. Coughs chorused throughout the room, and when Helena inspected the Conlis people scattered in the room, she noticed how their layers of clothing barely held onto their frail bodies, how their tired eyes were framed with dirtied cheeks and feverish brows.

With one swift decision, she'd found her purpose: a way to continue to witness Lume's life and defy the Chancellor. But the division between Lume and Petram was blurring again; with Petrans becoming more involved, she needed to be careful or else the old world would be lost once more…

Now she felt an internal pull, her subconscious keeping track of the passed time. She glanced around briefly, making sure attention wasn't on her, and stepped off the main road onto a smaller one dividing the buildings. Pulling the tempat from her cleavage, she opened a portal, for she had a king to check on.

Ally

is—wait, what? His sister? Maddox has a sister?" Rajveer's fury was almost entirely snuffed out with the information. "How do you know it's his sister?"

"Rajveer." Alouette started, drawing his name out.

"Ettie." He replied. He could say her name, too. "Don't play coy with me."

"She told me she was his sister. I don't think that's something someone would share if it wasn't true. Plus, she—"

A creak sounded from the direction of the stairwell to the main castle above, and immediately they all froze. They couldn't assume it was someone to be trusted. Shuffling quietly, Rajveer pushed Alouette into the shadowy corner of the alcove, in this moment realizing he carried no weapon.

Miles slid in front of them both, slowly dragging his stelgladio from its sheath to avoid the metal zing.

He heard multiple footsteps, and Rajveer tried to calm his breathing to focus on what his ears could inform him of the situation. A slow whistle started; a tune he was certain he'd heard before. It morphed to the words of the song, the voice deep. "*Miles, miles away, I saw the lady along the shore, the one to guide me home.*"

"Amicus," Rajveer whispered out in a rush, and Miles peered around the corner, edged in shadows.

"Amicus," Miles confirmed, stepping out and returning the blade back to its place at his hip.

Rajveer followed behind and saw Cora approaching with Amicus. He hesitated, trying to decide whether to rush forward and hug the captain, as hurt and betrayal continued to clamor around the forefront of his mind. The choice wasn't apparently his though, because Amicus clapped a hand roughly onto his shoulder, causing Rajveer to grimace.

"Bad shoulder," Miles acknowledged.

Amicus was quick to apologize. "I'm glad to see you back on your feet, sir. Had us all a little bit worried." He glanced nervously behind him. "We can't stay long. Keeping to one place is a sure way for us to get caught, which is why we need you out of here and to Amabel's by tonight."

"Is Amabel," Alouette pressed, "still over by—"

"Nope," Amicus said. "She moved closer to the market. Her new place is actually—"

"I'm sorry," Rajveer interrupted. "No, I'm *not* sorry. We have a more urgent discussion going on right now than where Amabel currently sleeps. Ettie has dropped on Miles and me that the person she's been in contact with is Maddox's sister."

"I wasn't aware he had one." Amicus' voice was slow, as if marinating on the information himself.

"Exactly! What if she's like her brother? I don't know if she is someone we can continue to work with."

"Well, sir…" The hesitation in Miles' tone had Rajveer turning his glare slowly in his direction. "I met her earlier. When you were going in and out of consciousness."

"She knows where we are?!"

"She's the one who—" Mile started, but whatever words came next faded from Rajveer's ears. A sphere of light broke into the dimmed glow of the tombs, a frame of white surrounding a lush green backdrop. The image was jarring and completely at odds with where they currently were.

"What in the fates?" Cora whispered behind him, while Amicus immediately shifted his stance, angling his body more protectively in front of Rajveer.

Rajveer blinked again before pressing his fingers into his eyelids, as if that would correct the vision in front of him.

A woman strode from the frame, her long hair of raven feathers and her violet-black eyes looked vaguely familiar. Alouette's own eyes batted in recognition, and Miles twiddled with a loose thread in his tunic.

The unknown woman spoke, and her voice was light, but death serenaded each word. "Oh, he's finally awake."

Rajveer's brows furrowed at her audacity, but he couldn't find his voice or words. He was still in utter disbelief over the sphere behind her, until on a silent command, it disappeared completely. There were so many questions bubbling for attention, each one rising to be the first to break out of him.

"Identify yourself and kneel before the King of Lume," Amicus commanded. If he was surprised by what they had just witnessed, he quickly pushed it aside, his duties as captain first.

Alouette opened her mouth to speak, but the unknown woman's laugh stopped her. The dark haired one's voice was sharp and vicious, as if it were crafted of blades. "Helena." She paused, clearly for dramatic effect. It all felt eerily similar—her face, her stance, her confidence—and an unnerving feeling skated along Rajveer's spine when the realization finally clicked.

This was Maddox's sister.

She spoke again and it confirmed his suspicions. "I'm Maddox's sister and your greatest ally. And I bow to no man."

Escape

Theodora immediately shifted to the closed door, pressing her ear against it, listening for the resounding click of the lock to ensure Maddox did indeed imprison her here. It wasn't necessarily like him to lie, although after his most recent betrayal, the argument could be made, yet she still hoped for an easy route out.

She let her head fall back against the solid door, and almost immediately her brain flooded with thoughts. Not only had Maddox (and Valix for that matter) completely betrayed her for their own purposes during the late king's assassination, but they had fucking portals?! They weren't even Lumens?! What did that mean for Seclus and her so-called fellow Seclusians?

And not to even mention that she *knew* she'd been dead. No one could tell her otherwise; she knew whatever spirit or soul she had had left the world and had started to drift in the direction of the fates until she'd been pulled back to Lume. Who did she owe for her second chance at life?

Hot tears burned at the corners of her eyes, and they fell quickly past her cheeks, eager to be felt. When they slipped down her skin, for a moment, she allowed them, counting slowly down from ten. She reminded herself when she made it to zero, she'd sweep the feelings, the *emotions*, the unending questions away from her mind and focus instead on her current predicament—escaping this prisoned room.

Zero.

She swiped the tears and blinked away the lingering ideas before she quickly glanced around the room she'd been hidden away in, realizing it was much different than her Lumen home and double its size. From where she stood, natural light poured in through the floor-to-ceiling windows. The top of the glass darkened slightly where fiedelight touched it.

Did they even still call it that here? Or did Petrams or Petrans...? Fates, her head instantly hurt, and her mind felt like stew trying to understand what had just happened. She couldn't even say her world had been turned upside down because this wasn't even her *world* anymore.

A small table sat before the windows displaying the courtyard she'd walked through with Maddox. To her right, a bar-like counter with stools divided the room. She glanced around, curious at the lack of décor or trinkets. No pops of color, merely a swarm of grays and ivory accented with black and metal, aside from the bright green of the flora outside.

She shifted, an uncomfortable tug pulling at her middle where her wound was, but she brushed it off. Although she was uncertain about this confinement, she'd concoct a plan to escape. She really wanted, no, *needed*, answers, but she promised herself they would all come in time. Time was the creator but also the destroyer of all things. Even secrets and vows broke under the perpetual ticking of a clock— though maybe that rule didn't apply to Madox and his ridiculous portal pocket watch. Maddox told her not to trust anyone and to stay in the room, but she didn't even know if she could trust him.

∴ ⋎ ∴

Theodora was fairly certain she would've worn a path in the ivory rug had it been made of actual fabric and not stone.

She'd spent most of the time pacing in front of the glass walls before she investigated the kitchen in search of food.

It was small and odd. No cabinets lined the walls, only a sleek counter that was bare except for a metallic cube with a faucet-like dispenser and a handful of nearby mugs. After a few attempts at pushing the buttons in varying combinations, a thick sludge pumped out into the mug underneath. She assumed it was warm from the steam escaping out, but nothing looked appetizing about the grayed goo and it had no real scent to it. *Was it even edible?*

Being hungry and irritated didn't help her situation as she explored the remainder of the dwelling. She found nothing useful. It frustrated her how Maddox offered no answers. Instead, only questions continued to sprout from his secrecy like unwanted weeds. Theodora didn't know why Maddox was so arrogant. He might be a committer or some high-power person on Petram, but on Lume, she was just as competent.

Unfortunately for him, she wasn't going to stay imprisoned in some room merely because Maddox had wished it, the same person who had planned to shoot her.

You hesitated, sir.

It rang in her head, like the sound of the shinegun blast, taunting her with a fragment of possibility that Maddox was on her side. No, she wouldn't let that thought deter her. Although he might not have been the one to shoot her, he at some point had the intention of doing so.

She'd found her way back to the front door in hopes of picking the lock, but even locating the lock itself proved far more difficult. No square pad, like the one on the other side Maddox had palmed, showed before her.

She turned away from the door, scanning the glass wall once more. Moving closer, she pressed her forehead against it, peering down and around the edges of the glass.

The building was all glass except the metal lips around the edges of the windows and along the corners of the structure.

The height where she stood made her heart fall to the floor. Looking at the other buildings from her vantage point, she could count she was at least thirty floors up, green vines climbing from the ground to meet her. It was the highest she'd ever been before. The few buildings and walls she had scaled on Lume were at most six stories. This was astronomical in comparison.

And it was simply breathtaking. The pale blue sky held a small scattering of wispy clouds which offered a backdrop to the tops of the buildings where the greenery hadn't spread yet. The buildings speared through the ground upwards, like hands reaching to the pearl of Lume in the sky. Vines like those surrounding her own glass cage could be seen framing other windows, hiding the structure beneath waves of green.

Her hand went to her waist until she remembered her tools and gear were still at home, on Lume. She'd gone to assassinate the king with only her weapons. Her reflection smirked back at her at the realization.

Reaching into the waister of her trousers, she removed the shinegun and stood at an angle facing the glass. She fingered the safety, her aim locked, and held the trigger. The charge brightened and launched at the glass. Within a heartbeat, the charge ricocheted off and flew into the couch. Theodora stared at the blackened chasm in the fabric for a moment until she directed her attention to the glass. It remained entirely unmarked: there was no dent, scuff, scratch, or even the smallest difference in color.

She scoffed at the gun, which hung greedily in her hand. Having been designed in Seclus, it wasn't entirely outlandish that Petrans would've created windows that were immune to such ammunition.

But what if….

Tucking the shinegun away, she pulled out her dumgun from her boot instead, the filigree of the barrel catching against the brightness of the room. Maddox always jested at her use of old technology. Could it be their world wasn't designed with protection against such technology? It was worth a shot.

Standing at an angle again to avoid any possible ricochet, she aimed at the glass and fired. A small puncture and crackling of glass met her gaze. A high-pitched ringing began in the room. It had to be some type of alarm system reporting the breech. It was overwhelming, taking control of her every thought, but she didn't want to find out what the alarm would bring her.

She aimed again, attempting to drown out the blaring of the alarm, and gambled on another two shots, barely offset from the first: a terribly skewed triangle with a cascade of fissures. Without risking any more bullets she hoped the damage she'd already done would be enough. A couple steps brought her to the stool tucked into the counter she'd seen earlier—light enough for her to lift, and hopefully, strong enough to use.

In a mighty heave, with every amount of force she could muster from a dehydrated, tired, and hungry body, she threw the chair at the cracked glass. It tumbled back, but not without first deepening the breaks.

She knew she'd run out of time quickly and she hadn't even thought of how she'd get down from this height. Picking up the chair again, she threw it. This time it crashed its way through the glass. She shifted to the edge of the room, teetering between the stable floor and the drop before her.

Flowers crept along the corner of the building, racing along the windows in all directions. A gust of wind pushed past, and a swirl of lavender petals danced in front of the buildings, floating down gently to the ground below.

The front door burst open behind her, and she glanced back to spot soliders. In a blink, she'd counted at least four who entered the room, covered in all black, head to toe, with masks shielding every inch of their faces, but before what she'd witnessed fully registered, Theodora jumped.

Relief

Rajveer was immediately intimidated. He hadn't felt that type of emotion or power since—*well, shit.* "You've got to be kidding me," he whispered, the words barely a scratch from his throat. The smirk that spread across Helena's bloodred lips was confirmation enough. His eyes shifted to Alouette, quickly glancing at where Miles hovered nearby.

"Raj…" Alouette's tone was hesitant, like a child trying to catch a bird. Soft and smooth, as if her words alone might scare him away. "I'm sorry. I tried to tell you."

"Oh, come now, Ettie," Maddox's sister spoke, "It's unbecoming to plead before a man, especially one like him."

"One like me? Don't begin to act like you know who I am." Rajveer placed a hand over his chest. He found those words quickly, engulfed in fury as they left Rajveer's mouth.

"Ah, maybe you should watch your tone and mind your manners because I know exactly who you are, Prince Rajveer Iyer Klauduisz, son of Richard and Lorelei."

Rajveer stopped. So few knew those details. She'd clearly known Alouette long enough to garner some details of his life, but Iyer? That was a secret of limited knowledge. "How do you know that name?"

"What the fuck do you have on your feet?"

Rajveer baffled by the subject change couldn't help but drop his gaze to his shoes. "What do you mean?"

Helena stared at him for a moment as if preparing to speak. "Never mind. I know a lot more than you can imagine, young prince. Your father is not the man you thought he was."

"You mean king," Amicus spoke at the same time Rajveer said, "An ass? No, I figured that part out."

As if venom laid on her lips, her smile was predatory, all gleaming teeth. "Would you like to know the story?"

Rajveer wasn't sure he did, but if he was going to attempt to save Lume from this plot for power, it seemed he had to. Even if it meant soothing whatever hard feelings were currently bubbling toward Alouette and Miles. He'd be damned if he didn't try.

"Yes." It sounded weak even to his own ears.

"Just remember, Lumen Prince, we haven't even gotten to the worst part. To save your capital, you'll have to destroy yourself." Rajveer slid down the tomb wall to the floor, dropping his head into his hands to listen, as Helena continued. "Maddox was required to provide reports of his accomplishments here. One such document I was able to intercept before they delivered it to our Chancellor, our king of sorts where I'm from. It identified the expected day of your wedding, and Maddox reported he was able to gain an audience with King Klauduisz with a simple offer of a shinegun. The king was given one as a token of their agreement. In exchange for the king releasing the throne to the Lawless, he requested a list of people to have murdered. From that moment, a long and detailed plan was established, one which has been in progress for fiedations."

"That doesn't make any sense. It was before my mother died. And I'm the one who decided to have my father murdered, not Maddox."

"All part of his plan." Helena waved a hand for dramatic effect. "The king knew of your mother's illness. They hadn't shared the news with anyone else and he had persuaded her not to tell you. Knowing they would bear no more children, the king needed to find someone else to secure the throne. Maddox was his opening. Lumens would never follow the coup of some Seclusian Lawless. They needed Seclus to appear as their salvation. The only thing left in their way was Alouette, an observant woman who started to notice things going astray. But removing her was easy once the king threatened her, her family—even you."

Rajveer let out a strangled breath, unsure if he was holding back rage or sorrow.

"But I'll let her explain all that fully later." Helena gestured a hand toward Alouette. "They patiently waited for your mother to pass. After her death, the king focused on causing you a miserable life; making ultimatums and broken promises to have you turn against him. Once the king had learned you were going to court Theodora, he recognized the plan was in motion. You know the rest."

Rajveer was quiet for a long time. He didn't know how long he let the silence fill in around him. His Satelles shifted uncomfortably nearby. He assumed they had questions of their own but mustn't be voicing them to allow him the time to think, yet he only came up empty-minded, at a loss for words.

"I am sure you're rummaging through a list of questions," Helena broke the silence. "Unfortunately, I'm only here to get the information I need for tonight."

"Information for tonight?" Amicus asked. "What're you talking about?"

"Helena isn't the enemy here," Alouette said. She must have sensed their irritation. "She's been a friend to me through the last few fiedations. She was here earlier to help Rajveer and Theodora."

"Wait, no. Let's go back to the beginning of this." Rajveer's words finally caught up with what he'd just learned. "What do you mean where you're from? Where are *you* from?"

"Why, Petram, of course," Helena offered, like she'd given them the answer to the universe.

"Petram? As in that thing in the sky?" Rajveer pointed over his shoulder as if there were windows in the tombs. "How is that even possible?"

The way the words were rushed, it could've been a rhetorical question, yet Helena apparently didn't see it as such. As she spoke, Rajveer felt his mind flash to his own youth. While Rajveer spent time eating peppermint sticks, following his father like a loyal and obedient dog, Maddox, Helena shared, had found a way to use aximum—a resource common in shallow water beds and used for their tempats, or portals to new worlds, like the golden ring they'd seen her walk through earlier.

"The resources are depleting on Petram. Maddox was dubbed as committer, a leader of a small group with a specific purpose of finding more of this limited resource, hone the current tech, and start exploration."

"So, how do you have a tempat? Why are you here?"

"My tempat is a backup—a safeguard as Maddox calls it—to his. After his glory of obtaining his own committee, and especially at a young age, I was quickly forgotten by my family. I became bored with their ways, the mundane of every day. I came to Lume on a whim to explore and witness this world for myself. I immediately fell in love. Petrans live life like fates, expecting to be worshiped for their tech and so-called intelligence. While Lumens are utterly human with old tech and a king unmotivated for change. I started helping some, talking to others, offering food and remediux, and sometimes information if it helped undermine my brother."

"And now?"

"You wanted to free Lume from its slavery to your father. I want to help free Lume from its Petran cage."

"What do you get out of all of this?" Amicus asked, stroking at the stubble growing along his jaw.

"Do not misplace my kindness. Though I've divulged enough for today, attempt to betray me, and you'll remember my name in your nightmares."

∴ ∵ ∴

Helena left shortly after, confirming with Alouette she would arrive at Amabel's that evening. How Helena knew who Amabel was or where her house was located still didn't sit right with Rajveer, but Alouette and Miles both shared that without Helena, neither him nor Theodora would be alive.

The Petrans' medicine and tech had salvaged Theodora's shinegun wound and fixed his shoulder. Given that his arm was built from Seclus, it shouldn't be surprising. But with Helena and Maddox, Miles and Alouette—not even including Amicus yet—this new information was like adding salt to an already festering wound.

With Helena's departure, Amicus and Cora were quick to follow, planning to ensure everything with Amabel was secure enough for Rajveer to leave the castle. He knew it pained Amicus to abandon him here, but there were things that had to be addressed and Amicus certainly didn't trust anyone else to do it. When it was the three of them again, Miles didn't stay long before he slipped further down the hall.

Rajveer stood silently in front of the stone patchwork of his mother. To learn his father had stripped him of his mother and his wife made Rajveer angrier. His father made these grand and elusive plans, but to what end? Could it be true it was all to ensure Rajveer never took the throne, or was that him merely being selfish and failing to see the bigger picture? What did his father fear from his only son; so much so to choose a Lawless, Petran scum instead.

"I'm sorry, Raj." Alouette's hand touched his shoulder and he immediately stiffened, his heart a quick thump within his chest, so loud he was certain she could hear it in the stillness. He turned towards her and didn't know where to begin. He hadn't abandoned the love they had had, but would they be able to move forward as if her leaving had never happened?

"No," Rajveer whispered. "Don't you dare apologize to me."

"You're being ridiculous; my apology is necessary. For all the pain I've caused you; you don't deserve this."

Wasn't she speaking the truth? If he spoke with any of his Satelles, wouldn't they say the same thing?

"I don't care what everyone else thinks." Rajveer let his right hand touch her cheek, his fingertips trailing lightly along her skin. The sensation was like lightning through his hand, up his arm, and straight into his heart. "I don't care if everyone expects me to be mad at you. I don't care if anyone thinks I don't deserve this. I've spent too long without you, and I'll be damned if I'm going to let proprietary and expectations come between us."

He hesitated; should he be this brash this quickly? "Kiss me, Ettie." Before she could question it, he repeated himself. Softer; barely a whisper over his thunderous heart. "Kiss me."

He could see her reservation in her eyes as they searched his own. He'd spent fiedations unsure of their future or if she were even still alive, while she must've dealt with grief.

She tugged him forward, but not in the kiss he'd demanded, instead folding her arms around his neck as he pressed his face into where the cloth of her headscarf fell about her neck. He buried deeper until he found her uncovered neck and immediately peppered her bare skin with his kisses. His name rushed out of her in a whisper.

Elation threatened to escape from Rajveer, in either a sob or a growl—he wasn't sure—and he pulled in deep breaths, inhaling in her vanilla scent he'd never forgotten. She pulled away from him, placing hands on either side of his face. He felt raw and vulnerable and exposed before her.

"Sir?" Miles reentered their terrible hideaway with the assuming grace of a cat. Rajveer let out an audible groan of annoyance as he placed his head on Alouette's shoulder, feeling her light chuckle beneath him.

"Oh, I'm sorry, sir. I didn't mean to interrupt."

"You know, Miles, I don't entirely believe you," Rajveer spoke as he pulled out of Alouette's grasp, but she shifted closer, weaving her fingers into his. Her skin smooth against the callouses of his non-metallic hand. He glanced down at her, flashing a brief smile. He could face the world if she was by his side. "What did you learn, Miles?"

"It appears that Maddox is er—not on Lume? We assume one of the Seclusians, if that's what we're still calling them, in the throne room is acting under his orders. But it's almost time for us to find our way to the capital. I expect this isn't going to be an easy escape."

"I think it's clear Seclus was always a ruse. We can call them scum for all I care."

"Well, the scum in control of the castle have been talking and it seems Maddox is trying to find you. They appear to be focusing most of their efforts near the Digere. I guess they assume you'd find your way there."

"Why is he looking for me?"

"Besides the obvious? Because no one knows whether you are dead or alive. Right now, you're a loose end."

"Great," Rajveer said with a sigh. "Well, like you said, let's get moving before they decide to search down here again. We get to Amabel's and then we can regroup to think about how to get them off my fucking back."

"Yeah, so you can get me on mine." Alouette's voice interrupted his train of thought, forced him to double take and he only stared at her until his brain restarted.

"This is why I've missed you, Ettie."

Miles cleared his throat as the two gazed at each other before he turned. "We're going to have to be quiet." Miles began as he started walking in the direction of the stairs. "And it's going to be slow, so just keep..." His voice trailed off, turning to see Rajveer hadn't attempted to follow him.

Rajveer jerked a thumb behind him. "We're headed this way."

"What's that way?"

"Access tunnels."

"To what?"

"Lots of places, but right now, the most important one is to Amabel's house."

"How...when did you learn of this?"

"I've known it, Miles. Rule number one of being a prince: always have a second way out."

"You aren't a prince anymore," Alouette reminded him. His attention dragged to her again, every word from her bolstering his ego. Fates, he wished she'd kissed him.

"I thought rule number one had to do with keeping a steady hand, so you didn't spill your drink," Miles quipped. Rajveer rolled his eyes at him.

Rajveer barely had a moment to process everything he'd learned from Helena; a blink to absorb all the information he'd been provided, and he was about to take his first steps into a fatherless world, but Rajveer decided with Alouette and Miles by his side, they'd figure this out and get Lume back. Rajveer didn't know if he felt happy or sad, but relief settled into his chest knowing he wasn't alone.

Gone

Theodora felt her stomach rise up to meet her throat as she fell. The adrenaline attempted to betray her hands as she sought one of the vines wrapped around the frame of the building. The vine pulled away from her and she fell further as she grasped for a thicker one. She grabbed another and it held, pulling at her shoulder before stopping her fall.

She took a deep breath, calming her nervous energy, and she adjusted her grip. She glanced around and noticed she hung in front of one of the windows, a stunned family of Petrans sitting around a table, cards skewed it, their game paused as they gaped at her. Theodora gave a small wave before securing her footing in more tangled vines.

As she descended, careful to settle each hand and foot before shifting her weight, she glanced upward. Vines she'd ripped away during her fall swung loosely in the slight breeze. Theodora lifted the collar of her shirt to wipe the dots of sweat that formed along her hairline. It was significantly warmer here, especially in the long-sleeved tunic Alouette had given her earlier. The pressing fiedelight didn't help either.

The process was slow, yet her descent gave her pounding heart time to settle into a more comfortable rhythm. It stayed there too, until she accidentally glanced downward and realized how much more she needed to go. After a few moments of forcing herself not to look, her brain wandered back to what she'd seen before she jumped: those masks.

To confirm their existence, she gazed up at the height of the building to where the window yawned open, and she saw the four masks where they peered down at her. They were speaking to each other yet made no movement or accusations toward her. The men, if that's what they were, wore black metallic masks of piping and gears. The masks that had haunted her for countless petriks, unable to be found again.

If the masks originated from Petram, was Rajveer, or fates, even Maddox, behind her parents' murders? Question upon question surfaced in an endless cycle, leaving Theodora without any more information, only more damn questions.

The slight distraction caused Theodora to lose her footing. She was still a good four stories from the ground, and her hands screamed from the scrapes and cuts decorating her palms. Gravity was a bitch and Theodora was losing against her. Her hands slid down, leaves from the stems ripping off and floating to their deaths. Theodora gripped harder, her palms burning as her boots clamored against the beams, trying to find footing once more.

Against her lungs' will, she forced them to breathe the air, compelling her arms to stop shaking. She reminded herself she'd climbed countless times before; she just needed to focus on the task at hand. First, get down the side of the building, preferably without significant injury.

Theodora made it close enough to the ground that she slipped off the vine, dropping the last few feet. She gazed back up the building, admiring herself for the height she'd overcome, before brushing the stray leaves and grime off her tunic and trousers and pulling a stem from where it had tucked itself into her boot.

Proud of herself, she turned to locate a place to hide until she could plan out her next move. She knew she needed to find Valix. She stopped short on her heels at the person nearby. Maddox leaned against the building; arms crossed over his chest. Although his cravat was still present, the smirk he typically wore on his lips was gone.

Interruption

Maddox had been in the meeting room, listening to the Fifth Committer speak on possible changes they were initiating along one of the local cities, Mexnar.

"As you see in the COE report, we remain on course to produce the appropriate number of wind mines. We are aware of the NTP date and do not anticipate needing to request any delays at this time." The screen behind the woman changed, shifting to projections and cost analyses. "We would recommend however to request authority to proceed with expanding—" Her voice was interrupted by an alarm blaring into the room.

The screens flashed a window providing information on the disruption's source. Those around Maddox who read the notation turned in his direction. Of course, it would be his building and his floor. If there was ever a moment for Theodora to follow instructions, it was today.

"Can you handle this, Second Committer?" the Chancellor asked with a hardened look in his direction, irritation narrowing his eyes.

"Yes, sir," was Maddox's only reply before he rose from the table, buttoning his jacket as he exited. As soon as he was out of the room, his hand immediately shoved into his pocket in search of his pocket watch. He continued walking down the hall as the portal rippled open before him. Maddox did not slow down his pace until he was through the portal and at the corner of the building. Dragging his gaze upward, he saw Theodora clinging to the vines.

The portal snapped closed behind him and he settled himself against the wall of the building, the metal beams digging into his shoulder as he watched Theodora fight with the vines and leaves on her ungraceful descent. She dropped to the ground, swiping at her clothes before turning around.

She noticed him and, to his surprise, was unable to hide her emotions from her face. "I mean, for fuck's sake, Maddox. Seriously?"

"You couldn't just wait, could you?"

"You ignored the question."

"Was that actually a question? I have the ability to portal. You are in my home world and with unmatched tech. Did you think so little of where I was raised?"

"If it was so unmatched then I wouldn't have been able to escape." She swiped more leaves off her shoulder. "Besides, I'm not going to sit caged like some prisoner."

"I told you we don't have those here." He released his irritation in a breath and gestured for her to follow. "You wanted to meet the Chancellor? Now you're going to."

He noted her obedience in his peripheral vision as he turned and headed in the direction of the main building.

The walkway was surrounded by more tall buildings of glass and metal, greenery scaling the metal beams and framing the glass windows. Petrans walked with purpose around them, some occasionally tipping a hat in his direction. Most were engrossed with their screens strapped along their forearms, continuing their required work while on the move.

"The high community is wrapped in a circle," Maddox began explaining, "made into smaller units divided by the walkways. Each unit has a number of buildings ranging from five to seven given their size and function. The units are grouped in a circle all leading to the main paths. Those larger paths funnel inward to the center, which you will be able to see shortly in our view, containing the main city buildings. It would be a similar layout to Lume, except we are by far more efficient." He paused, letting the information settle. "Ask, Theodora," he prompted, knowing the many questions which were rattling her brain.

"First, why are we walking? Didn't you portal here?"

"I did. Unfortunately, we have not yet mastered multiple portals successfully. The unit needs a few minutes to recharge before we will be able to portal again. Not a lot, but enough time that we cannot simply portal back to the Council building."

"Can't you carry multiple portals to allow you to do back-to-back portaling?"

"My sister and I remain the only ones with units."

"Two? Out of how many people must be here, only two were commissioned? Seems rather odd."

"Maybe to everyone else, but not to those in charge of the capability," Maddox said. "I don't know if I could explain it all without telling the full story, which we don't have enough time for right now."

"How does Seclus play into all of this?"

"It's a city on Lume under my complete control, an extension of Petram."

"Was any of our relationship real?"

Maddox had to tell himself not to stop moving his feet forward. Of all the questions, this was one of the first she was concerned about?

"What do you mean? Everything is real, Theodora," Maddox said, and she frowned at him, those green eyes reflecting the tumbling of greens behind her. "The short version: I was sent to Seclus. I eventually was instructed to gain control of the throne in hopes of securing Lume itself. I've never lied to you. I may have kept information concealed, manipulated others around me, but I've never lied to you. I told you I've always put myself first before anyone else."

"So, the assassination?"

"It was an agreement between me and the king for many fiedations. He wanted his son removed from the lineage and Petram needed the throne. Our wants coincided."

"And what of Rajveer?"

Maddox shrugged, unsure of his correct definition. "A martyr?"

"So, he *is* dead?"

"We don't know yet. My committee is actively searching to confirm his death, to ensure only the necessary information is revealed to the Lumens."

She fell silent beside him, and he knew the Council building would peer down on them momentarily. Above the buildings, poles poked upward into the blue sky, used to help provide access to the screens across their capital and to the other cities as well, allowing them to communicate across vast distances. As they continued around a curve in the walkway, a small garden expanse revealed gray-blue ponds.

"What of me?" Theodora's voice was barely a whisper over the crowds of people they now ventured through, the closeness to the city filling every crevice of space and noise. Chimes and beeps from screens as well as announcements over intercoms almost drowned out her voice.

"That's precisely what we were prepared to discuss today until you boldly interrupted."

Fatherless

At a fork in the tunnels, Rajveer instructed Miles to take the left branch. Alouette's thumb brushed along the back of his hand as they remained interlocked. They hadn't spoken, and they continued their silence as they began walking again. An unspoken acknowledgment amongst the three that the questions would begin soon enough once they arrived at Amabel's.

The tunnels were filled with cobwebs, dust branching out from their corners, while small soft globes jutted from the misshapen dirt walls, their only source of light. The scent of death suspended around them with the lack of airflow, knowledge of these hidden passages dying with each generation of Satelles.

In his father's later years, the king's idea of security was to never have someone close enough that would require such fanciful notions of darkened tunnels for quick escape. If no one was ever invited to the castle, an escape was no longer necessary. When his mother was alive, his father had a wider presence within the capital and the Lumen cities, but it had always been from a distance, viewed from a horse or carriage or dais, the tunnels remaining hidden and unused.

As a young boy, when the Satelles were training and he wasn't yet granted permission to be involved, Rajveer was left unattended to wander the castle. After a point of searching the same rooms endlessly, he finally garnered enough courage to investigate these tombs. Initially he spent his time looking through the various books shoved down here, left to be lost. Yellowed pages of blurred text and faded images of weapons and tools of an ancient time, and some newer ones with the initial drawings of the stelgladio plans.

When his younger self shifted to exploring the tunnels, he'd learned the left route took them to the underground web connecting the castle to various shops within the capital, some providing more advantages than others. Rajveer never learned where the right tunnel went. Every time he'd ventured it, it seemed to be unending; and he either never had the time to fully explore or feared exhaustion, where he wouldn't have the energy to return.

Following Rajveer's instructions, they stopped at a panel of wood at a dead end. He knocked, the sound echoing. A moment later, when Rajveer was prepared to knock again, a metallic clank sounded, and the wood pulled away from them and into the room beyond.

Miles slipped past him to exit first before Rajveer pulled himself forward out of the tunnel, which dumped them unceremoniously from a hole in a cellar wall. Amabel was there offering a hand for him as she held the door open, a curtain of fabric pushed out of the way. As Alouette exited behind him, Amabel immediately shut and locked the door, the fabric falling back over the door, revealing it was a tapestry. Its woven, colored threads depicted a tired Satelle on horseback swaying back and forth as the cloth settled itself into position.

He anticipated some discussion upon his arrival at Amabel's abode, but she turned away and proceeded up the stairwell, rambling about others and bread. They followed her into the main house, entering a dining room where a long table impeded their path to the remainder of the house, standing guard over a large damask rug. They continued in the direction of warm scents of dough and cinnamon. Rajveer's stomach rumbled its acknowledgement of food. Alouette turned her head in his direction, her hand remaining intertwined in his as she playfully glanced to his stomach.

"Don't tell me you aren't hungry, Ettie."

"Ravenous."

Rajveer forced his gaze away and his feet to follow.

The snug hallway directed them to an even more cramped kitchen. Satelles filled the limited space around the cabinetry, and a butcher block took up the remainder of the room. Golden auras reflected onto the white cabinets where the light caught on the threads of their jackets.

Maybe it was his newfound relief, or being freed from the castle, but Rajveer couldn't stop himself from dropping Alouette's hand to embrace Amicus this time. He saw Cora and Danika standing off to the side and he offered them a small smile as he withdrew from Amicus.

"Are you okay, sir?" Danika was the first to speak. "How did you escape from the fight?"

"You mean before or after Amicus used a registered Lawless weapon?"

"You aren't going to drop that anytime soon, are you?" Miles offered softly. His willingness to question Rajveer, but reluctance to start conflict, was clear in his tone.

"Not until I'm told the entire story."

Amabel interrupted from her place near the oven. "As much as I am happy to see this reunion, there are way too many bodies in this kitchen and if you all want to eat, I'm going to need you to move." She playfully shooed them from the room and back to the dining room, where the remaining six of them took seats to continue their discussion.

"How many do we have?" Rajveer asked, accepting a glass of water from Danika as she poured out more for the others.

"At least twenty, not including us," Amicus replied. "It's not a lot, but I think the Lumens would be willing to help, especially once they learn you aren't dead. Most feel lost and uncertain. Maddox has fed lies to the masses, informing them the assassination was entirely Theodora's plan and that he and fellow Seclusians tried to save the royal family. Between that and their strong forces and tech, Lumens don't really have much desire to fight back."

"Fighting back seems a little audacious given they have an entire underground city of both foot soldiers and tech, tech we might not even be entirely aware of at the moment."

"Helena can help," Alouette murmured to Rajveer.

"Who's Helena?" Danika questioned, looking back and forth between the group.

"Let's not forget the bigger issue," Amicus directed to Alouette, "is you returning to the capital. Or that Rajveer is already back to snuggling up against you."

"Helena is Maddox's sister," Rajveer replied to Danika, quieting the other Satelles as he rubbed the center of his brow with his metal fingers.

Danika's shock showed on her face, but the others exploded into comments and retorts. He knew what their arguments would be. Yes, Helena might've helped save his life, but that didn't mean she was there to assist them further. The annoyance from Danika and Cora against the endorsements of Miles and Alouette were quickly subdued.

"Who wants some cinnamon bread?" Amabel chirped as she entered the dining room, holding a wooden plate piled with baked rolls. She nervously looked around at them. "I guess I timed that terribly."

"No, no, not at all." Miles was quick to rise and accept the plate from her. "Let me take care of this and you go ahead and sit." He gestured to one of the remaining seats as he walked to where Rajveer sat at the head to serve him. When he finished serving everyone else and found himself back in his seat, he lifted his mug and toasted, "Long live the king."

The mismatched mugs of his comrades clunked together, and everyone eagerly took a sip of the Lumen wine, but Rajveer merely held his. *King.* The one Seclus needed in order to win; the one who determined whether this game was over. Everyone returned their mugs to the table, waiting for him to speak so they could begin their meal and discussion. He drained his own mug before pulling a piece of the warm dough from the plate and taking a bite, the cinnamon and butter melting in his mouth. He licked his fingers, every pair of eyes still looking at him expectantly.

"Well now that *that's* all settled," Amabel voiced cheerfully, "let's dive into the bread while it's still warm and we can start this discussion from the top. Yes? No decisions should ever be made on an empty stomach."

"Alright, we'll start with Alouette and Helena," Rajveer directed, "but then we need to ensure Maddox actually believes I'm dead so we can stop sneaking away from him and start rallying Lumen support and organizing weaponry. I'll keep talking, but you all need to start eating."

As each person reluctantly pulled apart pieces from their own bread, he began.

Troubleshoot

Although Theodora expected to find some elaborate meeting room, she was surprised to see Petram, run by committees, was as vast as the Lumen throne room, but far sleeker and tech-heavy in comparison. The tiled floor was a smooth gray, almost forgotten beside the walls of slate blue. Display screens staggered the length of one of the walls. The room held circular tables, in a similar setting to the gambling ones she had seen in Ludi Votivi, yet these weren't made of wood, but rather some type of molded or cast material.

Theodora walked down the center of the room next to Maddox in the direction of two crescent-shaped tables. The sound of her boots on the floor seemed loud even among the low murmuring that began on their approach. She noticed the center tables angled to face both the assembly of Petrans present as well as the nineteen other committee members, one chair remaining empty. Valix stood between the assembly tables and those she presumed were the Council.

As they continued their slow march, Theodora noted everyone in the room wore various shades of black, accents of color dotted throughout. The fabric difference was subtle compared to Lume, but apparent as the material stretched over the shapes of their muscles. The most notable difference was the lack of dresses and full skirts, yet what grabbed Theodora's attention first were the accessories: one person wore glasses that merely appeared to be a wide band of metal across their eyes; another sported thick cuffs of colored metal around their biceps.

Maddox stopped shortly before reaching Valix, who turned to face them. Theodora didn't slow her gait, only shifted around Maddox and punched Valix square in the nose. Slight gasps filled the room, but she gave none of them the chance to realize what she was going to do. Fates, she barely thought it through before merely following impulse.

Her hand throbbed and she shook it out next to her as she turned back to stand next to Maddox, facing the Petrans where they remained seated. She saw some with a slight twinkle in their eyes, and she noted which ones they were as well as which ones looked at her with only disdain.

"I think she broke it," Valix murmured, his hands wrapped around his nose, his long digits covered in blood.

A member closest to the center of the assumed Council rose, his height close to matching Maddox's own. He wore a suit like Maddox, except a tie fell from his neck into his buttoned vest rather than a cravat. Theodora noticed the gloves he wore on his hands, the tops of the knuckles gleaming with gold buttons.

The unnamed man said nothing, merely stared at her, and then the pain ignited. The slap across her face took a moment for her to recognize. The leather of his glove left a lasting tingle on the outside of her face. She slid her tongue to the inside of her cheek, checking her mouth and her teeth. The metallic tang confirmed the blood in her mouth. Theodora spit the wad out, letting it splatter on the tiled floor beneath her, before raising her eyes to meet his.

The man gestured to someone behind her and spoke. "Have Tommee come in and look at Valix for a moment. We also need a cloth for Theodora to clean up this mess."

Someone from the assembly, presumably Tommee, walked past her to look at Valix, examining his face as another individual came forth jutting out a hand with a cloth.

Theodora yanked the cloth out of the unknown's grasp, staring at the fabric, the white threads stark against her skin. Although not entirely filthy, she spotted dirt under her fingernails, grime along the inside of her wrist. She let the cloth fall to the floor, just barely covering the blood she'd spit before she ground the toe of her boot into it. She glared at the one who'd slapped her and spit again, narrowly missing his shoes.

Theodora expected the reaction, though it didn't ease the pain. This time it wasn't a slap but rather a closed fist to her cheek. Her face jerked toward the ground, but Maddox barely flinched next to her. Taking a deep breath, she willed the tears that burned unbidden in the corners of her eyes to dissipate.

"I think he'll be okay, sir. No broken nose," Tommee reported.

"I guess I didn't hit him hard enough, then. He certainly whined enough." Theodora didn't let her voice shudder as she faced the unknown man again. When she met his intense stare, Theodora realized his eyes seemed vaguely familiar. She glanced to her left, where Helena sat in the assembly, then quickly shifted her gaze to look at Maddox, when the sneaking suspicion formed. "And who might you be?" Theodora directed her question at the unknown man.

"Chancellor Umberto." Arrogance wrapped his name. "And you must be the infamous Theodora, who has such difficulty staying out of trouble."

"I'm not entirely sure if that's true. I did what was requested of me by your men and was betrayed. It's not my problem your people are terrible shots and here I stand still alive."

"I'll show you what type of shot I can be." Valix turned in her direction, taking a step before being stopped with a simple gesture by the Chancellor.

"Try reading the troubleshooting section in the manual next time," Theodora returned, slipping one of Maddox's smirks across her face.

Before Valix could reply, Maddox stepped forward, placing a hand on his shoulder to interrupt him, whispering something in Valix's ear. Valix let out a low growl in response but turned on his heel and exited the room.

Theodora opened her mouth to throw another insult when she was cut off by the Chancellor. "Now we were about to discuss what to do with you, but since you were so determined to interrupt with your escape, you can now listen in. Please, have a seat." He gestured behind her to an empty chair in the assembly.

"When your second has gathered himself enough to return, we'll expect him to finish his report," the Chancellor demanded, giving Maddox a weary look before turning back to his position in the center of the room. Maddox trailed behind, sitting to his immediate right.

Theodora slid into the empty chair she was instructed toward, but not until she'd looked at the members of the Council and stared them down. They might believe they'd decide her punishment, but she wouldn't let them think she was afraid of any of them.

Umberto

The Chancellor called the room to order and Maddox forced himself to keep his attention away from Theodora, although he felt her gaze upon him like a branding iron.

He shifted his suit jacket around him, bringing his foot to rest on his knee, and angled himself toward the middle of the room. It was a slightly awkward view with the Council seated on either side of him.

"Tommee, have Valix brought back into the room, please," the Chancellor ordere. It was barely a moment and then Valix returned to his position before the Council, hands tucked behind his back. The Chancellor waved a hand and spoke. "You can complete your report, second of the Second Committee."

"We've been able to secure the throne, castle, and the surrounding capital of Lume. This was achieved with very little leverage on our part, and with the rumors of both a deceased king and prince, the few who had initially resisted have begun submitting. We are planning a funeral for the royalty in the coming days. Nothing too fancy, just enough to help soothe any remaining ill feelings, and then work to introduce the necessary tech to begin making changes to the infrastructure and gather resources in the same manner we have here." Valix paused to clear his throat. "We had initially assumed the assassinator, Theodora, had been killed in action. However, as you are all very much aware now, she was not. Unfortunately, we have secured our favor with the Lumens by claiming Theodora was the sole Lawless responsible for the royals' murders. With her survival, she can now destroy our entire foundation and work for the last several fiedations."

"We clearly need to have her removed immediately," Alivia interjected, her short blonde bob swaying as she spoke.

"She is removed," Paal started, jutting his hand forward, the bracelets on his arms tinkling as if to accent his statement.

"I personally believe," Valix began, "we should have her sacrificed. The entire rebellion of Lume hinges now on her life. It's an easy decision because we know she will refuse compliance."

"Who do you—" Theodora started.

"If I may—" Maddox could barely hear his own voice over Theodora's aggressive insertion. He glanced in her direction.

"I don't need you to speak for me, Maddox," Theodora said as she rose from her chair. "It's clear Valix cannot remain unbiased in this decision. He is being emotional about the fact that even with a shinegun blast he was unsuccessful in killing me. Am I not Lawless? Did I not help Seclus over the past few fiedations? Did I not work with them over the course of the past few days to willingly assassinate the Lumen King on Maddox's order?"

Maddox searched her face. She was surprisingly level-headed and adapted quickly to the discourse that was beginning to form. Any of her true feelings on the matter, he assumed, were buried deep under the surface, and she showed only a mask, as if on display.

"Second Committer, I would like to know your recommendations on the matter at hand, as you are in charge of Lume in this regard," the Chancellor directed.

"Seeing as Theodora is now on Petram with no ability to return to Lume without the assistance of either myself or

Helena, I think it is agreed she no longer poses a threat. I believe, given her history with Seclus, we should grant her the opportunity to decide whether she can remain an asset for Petram."

"And this has nothing to do with your other feelings for her, sir?" Valix said the words in a lowered voice, but with the shape of the room and attention of others present, Valix's allegation carried heavily.

Maddox didn't have the opportunity to respond before the Chancellor spoke again.

"I'm of the opinion we follow Maddox's recommendation for the time being. If it appears to be of further issue, we can reevaluate." The Chancellor's voice carried no sliver of emotion, remaining stoic and borderline digital like those showcased within the city. He waited a moment, allowing the others sitting around the table to consider, before requesting acknowledgement. It was a unanimous decision by the others, a small wave of three fingers for acceptance, and the relief flooding through Maddox was an odd sensation.

As the meeting transitioned to other areas requiring the Council's attention, Maddox shifted back toward the center so he could keep a better view on Theodora. He hadn't noticed how much he was staring at her until she glared back. It broke him from his trance and kept him focused on the other tasks facing Petram.

∴ ∵ ∴

Maddox portaled himself and Theodora to the doorway of the room he'd brought her earlier to. He watched as her shoulders slumped forward and she stared begrudgingly at the door. Maddox opened it, allowing her to walk in first. The windowpane had been replaced and the glass pieces cleaned up, as if her little tantrum hadn't even occurred.

"I'm sorry, charm." The whispered apology rushed out of him almost as quickly as the door closed behind him.

"Are you? Are you truly? You didn't appear apologetic before this council of yours."

"Unfortunately, it's your council now, too."

She audibly scoffed, crossing her arms protectively in front of her as she paced. "You know that has always been the issue—with everyone. Why do I need to be told what's mine? I'm told who my king and prince are, told which people I must avoid, told to act a certain way so I can abandon my Lawless title, and now told Petram's Council is the new authority I must follow. What if I don't want to? Is it so terrible to want to be alone, to live out the last of my fiedations in quiet solitude with enough shelter and food to last to the bitter end?"

"We can't let you go back to Lume. Everyone thinks you're dead. If you return, you jeopardize our entire mission."

"I don't care! It's not my mission. It never has been."

"I think you do care. You can yell and get pissed at me all you want. Glaring at me is fine, too, but I don't think you want to be alone."

"Again with the assumptions about what I actually want!"

"I don't think you even know what you want, Theodora. No one actively wants to be alone." Maddox debated whether to continue arguing with her, but he knew it would be pointless. She would have to come to these conclusions on her own. "If you'd prefer, you can join me in my rooms. We don't have to share a bed; the couch is spacious enough for me to lay on, since sleep eludes me most of the night anyway."

When she said nothing, letting the late afternoon view hold her attention, Maddox turned and left. He stopped, though, when he didn't hear the click of the door shutting. He turned slightly to see Theodora's silhouette outlined in the doorway. After a few breaths, she exited and hurried until she caught up to him. Without a word, he merely turned and continued in the direction of his quarters.

She didn't take long to break the silence. "What's your family name?"

Maddox hesitated, feeling as though Theodora already knew the answer. "Umberto." It was like a weight, both heavy on him and yet also lifted from him.

She let out a sigh. "We really don't know that much about each other."

"Aside from living on Petram with committees and a Chancellor, which you know now, I am the same as I was in Seclus." They slowed at his door, and he was unsure of what would happen next between them when she entered.

"I'm surprised you didn't strike Valix after his comment about your feelings towards me."

Maddox didn't reply; there was nothing to say. And he felt if he did, the conversation would circle into an area he didn't want to discuss with her.

"Do you have feelings for me?" Her voice was soft, reserved.

Nope. Leave it to Theodora to broach topics he *really* didn't want to consider. "Charm," he said slowly, trying to keep his voice full of indifference and warning.

Theodora shook her head. "Never mind." She bit at her bottom lip. When was the last time Maddox had she'd her this nervous? "I just meant Valix really wanted you to appear weak."

"Reacting with violence is a sure way to show weakness. Being impulsive means being careless."

"But it would have helped show Valix he is only a man, not some fate he believes he is to Lumens."

"Does he bleed?"

"Who?"

"Valix."

"Well, I guess so," Theodora responded slowly.

"Then he is a man, and he can be killed."

"What are you saying? Speaking in cryptic riddles is a skill I believe only you have mastered."

"Being cryptic is the very nature of a riddle. And I've mastered plenty."

"Alright, keep your secrets."

Maddox let a smirk form on his lips as he unlocked his door and held it ajar for her. "How about a new assassination plan?"

"I'm listening."

Trapped

"Explain to me *again*, the logic behind removing another part of my body?" Rajveer rubbed his right hand along where the metal of his left hand met his wrist, moving it up his forearm, feeling where the contraption became a physical part of him.

"We need to make Maddox believe you're really dead," Helena said. "Otherwise, he is going to continue to keep his people searching for us. *And* we need their attention directed elsewhere if we're going to take control." Although Rajveer assumed Helena was trying to keep the irritation out of her voice, her face wasn't as masked.

Miles interjected. "But why can't we remove the one he already has? Just like, creak it off?" He made a jerking motion, attempting to mime twisting his wrist off.

Helena sighed again, as if everyone in the room was incapable of keeping up this seemingly technical discussion. "The metal that extends from the hand, connecting it to his arm, is fused to his bone. There are also intricate conduits connecting to various nerves within. If we merely detach it, which will take a significant amount of time, it will also be obvious Rajveer's death has been staged."

"But how does cutting my arm off make it look less staged? Maddox won't think this is possible?"

"No. Well, at least not initially. He doesn't know you're working with Seclus, or Petram for that matter, and I'm assuming he won't consider you'd come up with an idea like this on your own. Which is true. You wouldn't have."

Amicus, Danika, and Cora had long since left before this discussion began, needing to set up hidden watch points and to pick up more gossip around the capital that might provide any possible advantage. All of this would be for naught if they were ambushed by another Petran plot. But with the new direction Helena brought the conversation, Miles shook his head and left the room as well.

Alouette merely stared at Rajveer, her face unreadable, but he wasn't sure if it was because of their time away from each other or if she was forcing a wall between them.

"Can we have a moment?" Rajveer asked Helena. She mocked a bow in his direction and followed Miles out of the room.

Rajveer took a long breath, turning away from Alouette and to one of the front windows of Amabel's home, which looked out onto one of the capital alleys. The cobblestones wet from the morning rain. Fiedel peeking over the roofs of the buildings across the street. He watched as leaves twirled with each other from a gust of wind.

"I'm assuming you think I should do it," Rajveer said into the void of the room as he traced his arm and continued staring out the window.

Alouette was silent and then he felt her arms wrapped around him. He savored the warmth her body pushed into him. He felt her cheek against his back as she said into his shirt, "Rajveer, you can only do what you want to do."

"But you can still give me your opinion."

"I can, and yet you already know it."

"I don't know if I can do this again."

"You survived the first time. You can survive this again. And besides," Alouette continued as she shifted around his body, forcing him to wrap his arms around her, "Helena knows just as much of this Seclus tech as Maddox. There is nothing to worry about."

But that was precisely what he *was* worried about. Rajveer leaned forward, tucking his face into the space between her neck and her shoulder, her bare skin warm against his face. He pulled her tightly, and when she attempted to pull away, Rajveer spoke. "Don't leave me, again, Ettie." The words rushed out in a breath.

"I won't, Raj." She shrugged her shoulder upward, forcing him to lift his face to look down into her warm eyes. "Until the fates remove me from this world, I'll be here."

"Forgive me, but you've left before."

"We are but only human."

Rajveer let out a sigh, his brain unable to process through the thousands of emotions and doubts and worries racing through it. "I can't keep doing this. I need to know this isn't another plot or some fake part of some grand plan. I've missed you every single day you've been gone."

"It's none of that, Rajveer. I didn't want to leave. I thought by doing so, I'd be able to *help* Lume."

"It didn't. And even if it did, I'd rather see her destroyed than live another day without you by my side."

"And I want to spend those days with you." She offered him a small smile. He wanted to say more. To tell her he still loved her and confirm she did too. But they'd had fiedations without each other and since she'd returned, he still hadn't been allowed to kiss her.

He glanced down to her lips briefly before meeting her gaze once more. He was hesitant, the storm in his gut making him embarrassed she might feel his hands start to shake, but he leaned forward slowly before touching his lips to hers.

Her lips were soft, and her mouth tasted sweet Like peppermint sticks and a cold dip in the lake during solta; like the giddy laughter of the Lumen children and the raging bonfires during heim. It was a rush of every euphoric moment of his life flashing between the movements of their mouths. Rajveer pushed harder against her, urging, wanting…

Alouette slowed the movement, forcing the kiss to stop. Rajveer obliged, but for a moment kept his eyes closed, as if by not opening them, time would be forced to stand still for a moment longer.

He exhaled and opened his eyes. "This better be worth it, Ettie."

"Every moment with me is worth it," she replied brightly.

Rajveer called Helena and Miles back into the room, and the latter entered with a face ashen from grief and disgust.

"What do I need to do?" Rajveer's voice was soft, hesitant. Any confidence had long since seeped out of him. Alouette slid her hand into his, giving his fingers a squeeze.

"You are the drinking prince, are you not?"

"The reputation precedes me."

"Whatever you do, *don't* drink. I know you have difficulties following orders, but you cannot drink. It will only thin the blood, making a greater risk of death. I am going to try to get some sedatives from Petram, but it will be difficult. Everything is documented when it is removed. I'll return at this time tomorrow."

The portal rippled into the room and was gone within a blink as Helena stepped through. The three of them begrudgingly returned to the kitchen. Rajveer didn't take a moment to announce his disagreement. "Don't drink? Does she not know who I am?"

∴ ∵ ∴

The next morning, Amicus and Cora left again at the cusp of dawn, as the smell of bitter coffee roused Rajveer from where he slept on the floor of one of the spare bedrooms. The blanket provided little comfort, and although it was worn through, the draft of astrum seeping in through the cracks along the window frame, he was hesitant to move—afraid of how his bones might creak and his muscles stiffen.

When he finally pulled himself upward, he slowed his departure, glancing at where Alouette remained sleeping in the bed. He'd wanted to join her but felt it might be too soon. Desperate not to scare her off again, or ruin whatever this might be blossoming into once more. A slight shiver caused her body to jolt, and Rajveer grabbed the blanket from the floor and draped it over her. Her hair fell into her face, and Rajveer couldn't fight the temptation to slip it behind her ear.

He descended the stairs, the wooden steps creaking from his movement, and strode across the living space. It was mostly quiet, the occasional gust from outside reminding him of the cold temperatures, muffling the little bit of noise from the kitchen. Rajveer peeked in before entering and noticed Amabel busying herself with decorating scones on the center butcher block.

"Good morning, King," she greeted him with a small bow. "Would you care for some coffee?"

"Please." Rajveer settled himself against the countertop. "What are those?" He nodded his head in the direction of the pastries, accepting the mug from her.

"Pecan braids." She brushed something along the top of one, giving it a glossy finish before strategically placing pecans into the dough. "I made a couple extras for you today. I need to get ready to take my cart to the market square unless you need me to stay here with you."

"No, not at all. I'll be alright. I wouldn't want to take you away from your work."

She offered a wistful smile. "I'll be back around dinner. Albani might be back before me, but otherwise, I don't expect any other visitors."

"Is everyone else gone?"

"Aside from Miles and Alouette? Yes. Danika left in the middle of the night—mumbling about forgetting something—and Amicus and Cora just left." She paused, packaging the dough into little boxes. "Do you need anything else before I leave?"

"No, this should be good enough."

"Okay. I left some sandwiches in the chiller. I'm sorry if it isn't much, but it's the best I could do at such short notice. I'm trying not to draw too much attention to myself with Seclusians on guard."

"It's more than enough."

"Well, I'll get ready to leave. If you need anything before then, don't hesitate to ask." She turned away from him and walked out of the kitchen.

∴ ∵ ∴

It wasn't long until Miles woke and entered the living space where Rajveer sat, sipping his mug as he stared out the front window, catching small glimpses of his citizens headed to and from the market square.

"Where did Danika leave to?" Rajveer said over Miles' yawn.

"Not sure. Before I woke Amicus for night shift, she said she needed to check on someone."

"Do you think we can trust her?"

"Rajveer." Miles let out a sigh, looking into his own mug, before returning his attention back to Rajveer. "You have to trust us. There are very few we *can* trust and when we start questioning everyone, it's only going to make things worse. Amicus, Danika, and I swore an oath to *you*. We helped *you* when you wanted to kill your father. You need to trust us now too."

"And what of these other Satelles that we're trying to round up?"

"You'll have to trust our judgment on who we believe is warranted to learn this information. But being afraid you'll always be betrayed means you'll never fully live life."

"How am I supposed to allow that? The ones I *did* love deceived me."

Miles shrugged. "Isn't that what love is? Sure, you adore and care about someone, but without being scared or afraid of getting hurt, it never ascends to something more."

∴ ∵ ∴

By the time Fiedel began to set, Rajveer was losing his mind. Everyone had the opportunity to leave the house, Miles albeit briefly around lunch while Cora returned to stand watch. Even Alouette left and returned with a discreet bag claiming some necessary shopping.

Having Miles and Alouette with him for most of the day meant people to talk to, but being forced to stay indoors, after being trapped in the tombs of the castle, made Rajveer feel claustrophobic.

Alouette sat in a chair, tucked in with a book. He'd watched her for a while as Fiedel set beyond her. The way the golden rays cast her profile into a silhouette, highlighting the slight point of her nose and curved cheeks. It was a small moment, offering him a bit of distraction before his nerves racked up again. He felt like every part of his body was shaking, yet when he held out his hands before himself, they looked utterly still. Rajveer tried to remind himself it was almost time. Then they could start this process and he could drink again. But as Miles sulked into the room to begin a solo card game on the coffee table in front of the sofa, it reminded Rajveer of how long they'd been here waiting.

Rajveer stood up to begin pacing the perimeter of the room when the front door burst open. The chilled air brought in a swirl of small snowflakes as Albani stepped in, quickly pushing the door closed behind him.

"It's about time!" Rajveer's irritation was unable to be controlled. "Amabel said dinner. Where is she?" Albani ignored him, shucking off his jacket, any snowflakes looking like only rain drops. "I asked you a question."

"My king, no reason to fret. She's on her way home. I don't like to spend my time at work just to be criticized as soon as I come home, especially when I still have to return to the tavern shortly for the dinner rush."

Not a moment later, Amabel arrived. She let out a shrill cry. "I can't believe it's snowing! Heim is going to make an early arrival. It's a shame the citizens aren't going to be able to build their bonfires for the festival this fiedation."

After discarding her own jacket, she immediately replaced her dirty apron with a new one, which hung on a nearby hook. Amabel moved into the home to draw the curtains closed. "What are you reading there, miss?"

"A tale of a fate fighting against time." Alouette flashed the cover to Amabel.

"I absolutely loved that story."

"Why is everyone so calm?! Amabel showed up late and yet you merely waltz through the front door."

Amabel appeared startled at Rajveer's outburst, while Alouette and Miles merely looked in his direction. Concern buried into Alouette's eyebrows, but no one seemed eager to calm him down.

"My king…" Amabel began, bowing and stumbling over her words when Albani interrupted.

"Look, I know things are difficult right now. You haven't had a drink and I'm sure it's causing you to be short-tempered, but—"

"Short-tempered? How dare you speak to me like that? I'm your king."

Albani showed his palms in submission. "I'm telling you this as someone who has lived many fiedations. As much as you think you know everything now, you don't. You may have the title of king, but you haven't inherited the qualities yet." Rajveer stared at Albani in disbelief. "Yes, everything turned to shit, but that doesn't allow you to attack everyone else. You were a spoiled brat who drank time away. You *are* the Lumen king now. Start acting like one and not a petulant child who merely throws a temper tantrum because someone who is *helping* you is a few moments late."

Rajveer continued to stare, the room falling into an uncomfortable silence.

"Let me get dinner cooked, dear." Amabel attempted to smooth the tension.

As everyone appeared to look busy, Rajveer was left to his thoughts. He had no choice but to hope this ridiculous act would get Maddox off Lume and back to Petram, keeping his guard down long enough for them to take control of the city again and save it.

Darkness

The Lumens really were fools. Helena didn't expect persuading them of her plan would've taken as long as it did. Their suggestions and ideas they'd come up with weren't totally ridiculous, but her plan would be the only one that would succeed in distracting Maddox. It also didn't help they didn't fully understand; not only how the procedure behind removing Rajveer's hand worked, but also how underestimating Maddox would be their inevitable failure.

Helena knew without a body for Maddox to find, he wouldn't fully accept the premise that Rajveer was dead. He needed something; otherwise, he would move forward expecting Rajveer to miraculously appear. And they desperately need his attention elsewhere, like on accepting his position as king regent.

Maddox as king? It was a thought that made Helena snort as she continued walking through the market square of the Lumen capital. The tempat was charged, so she could return home, but her mind kept buzzing with endless possibilities. Sorting through them until she could find the one with the greatest chance of Lume's survival.

Helena preferred walking at night, although here in the capital it was very different than her strolls through the port. All the cities had their own uniqueness to them—their own quirks, making Lume a wonderful place to tour. But something about Freta brought her back again and again.

During the day, the port town was frantic. Yells and curses flowed along the constant soft breeze, clanging against the metal strappings and riggs. Sails and fabric whipped with the sporadic gusts, the incessant crashing of waves making the wood groan when they got a little too rough. And at night, all those people who'd been running up and down the docks, loading and unloading boxes, filled the dirt-covered streets. Lumens traipsing along looking for goods to barter for and pleasure to trade with, well into the darkened nights. Quiet only settled when Fiedel began to dawn across the sky.

Here in the capital, it was oppressive. Especially this late at night, she barely saw two people, and they happened to be Seclusians on patrol, whom she was able to avoid when she quickly tucked into the shadows of a building stairwell. Her boots sounded loud against the cobblestones until an occasional gust would force leaves to tumble across her path. Most buildings, even the resident dwellings, were darkened, only the lampposts offering small traces of light or hint at life.

She still needed to rummage through her ideas. Really, she needed to find someone to talk to, but who? Helena needed to think of a person who could fully understand the gravity of their situation.

Amicus wasn't an option. Her brief encounter with him grated Helena in a way she couldn't quite place her finger on. Maybe it was his sense of questionable loyalty—how could one guard and protect the late king's life yet also fully support Rajveer's?

Rajveer wasn't a possibility either. She liked the Lumen prince—*king*—well enough. Watching how quickly he could be annoyed, and the shortness of his temper offered Helena easy amusement, but he was controlled by his emotions. And she knew, soon, grief would join and overwhelm him.

Helena turned a corner and realized she couldn't keep putting off her return. She not only needed to get the remediux unnoticed, but also the tempat would need time to recharge so she could return for the procedure. Tugging the tempat from her cleavage, she turned the dials, making the portal appear outside of Petram's Twelfth Committee building. She sighed as she began unlocking the main doors. Here on Petram, nighttime wasn't anything like Lume. It seemed more sterile than the closely guarded Lumen capital.

Of course, the easy person to discuss her ideas with would be Alouette. Her brain flipped back to her prior thoughts as it went through the monotonous movement of unlocking the building's doors. After so many fiedations, Helena did consider Alouette a friend. Watching her as she found Rajveer alive (and mostly well), she'd seen happiness begin to fade the dark circles under Ettie's eyes and breathe life back into Ettie. Helena didn't want to burden her any more than necessary.

There was also Miles. A smile formed unbidden on her lips at the thought of the young man. His cheeks, still round from his youth, contrasted with the wisdom he held in his eyes. Watching Miles as he cared for Rajveer and Theodora in the tombs had been entrancing. An idea flickered to life.

Helena merely needed time to speak with Theodora. Helena knew at some point there was love, or maybe merely adoration, between Theodora and her brother; but in the brief moments she'd spent around Theodora, Helena felt she would not be so willing to forgive Maddox. It was hard to—Helena knew from her own experience.

She cracked the door open and slipped inside, prepared to override the main system. As she began swiping away alerts and entering new run commands, the idea of using Theodora grew in the darkness of her subconscious.

With a gray blanket fluffed up around her, Theodora sat tucked into Maddox's bed, as if the fabric could shield the chaos out so she could think peacefully. She rubbed her fingers against her temple. She still hadn't eaten anything, and her body felt drained. She'd assassinated the king barely even a day ago, her last meal the brew she drank from Alouette that morning, and Maddox was already discussing another one, or merely mentioning it.

Maddox said he needed to remove Valix from his position but didn't have a plan crafted yet—which Theodora readily admitted wasn't typical for him, wherein he claimed he was *keeping her involved.* Shortly after that, Theodora told him she needed to lie down. She didn't know if she could believe this wasn't another attempt to kill *her.* Trusting him was difficult, but she had to admit, she couldn't recall an exact moment when he actively lied to her.

She scoffed as she shimmied her body deeper into the blankets, embracing the weighted feeling around her. He distorted reality, sure. Withheld information, absolutely.

She *should* go back out there, to where Maddox was presumably on one of the couches, and demand food and water—she glanced down at herself—and probably even a shower and change of clothes, but it made her exhausted thinking of doing anything at all.

What she really needed was a moment away from him. She was afraid to admit it, but she missed him fiercely. She wanted him to put his arms around her, to provide a safe place where she could fully relax, even if for a moment.

A knock sounded on the bedroom door, clearly conjured by her fleeting thoughts. She pulled herself upright as she told him to enter. The door pushed inward slightly, showing Maddox's face with the most hesitant look she'd ever seen.

"You can come in," she acknowledged again.

"I realized you probably haven't eaten. I brought you some food."

Theodora raised an eyebrow at him as he entered the room with only a mug in hand. She took it from him. It was warm to the touch, and she peered in, seeing the gray goop she'd created earlier in the other room. "What in the fates is this?"

"Food." He shifted away, palming another square inset into the wall she hadn't noticed. "You eat and then I'll show you where you can bathe."

Theodora eagerly gulped down the thick *food*. It reminded her of warmed oats, except it tasted of nothing. The texture and the fullness in her belly provided the only indications she'd eaten. She rose from the bed and followed him into the other room. It was just as sleek and far bigger than she imagined. She found Maddox in the closet, pulling out clothes from drawers, which he brought over to her.

"You can sleep in these tonight. I'll have someone take you around the shops tomorrow so you can get some new outfits."

"Thanks." Her voice was surprisingly soft. When he didn't move, or say anything more, she spoke again. "Is there something else you wanted, Maddox?"

"I can sense the tension between us, charm. If there is something I can do…" His voice trailed off.

"You betrayed me. That's not something forgiven overnight. Or just because you told me to. You may think everything is okay now, but it's not."

"You are treating me like some ex-lover, Theodora. I'm not Danika. I never lied to you. Did I not hesitate to fire my weapon? It's proof positive I didn't agree with the decision, regardless of the plans we initially presented to Petram. You're acting as if this is something I need to fix, and I'm not entirely sure that's within my expertise to do so. I've offered answers to your questions, offered you an escape from the life you so bitterly hated, and presented you with the opportunity to take your revenge against Valix."

"Is that supposed to make me forgive you? Because that was by far the worst apology I've ever heard."

He said nothing, only rubbed his hands up his face and through his hair. She knew he wouldn't—couldn't—find the words. So, against her better judgment she went to the core of her feeling of betrayal. "Did you ever love me?" The question fell faintly from her lips.

"I..." Maddox sighed, "I don't know if I can answer that. Love isn't a definable term. It's emotions and ideas, dreams and possibilities wrapped up in such a small word, with a varied meaning for each person who loves and is loved." Maddox stepped closer, placing his forehead on hers, but didn't touch her anywhere else. She craved his touch, wanted to feel it. His voice was gruff. "I don't know what I'm feeling. I can't grasp these flimsy emotions. I adore you; I'm fond of you. I find myself thinking of you more times than I should and even more times wishing you here with me. It feels like a weakness, like I'm suffocating and the only way I can breathe is with you nearby. Is love merely a flaw?"

A tear slipped from her eye, skittering along her cheek. He reached up, wiping it away with his thumb while his hand cupped the curve of her neck. She raised her head further and he lifted his head from hers, enough so she could meet his gaze, stare intently into those darkened eyes. Maddox bent lower. his eyes dropped to her mouth before meeting her stare once again, and she knew where he wanted this to go.

She put her hand on his chest, pushing him away. "I can't do this yet, Maddox."

"Fuck, Theo." He pulled away from her quickly, a hand twisted into his hair. "I told you my feelings."

"Did you? If you think that is some kind of love declaration, you are mistaken. I can give you a list of novels providing examples if you need them."

"This isn't some wild, fantastical world. Those declarations are all bullshit."

Theodora's laugh weaved in between her words. "You've never said you loved me, Maddox. Those words have never left your mouth, and if I'm being entirely honest *with you*, I don't think you are capable of such feelings."

Maddox stormed across the room, turning a knob on the wall. A gush of water immediately fell from the ceiling. He said nothing more as he pushed past her and out of the room. She turned away from the empty doorway and looked longingly at how the water cascaded down like a rainstorm. She glanced at the clothes she still held and smiled sadly at the memory of the Astrum Festival—how he'd kissed her. She leaned forward and breathed in the scent of him threaded into the fabric.

Although Maddox, in his own way, was trying to bridge the distance, mend what little emotions existed and warmed within Theodora's heart, she knew it would never be enough. What he felt would never amount to or equal anything she felt for him.

Felt.

Because she did feel and would.

Falling in love with Maddox was nothing she ever wanted, but she could no longer wish it away, either.

Protocol

*C*ontrol was an absolute Maddox desired at all times, and Valix's impulse to shoot Theodora, without waiting for his order to do so, threatened that. Although Valix may have been using his hesitation as an indicator of weakness, Maddox knew he could persuade any person within the committees that his actions were valid.

Theodora was an essential asset, and one they shouldn't be discarding carelessly, especially when the Lumen throne remained at large and not entirely secured, at least not until Rajveer's death was confirmed to the Lumens and Maddox fully took over command as king regent.

The more he allowed others to make their own decisions, the more damage control was forced onto him. He felt within his gut he could trust the Gems, but Valix was questionable at best.

He sat idly, combing through his recent conversation with Theodora. He didn't understand how she could throw his feelings back at him the way she did. He loosened the cravat around his neck when a subtle chime echoed into the room, a blue light pulsing at its corners.

"Accept," he said.

"Second Committer, your presence has been requested by Chancellor Umberto immediately," a robotic tone announced throughout his quarters, the pale light continuing its rhythm.

"Acknowledged," Maddox replied, and the light stopped abruptly. He glanced in the direction of his bedroom and saw Theodora leaning against the doorframe, a pair of his trousers and tunic hanging loosely off her shorter stature. The question apparent on her face. "A way to communicate across vast distances." Theodora's expression didn't change, and their silence entombed them. "I must go to speak with the Chancellor now," Maddox said as he rose from the couch, "but I'll alert the Gems and allow them to escort you to the shops tomorrow morning."

"No."

Maddox turned back to face her. "What the fuck now? What do you mean by no?"

"Exactly what no means. I won't go to the shops with them, not after the incident in the Lumen throne room."

"I don't have a lot of choices of people you can be escorted by."

"Why do I need to be escorted at all? I'm sure I can figure out where to go. Just provide me with a map or point me in the right direction. I'll manage."

"You have no credits."

"I'll manage that, too. You forget, Maddox, I learned how to be a Lawless when I was child…on my own, without a whole other planet providing me tech and resources."

"Technically, it's not a planet, it's a—"

"I'm not stupid."

Maddox took a moment to let her frustration fade before he spoke again. "If you don't want to go with the Gems, I can ask Helena if she could be available, if only to provide you useful insight for your tour of our high community.

"Fine. Helena only. Tell her to meet me after breakfast."

"Should I tell her to meet you here?"

"Does it really matter? I'm sure if something changed, the ever-watching camera system will be able to tell her where to find me."

∴ ⸫ ∴

As Maddox strode down the hallway, he pulled the pocket watch from his vest, spinning the dial at the top. The portal opened in front of him, and he stormed through, entering the hallway of the Chancellor's chambers. He didn't slow his pace as he approached the door, which automatically swung inward as if threatened by his presence. In reality, there were guards located within a secure room watching the door for expected, or unwarranted, guests. He finally slowed his steps as he crossed the threshold and passed through the initial foyer, which deposited him unceremoniously into the open space. Wide windows, like those in all the other buildings, stretched across the wall, allowing for a complete view of the community. The only difference here was the Chancellor's view was far grander, as it was situated within one of the spires of the Council building, providing a higher vantage to look upon the citizens below.

The main living space was like Maddox's quarters, sleek metal with natural tones. There was no unique decor to indicate you were within the Chancellor's dwelling, the only clue the mere size difference. Maddox had requested a smaller unit, adhering to standard efficiency as well as the fact he rarely stayed, let alone slept in it.

Within moments, his mother entered the room, arms outstretched to caress his cheeks, which he quickly turned away from.

"Mira," Maddox acknowledged her.

"You mean Mother. It doesn't hurt for you to call me by the title, Maddox. I gave birth to you after all. It is the least you can offer me, especially within the confidence of our own home."

"What is he offering you?" the Chancellor, his father, asked, his voice familiar yet different from Maddox's own inner dialogue.

"He offers me nothing, Altair! He still won't call me mother! You've ruined my children's love for me as their dutiful mother."

"My apologies, Mira, but there is little room for love inside the Council. You know this."

It was an odd experience to see both the Chancellor and Mira discuss fleeting ideas such as love, especially given their procreation had been merely to produce an heir to their name, and hopefully, someone that might be able to rise to a level adequate enough to get approved as succeeding chancellor one day as well. Succession on Petram wasn't as easy as Rajveer had it; being born didn't automatically guarantee Maddox the position. His sister was, of course, the Chancellor's first choice until Maddox came along, and since Helena began to carry too many emotions of her own. Tantrums and screaming matches from the young child had sealed her fate.

"Where is Helena?" Mira questioned as she poured a mug of tea, the large bangles on her arms clinking together with her movements.

Maddox raised an eyebrow to Mira in silent response, as he hadn't known she was summoned as well.

"Not sure." The Chancellor's face gave no emotions—not that Maddox expected any at this point—as he reached over to push a button for the intercom situated on the wall.

"Yes, sir?" The robotic voice filled the room, a pale blue light encircling the speaker unit.

"Was a request sent to Helena for her presence as well?"

"It was, sir. We have continued to try at three-minute intervals, per protocol. She has not responded to our requests."

"What does the building log indicate?"

"Hold while we conduct voice analysis for authority… yes, sir, we have her exiting from the Council meeting earlier today. Helena Umberto has not entered another building since."

"Strange," Mira mumbled into her glass as she took a sip.

"Maddox, go ahead and sit," Altair gestured to one of the sitting chairs. "We can continue with our discussion with you for the time being, although we will need to locate Helena soon."

"Could she be on Lume?" Mira leaned back into the cushions of the nearby couch, draping her forearms over her knees, her glass clutched within her fingers. "It was the only time Maddox was undetected by our systems."

"She isn't undetected," Altair said. Maddox allowed them to continue the conversation without him, remaining silent until necessary. "She hasn't entered another building since the meeting earlier today."

"If she hasn't entered another building, what could she possibly be doing? Going for a stroll through the gardens? Seems unlikely, is all I'm saying. Did either of you want a glass?" Mira gestured to her own.

Maddox grumbled his dissent. The Chancellor shook his head and said, "But Mira, would you mind getting my desk pad from the other room? I must've left it there."

"Certainly, dear." Mira placed her glass onto the nearby table and swept out of the room.

"Before your mother returns," the Chancellor began. Although it would probably only be moments before she returned, the tempo at which he spoke remained unhurried. "I must say, I am not pleased with these interactions I am noticing between you and Theodora. I know this is difficult, and after so many fiedations, I'm sure you are exhausted, but we must remain mindful, especially you."

"It's always me. I'm always what it comes down to."

"Are you trying to be pitiful right now? Come now, Maddox. You knew what would be involved with this. I won't allow you to begin second guessing it now. We have worked too hard and for too long."

"But what would you want me to do?"

"What is with this whining? I would've expected this kind of nonsense from your sister, not you. I don't care about any fanciful notions of now, Maddox. Our one goal is to worry about our future. We aren't seeking to gain Lume's throne for pure fun. There is reasoning behind it."

"And I know of it, Chancellor!" Maddox couldn't stop the rise in his voice as the words let his mouth. He knew what he was being told—how Petram's resources, no matter how they tried to restrict their intake, would no longer be able to support their new world without those of the old one.

"Mind your tone! Or your mouth will meet the same hand that quick-tongued bitch of a woman you brought here did." The Chancellor wiped an errant hair that had slipped out of place. He sighed before speaking again. "At your mother's request, I'm allowing Theodora to stay here, on Petram. Otherwise, I would be inclined to follow Valix's recommendation. One wrong move, one toe out of line, and she is gone…sacrificed for the betterment of Petram. Do you understand me?"

Maddox lowered his head in submission. He knew his father was right—emotions and this unheard-of possibility of love was ridiculous. "Yes, Chancellor."

King

The portal charged into the room, with Helena hot on its heels as she entered their world, a bag draped over her shoulder and a mess of tulle thrown around her hips.

Rajveer stood, gesturing to Miles as he spoke to Helena. "Amabel has prepped one of the spare bedrooms upstairs for us. Feel free to get set up and I'll be up in a moment."

Miles followed in Rajveer's wake as they congregated in a study tucked off the side of the house, the wood floors barely aglow from the lampposts outside. Rajveer lowered himself into one of the chairs, the pillows molding around him, as he indicated for Miles to sit as well.

Rajveer clasped his hands, fingers twining together. "I know you don't agree with this, but unfortunately this is what must be done for Lume. If Amicus returns while this is still going on, I need you to tell him to get a staged incident prepped for us to deposit the arm."

"You still haven't told Amicus about this procedure? Don't you want to discuss this with him first to make sure you are okay with this plan?"

"No. With this," he waved beyond in the direction of upstairs, "whatever you want to call it, will be my final act as prince. We're going to start putting things in motion to take back the throne, gain the capital, and make my people safe. I need to do that as their king."

"What about Amicus? He's still the captain."

"He is. However, I'm unsure if I can entirely trust him."

"My king, we've already talked about…"

The fact that Miles used his official title didn't go unnoticed by Rajveer. He raised his hand to quiet him. "I know what you said. I stopped arguing this morning about Danika. But there are still questions Amicus needs to answer about the shinegun before I'll be able to entirely trust him. I know he'll defend the throne until his last breath, yet I cannot guarantee he will do the same for my life."

"But you trust me to?"

"No," Rajveer said quickly as Miles flinched. Rajveer continued, "But I trust you'll try. I also can't help but wonder if I'd listened to you, if we might not be in this predicament, or at least be in a far less precarious situation."

Miles' head dropped, and Rajveer watched as he wiped his hands down his face, witnessed as Miles shifted beneath the invisible weight he now bore on his shoulders. Miles lifted his chin, his brown eyes submissive. "I still don't understand how removing your arm helps anything anyway. Why are you so trusting of Helena, but you can't do the same for Amicus, a lifelong friend?"

"It's true that I've known Amicus my entire life. He has been a constant almost as much as my father was, but I don't know if Amicus' fidelity remains to the crown itself or to me. Amicus used a shinegun; didn't only carry, but used an active shinegun, registered with Seclus. I don't know what that means yet for me, but I know from what Alouette has told me, Helena has been helping Lumens over the past few fiedations, and I'm hoping that this plan she's helped develop will ultimately assist Lume as well." Rajveer sighed, dropping his head down to look at his feet for a moment before looking back at Miles. "My mother used to tell me, something I've clearly forgotten until recently, that you can't control others; you can only choose how you react to them. Amicus and

Helena are unknown factors right now. I'm navigating them the best I can with the little information I have. But I do know that if I have Alouette at my side and you on my other as…" Not captain. What could Rajveer call Miles?

"Your better half?" Miles proffered.

Rajveer smiled. "My better half. You two are inherently *good*. With you, I can't lose."

"What do you need me to do?" Miles asked, albeit still a little reluctantly.

"First, we need Amicus to tell Albani we're going to use the Digere to help convince Maddox and the Petrans of my death. We're going to plant my arm in the tavern and burn it down."

"What if Albani tries to put up a fight and doesn't agree to it?"

"I'll expect some push back, but Amicus can tell him his king requires it and he'll be heavily compensated for it. And if he still argues, you can remind him that we gave him the courtesy of knowing and the hefty payment instead of burning it without his knowledge and gaining no klaud as a result."

"Why not tell Albani now?"

Rajveer chuckled. "Why would I do that? It's one of the best parts of getting other people to do the dirty work."

"Okay… what about after that?"

"Hopefully, I'll have recovered enough that we can begin making the next arrangements." Rajveer rose and Miles followed suit before starting to leave, appearing both eager and hesitant on his next tasks.

"Oh, and Miles," Rajveer called after him. Miles stopped and faced him. "While they're doing that, I need you to get word down to Hakon. It's time we use his status in Seclus to our advantage."

∴ ∵ ∴

On reluctant feet, Rajveer headed to the spare bedroom where he knew Alouette and Helena awaited him. Amabel busied herself around her home since Albani had already left back to the tavern for the dinner rush. At least she'd have Miles to help. Though Rajveer realized he might appear harsher than usual, probably more confident than his Satelles were used to, he knew it was a necessity at this point. He didn't want to sit and watch his people forced into whatever society and rules Maddox would deem appropriate. Rajveer wanted to take over the throne to help Lume after his father's inaction, not allow them to be oppressed by Lawless. Lume could govern itself, make its own decisions, adapt, and create its own advances; they just needed the chance to do so.

A chemical smell assaulted him first when he entered the bedroom, followed by the agonizingly bright lights from large free-standing lamps scattered throughout, as if to scare off the shadows from every corner. The bed, which clearly had been in the middle of the room, was shoved against the far wall, the pillows and blankets removed to a shambled stack near the curtain-drawn window.

The fingers of his normal hand twitched, and he wished strongly for a glass of wine, if even a sip, to help calm the nerves which seemed to pulse through his veins.

His thoughts must've been more apparent on his face because Helena directed her question to Alouette, like he wasn't even in the room, "Was he able to stay sober?"

"He hasn't had a drink."

Rajveer wanted to interject, make it known he didn't need anyone to speak on his behalf, but honestly, he was incredibly nervous and creating words seemed like a difficult task on its own.

"Go ahead and make yourself comfortable on the bed," Helena instructed him, offering no appropriate bedside manners.

"Can I have a smoke and a few minutes alone to gather myself?"

"Sure, but you are pressing my patience. Some of us have other requirements." Helena didn't wait before leaving the room, Alouette slower to follow out behind her.

∴ ∵ ∴

The night Rajveer went out with his father to patrol with the Satelles was a balmy solta evening, the humidity sticking tightly with them, refusing to leave their world. Rajveer forced himself not to actively tug at the collar of his jacket, feeling as if it were some kind of noose around his neck.

Satelles he rarely mingled with were present and, although it made him slightly uncomfortable—if only because he was unsure how some of the elder Satelles would treat him for his decision to follow along—it allowed him the opportunity to meet and evaluate those making up his, hopefully, future guard.

Since he remained close to his father, Amicus had become an easy friend during most of Rajveer's childhood. Especially when, during the rare moments his father would take him around the continent and no one would keep him entertained, Amicus helped to occupy his restless, childish mind.

"Halt there, missus," a significantly older Satelle, whom Rajveer was convinced was on the verge of collapse from his countless coughing attacks, voiced in the direction of a woman.

The woman wasn't elderly, at least Rajveer assumed she wasn't, but the dirt and grime coating her skin made it difficult to gauge. Her dark hair was covered in an ashy gray, giving the appearance of a mythical spell caster rather than a typical Lumen.

She tucked her features deeper into a shawl she had wrapped around her head as she withdrew further into the shadows. "Yes?" A bare murmur, a simple acknowledgement when a group of five Satelles and her prince stood gathered nearby.

"Empty your pockets," his Satelle commanded.

Her response was gobbled up by Rajveer's own voice. "What are you questioning, Satelle?"

"This woman, sir," he turned slightly in Rajveer's direction, "has stolen food from the markets. I witnessed her take it from one of the vendors and have discreetly followed her here."

"Which vendor do you speak of? What did she take?" Rajveer hadn't seen anything and was curious why he waited this long to speak up.

"Am I under investigation, Prince?" The Satelle responded, "Are you going to believe a soddy old woman over me?"

"I'm merely requesting you prove you witnessed the act. If you did, in fact, this won't be difficult for you to answer."

"She stole a loaf of bread and tucked it straight into the pocket of her apron." He jerked a hand in the direction of her body. His mannerism was remarkably calm, which made Rajveer's mind race with possibilities of how to proceed if he was correct in his allegation.

Rajveer moved closer to the woman, blocking the path to the Satelles. "Go ahead," he directed her, wishing to the fates this man was wrong.

The woman began to reach for her pocket and Rajveer's heart went straight to his gut. She produced the alleged stolen loaf. The prince refused to drop his head in defeat.

"What's going on here?" the king bellowed across the cobblestones, his voice echoing off the surrounding buildings, where he caught up to their group.

The woman immediately dropped to her knees, bowing her head with a whisper of "my king," the loaf tumbling across the dirt. "My king." Her voice was louder, borderline hysterical. "Mercy, my king. Mercy!" Tears rolled swiftly down her grimy cheeks. "My king." She fell forward, her fingers digging into the dirt. "Please grant mercy."

"This woman has stolen a loaf of bread, and Prince Rajveer helped to confirm it." The elderly Satelle didn't hesitate to produce his response over the wails of the woman.

Rajveer flinched and turned slowly to witness his father high on his steed, Amicus flanking his left side.

"Well, what do you wait for? Punishment is to be rewarded, yes?"

"Yes, sir." The Satelle advanced, and Rajveer shifted again between him and the woman, bringing up his hand to stop him.

"Wait," he instructed the Satelle as he shifted his gaze to his father. "Father, if I may, I am sure there is a reasonable explanation. Why don't we allow her to share it with us?"

"It matters not."

"It matters to me."

The king paused for a moment. "If it pleases you." He gestured Rajveer to continue.

Rajveer knelt next to the woman, placing his hand on her back. She raised her face and streaks from where the tears rolled down her cheeks left lines across her face. An emotion he couldn't entirely name crossed her dark eyes, puckering her brows. He was unsure how his father would react to whatever Rajveer had planned. Yet the alternative was the woman immediately having her hand removed without question, especially given the crime had been confirmed when she removed the loaf from her pocket.

"Why did you steal the loaf?"

The question was faint, barely heard beyond their shared breaths, as if the transgression was whispered it might melt away.

"I hadn't meant to cause any trouble, my prince. I've been unable to find any local work since moving to the capital. I have two growing boys at home, and I wanted to give them food more substantial than the stewed cabbage we have been feasting on over the past petrik."

"I'm sorry to hear that. I'm sure securing food for yourself is difficult, and with two lads? I'm sure it is challenging at a time like this. I think Noble Zyair is looking for some help in the temples if that would help."

"Oh, yes. Yes. I'd certainly be willing."

"Come on. Go ahead and stand up. Meet me tomorrow at the temple and I'll secure the placement. We will get you a job and well on your way to giving your family much better meals for the foreseeable future."

"Oh, thank you, Prince Rajveer. How can I repay you?"

"Don't worry about that. A capital is nothing without its people." Rajveer produced a small wink and gently began

pushing the woman away from the Satelles, hoping to have her well out of their vicious claws.

"What do you think you are doing?"

The eldest Satelle's raspy voice caused Rajveer's entire body to tense. He gave the woman a reassuring nod before turning to face him.

"What I please. Although you are a member of the King's Satelles, you still respond to me, and your questioning of my authority will not be allowed."

"Ah, he may report to you, son," his father spoke haughtily from where he remained on his steed, "but you all answer to me. I don't agree with allowing her to be freely dismissed for such a crime."

"She is merely struggling with her recent travel to the capital. We provide her a job, she helps the city and our local businesses, and she'll soon be able to afford food on her own."

"And are we to pity every person who struggles?"

"In situations like these?" Rajveer answered. "Yes, I would think we should."

"So, what happens when the entire capital claims they are unable to pay for their bread for the week? We are supposed to continue to throw our resources away?"

"It's the price that must be paid. Will you pay it for her?" "Well, removing her hand limits her ability to work ever again."

Rajveer scoffed out a laugh, his chin turned upward to the fates. He could not be serious. *"You're serious?"*

"Son, when in your lifetime have I ever been known to make a joke?"

His father was serious. Rajveer was speechless.

The elder Satelle's ugly grin was plastered across his face, and Rajveer's stomach performed a somersault in response.

∴ ∵ ∴

That memory of the king had been so different and yet entirely the same as the man he last saw a few days ago. Following the incident with the elderly woman, Rajveer had lost his hand, with Amicus forced to perform the act after attempting to defend him.

As much as getting his hand removed had hurt, his father refusing to provide any herbs or even wine afterward *had* helped Lume. Once his mother learned of the event, she forced his father to pass a decree no longer allowing physical punishments. It was why Rajveer rarely saw Lumens walking around without hands or eyes.

The shuffling of feet pulled Rajveer from his thoughts. He snuffed out his cigarette as he looked up to see Alouette standing rigid at the doorway, tense with what he assumed were unspoken words. He slunk down onto the mattress and gestured for her to come in.

"I'm so, so, sorry, Rajveer." Ettie sank onto the bed next to him. She wrung her fingers together in her lap, looking at them as if they held some unspoken answers. "Raj, I don't—"

"Ettie," he spoke softly, gently to stop her. Because there was nothing she needed to say. She was clearly struggling to relay these feelings, and no matter what they were, he didn't want to be the source of any amount of pain in her life (having abandoned him or not). "It's okay. You don't need to say anything at all."

"No, I do. I need you to hear it," Alouette said. "You deserve to know. I was a terrible person. I agreed to be your wife and at the first threat, I ran. But I want you to know it wasn't you. I cared for you, still care for you so much. Your father threatened not only my life but also my family's life and your mother's. And when I found out she'd died, I should've returned. I feared for you, but I thought distancing myself would be best. I hoped it meant he'd move onto torturing someone else. But all it showed me was that I can never love you right."

"Then love me wrong."

"What?" And this time, Alouette didn't stop herself from looking at him. He would never tire of having the opportunity to stare into those round eyes.

"If you think you'll never love me right, then love me wrong. Ettie," he sighed, turning his body to grasp her hands in his, twisting their fingers together, and then let out another long sigh, the sensation of her soft hands in his almost enough to undo him entirely. "Ettie, although I've spent fiedations without you, and in some of those I'm sure I've hated you, or cursed your name, I never stopped loving you. I'd rather spend my lifetime knowing our time together was delayed than to never have the chance to be together at all. So, our beginning was a little rough. That doesn't mean for a single moment that I've thought of ever spending my life with anyone other than you."

"I don't deserve you, Raj." A tear slipped down her cheek, and he moved quickly to wipe it away with his thumb, cupping her face gently between his hands.

"Hey," he whispered. "I'll tell you a secret."

"What?"

"My mother…" Rajveer dropped his hands from her face and back into her awaiting hands as he choked down a knot in his throat. He cleared his voice and tried again. "My mother used to tell me that the strongest marriages came from two people who didn't think they deserved each other."

"What are you saying, Raj?"

"That I don't deserve you either."

"Anything else?"

"What do you mean?" Rajveer faked incredulousness.

"About the marriage part, silly!"

Rajveer produced an impish smile. "Nope, not yet. There are things I must fix about myself first." He tapped his forearm, where the metal rods protruded into his flesh, before he said, "Including this."

Alouette smiled at him, and he couldn't drag his face away from hers. He wanted to capture that radiant moment and live there forever. He said in a slightly raised voice, "Helena! We're ready when you are."

Helena returned almost immediately, appearing as a swift dark cloud in the bright room and Rajveer questioned whether she'd been eavesdropping just outside the doorway. "You're ready, Prince?" She faced the nearby table displaying all her tools as she swirled her long black hair up on top of her head, securing it with some cord.

Ready, although the nerves in his gut made him about as nauseous as a day filled with revelry and wine. He nodded; his mouth suddenly too dry to speak.

"Remove your shirt," Helena instructed.

When he moved to throw the shirt across the room, Alouette stepped back into view and drew his entire attention. He was Lume and she was Fiedel—or maybe he had it wrong because she was *his* world.

Rajveer laid down, the bed feeling entirely too soft. He kept his eyes on Alouette when Helena spoke, probably telling him what she was doing, and even though he felt a coldness around his shoulder and a slight pinch, he heard none of what she said, drowned out by Alouette's beauty and presence.

The numbing sensation, which he typically felt in his fingers and wrist, extended further up his arm to his shoulder. He attempted to force himself to embrace the feeling, because he expected this was what it would be like for the rest of his life.

Helena pulled a tube across his face and tucked something into his nostrils; it was foreign and irritating, and he detected a sweet scent. It was nothing like the delicacies from Amabel or even desserts baked by his staff. It felt inorganic and artificial, and he was unable to compare it to anything he'd ever smelled before.

Rajveer blinked against the heaviness of his eyelids. His entire body prickled with an odd sensation he couldn't fully describe, let alone try to explain to someone else.

He forced himself to focus on Alouette's face again, his vision faltered. She became blurred as small remnants of tears gathered in the corners of his eyes, daring to fall.

He'd been so afraid to find a wife, to take up the mantle as king, and he realized it was because she'd been gone. He never wanted to be anything if Alouette wasn't a part of it too. Her being here gave him courage, and now he knew she still cared for him. The prior removal of his hand, Alouette's abandonment, and his mother's passing were all pieces that dragged him deeper into oceans of despair, rage, and grief.

Although Rajveer was losing a larger physical part of himself tonight, and nothing could bring back his mother, he knew he would awaken stronger, with his betrothed returned to his side, and Satelles protecting his back.

He was Lume's king, and fates be damned if he was going to let someone else take the throne from him.

Proof

After earlier requesting the main system to alert him immediately when Helena could be tracked, he received a notification in the dead of night. He stood before the expansive window, staring across the darkened Petran sky, all indication of the day erased, only soft orbs from the building lights remained.

Family or not, Maddox couldn't ignore the warnings in his brain surrounding her disappearance. He assumed it happened occasionally since his parents didn't appear too concerned earlier when she wasn't located. With Maddox spending almost his entire life wrapped in the affairs of Lume, and remaining tucked away in Seclus, he had no information to identify how often this had previously occurred.

His sister was the eldest, born almost nine fiedations before him. She'd been well on her way to securing a committee for herself, discussing ideas and solutions with the Chancellor and Council.

Whether his parents intended to have another child was unknown to Maddox for a long time, having focused on his new duties and expectations as soon as he was weaned from his mother. Suits and appearance were a priority to combat quick assumptions and ensure a strong persona, so he'd always radiated pure confidence. He learned early in life that leaders were not merely born. They did not walk from the womb with these skills. They were molded into the person: the height of their stature, their inability to drop their gaze, a serene calm among the chaos of others. Those were the ones who rose to meet power, grasping it dangerously around the neck and making it bow to them. Maddox took to the task like a fish to water, and he quickly proved to be a shark.

Altair, with the pride of not only a father but also of the Chancellor, had pushed Maddox to continue his growth, bringing both him and Helena to the Council meetings. Maddox hadn't realized the exact moment when the change happened, when he surpassed his sister in rank, but murmurs about him nearly guaranteed the Committer title. Although Helena had lost her own position she'd been expecting since birth, she was still bestowed the title of Chancellor's daughter, granting her a trademark defiance that she alone held and somehow unpunished.

Now, utilizing the portal, Maddox appeared outside of his sister's quarters, two pounding knocks informing her of his presence. After a few minutes without response, he silently cursed himself, wondering if he should have simply portaled into her living space. Yet, after the first time he had done that—during one of his rare returns home when he was younger—he'd learned to never enter again without her knowledge after getting punched in the face when he was younger.

He knocked again. He debated leaving when he heard the door begin to open. Helena peered through the crack, and Maddox noticed the towel wrapped around her head, securing her hair. It was only then he realized there was another towel draped over her body. She appeared slightly frazzled at his presence. The skin under her eyes remained a normal color, although her cheeks were a bright red.

"You still crank the temperature on your showers?" he asked as an introduction before pushing himself into the room, invited or not.

"Yes, not like it matters. Did you forget we are provided an unlimited supply?"

"A luxury you have been provided with while remaining comforted here on Petram. Some of us—"

"Right. It's all about you again. We all know you were stranded on Lume with your ridiculous mission. Poor you." Helena closed the door and crossed the living space, standing in the archway dividing the kitchen and the rest of the house. Crossing her arms over her chest. "What do you want, Maddox?"

"Can't a brother come over to see how his sister is?"

"Maybe any other brother. Not you. Unfortunately, after a long time dealing with you, I know your antics. Everything you do is not without purpose."

"Fine. Where were you?"

"In the shower."

"You know I don't mean just now, Helena. You've been unaccounted for most of the evening. And given the fact that the Chancellor and Mira seem to recall the only time the system couldn't track someone was when I was on Lume, I'm assuming you are using the portal to visit. You know yours is meant as an emergency, a failsafe should something happen to me when I'm off-world."

"I know what it's for. A failsafe is useless if it isn't regularly checked to ensure its functionality."

"How long?"

"How long what, Maddox?"

"Don't play coy or dumb with me."

"Ask a full question, then."

"I became Committer for my ability to be efficient. Members of my committee earned their position by responding to questions when asked. *You're* the only reason you've been denied any of this."

"Is that why Valix undermined you in front of the Council?"

"How long?"

"I'll answer your question after you've answered one of mine."

"I won't promise anything like that."

"Fine, I'll go first." Helena looked at her nails as if examining their length, a vicious grin stretching upward from the corner of her mouth. "Did you fuck her?"

"Who?"

"Now who's playing dumb?"

"Not entirely sure it matters, but yes."

"Do you care about her?"

"Tsk." Maddox leaned back against the front door. "You asked yours."

Helena's face fell into a frown, leaning against the frame of the archway, each sibling mirroring the other in their half-attempted game for truth. She sighed as if she had lost. "Shortly after receiving the tempat. I would usually go and people watch, observe the Lumens and their interactions with each other."

"And now?"

"It's much of the same. I watch them from afar, very occasionally mingling to see what they are thinking. I visit the other cities to see what their opinions are, or were, of their king. Their aspirations for the continent, things they wished were different."

"What about tonight?"

"I started in Freta and had dinner at the local fishing tavern. They have a dish which I find delicious, a cream soup with shellfish. After watching Fiedel set at one of the piers I went to the capital to check how people were feeling with the recent assassination and Seclus's work to secure the castle. Within the capital there was a building on fire so most of the Lumens were focused on getting that under control, but the

Seclusians finally arrived and got it resolved. After which, I merely waited for the tempat to charge enough to return here."

Maddox looked deeply into her dark eyes, a reflection of his own, to determine if his sister was decorating her story with truths or lies.

"I also heard rumors of the prince's body being found."

Maddox refused to let his face react, choosing to ignore the last statement entirely. "No more. You are not to visit Lume anymore."

"Maddox, I'm not a child to be scolded and prevented from doing what I please."

"You're right. You're not a child. I will not have this mission compromised. We can discuss whether to grant you additional privileges in the future, but for now do not travel to Lume again. Just don't use the portal." Maddox stared at his sister, deciding whether to proceed with his reprimand. He turned as if to leave, dismissing the conversation entirely, but paused at the door. Helena hadn't moved from her spot. "As punishment, you're to take Theodora out tomorrow. Show her the shops, teach her to make purchases, and help her select appropriate attire." He threw back a smirk. "I know how much you love interacting with others."

∴ ∵ ∴

After Maddox's late-night meeting with Helena, sleep was hard to come by. His was brief and fitful, and he rose before Fiedel barely broke over the horizon, a faint pink reflecting off the water droplets from the scheduled morning rain. He turned from the window and glimpsed his shut bedroom door.

Without a second thought, he slowly opened it, finding Theodora still asleep with the bed sheets wrapped around her body. One of the pant legs of her trousers hiked up past her knee, revealing her tanned skin. With a sigh, he closed his door quietly before he reached into his pocket. After a spin of the dials, the portal opened, showcasing Lume's throne room; he stepped forward and through.

He found Valix, his body lazily draped over the arms of the throne, his head hanging over the side. He didn't even bother to straighten himself. "It's been an evening, Maddox. You wouldn't believe what has happened."

"Let me guess, one of the capital buildings was on fire?"

Questions knitted Valix's brows together, but Maddox merely shrugged. After Valix's incident during their council meeting earlier about Theodora, he wasn't entirely sure how much he could trust him anymore, if he ever really had.

Valix lifted his head and rose from the throne, adjusting his jacket. "Yes, the Digere. It was fully ablaze by the time we were able to dispatch Seclusians there. But there's more." Maddox didn't even deem his hesitation worthy of asking him to continue. "One of the Seclusians was walking along the rubble, and metal caught his attention as it reflected some of the remaining flames and embers. It was Rajveer's metal hand."

"His hand?"

"Yeah, the hand and the metallic bars that connected to the bones of his forearm. We had Mekari examine it and it appears there are some charred remains attached to the metal. It's proof Rajveer is no longer alive."

Maddox remained slightly skeptical. He knew the wrist could be removed; it had been upgraded a few times by himself. But without someone from Seclus to help him, how would it have successfully been removed? And if it was true what Mekari was presenting, it hadn't been properly removed.

"I want to meet with Mekari and go over the wrist and rods myself. I'll bring the Gems to Lume to help you and your team as they continue to investigate."

"Investigate what? Wait, you don't think he's dead." Valix waved a hand dismissively. "Look, Maddox, he probably killed himself—drank himself to oblivion and lit a match. He never handled grief well."

"Why are you even lounging here?" Maddox ignored Valix's ramblings completely.

"I was having my own discussion with the security team about increasing patrols. Although I don't anticipate another building fire happening again, the fact it did shows a level of incompetence on our part." Maddox watched as Valix pulled cigarettes from his pocket, his hands shaking slightly. "And we need to get teams moving to the other cities. The capital might be complacent now, but we must prevent further chaos from spreading."

"Are you making the decisions now?"

"No, sir," Valix said, "merely making a recommendation."

Maddox watched as Valix took a long pull on his cigarette to light it. "You've been making a lot of noise recently." Maddox shifted closer, using his full stature. "I will dismiss you from this position, Valix. Even though the Gems don't want it, I can easily find someone who is able to obey instructions and not question me in front of the Council."

"My father is beginning—"

"Your father answers to mine, just as you answer to me," Maddox said. "He has kept his position for so long due to his loyalty and obedience. You are not irreplaceable; let's make that clear."

"Sir, if I may, Theodora is a liability."

"Theodora is not part of this discussion. But if you want to continue to bring her up, *she* has followed the orders she was given, unlike you."

"Yes, and the plan was to kill her once she succeeded."

"Plans change, Valix. If they never did, we would never adapt when presented with unexpected results. They're mine for the changing, however, and mine alone." Maddox paused, waiting to see if Valix was going to continue to push on this topic. "Arrange for announcements to be sent out in the capital and the cities, letting them know of the funeral ceremony. Let's lay the Klauduisz line to rest."

"Fine, I'll handle it." Valix waved a hand around.

Maddox glared at him.

"I will have it done, sir," Valix said, dejected.

"That's right, you will."

Sister

A dim light filtered into the room, waking Theodora from her sleep. She couldn't believe how quickly she'd fallen asleep, but the soft bed and food in her belly had eased her enough to calm her. It was admittedly the most restful night she'd had since, well, probably the night she had been with Maddox.

There was no indication of him having slipped into the bed in the middle of the night, either. Theodora had considered locking the door the previous night, yet with his ability to portal it seemed pointless. And, she did have a little bit of hope, if that's what it could be called.

Maybe not hope; it was wishful thinking, wrapped in regret.

When she removed her feelings, she saw the similarities between Danika and Maddox, both relationships stemming from manipulation at Theodora's expense, the difference being Theodora had never learned to love Danika. She cared for her and wished her the best, but her feelings never blossomed into something more. Could Maddox have the same thoughts about her? He said he had *feelings*, that it might be something similarly defined as love, but would that definition ever match Theodora's?

It didn't matter though. He had betrayed her. He might not have outright lied to her, but he'd denied her, used her, and mocked her. If she allowed herself to forgive him, to sweep it all under the rug, what did that say about how Theodora felt about herself? She'd prepared herself to live a lonely life, but when Maddox had shown he might reciprocate her feelings, she'd entertained a far more fanciful idea than hope. It was a wish she had tucked close to her heart, the only problem being that wishes weren't tangible; they weren't items you could hold onto, keep inside a pocket. They could disappear as easily, or even more quickly, than they'd arrived.

She took a moment to raise her oversized tunic over her stomach and investigate her should-be healing wound. The angry red had dissipated to a pale pink, the coloring typical of an injury just before turning into a scar. She was baffled by the intensity of how she'd not only been snatched from the clutches of death, but of how quickly she'd also healed. Curiously, she poked along the wound's ugly edges, discovering a mute soreness in its center; otherwise, it felt normal.

There was a soft knock, too soft to be coming from the bedroom door she hid behind. She ignored it until it came again. Without hearing anything from outside the bedroom, she peeked out to investigate. The living quarters were empty, and the knock came again. She walked over to the front door but still found no way she could open it. *Fucking fates.*

"Erm–who is it?" Theodora called through the door. She slapped along the edge of the door, trying to find the square Maddox used to palm every other door open.

Almost of its own accord, the door started to push open. She expected to see someone she didn't recognize, maybe someone who served Maddox like the royals on Lume had. Instead, it was Maddox's sister.

Although Helena's face was softer than Theodora had seen previously.

"Why didn't he teach you how to use the door?" Helena teased as she shut the door behind herself.

"Probably because he's an arrogant bastard."

Helena smiled at that. "I can see why he likes you." She stepped closer, and Theodora noticed she was carrying a bag. "I'm Helena."

"I know who you are. I guess Maddox was able to command you to come over to take care of me."

"Ha, I don't take care of people. But when he gives me the opportunity to shop on his credit" —Helena shrugged, a gleam of interest twinkling in her eyes— "I can't say no." Helena tossed the bag onto the center table. "Maddox did say you didn't have another set of clean clothes, so I brought over one of mine. Due to our height difference, I think this one will have to do."

"Do you know where Maddox is?"

"My last information was he was on Lume, investigating a fire and planning a ceremony."

Theodora squinted her eyes at her. "What type of ceremony?"

"Funeral for the king." Helena picked at her nails. "Oh, and the prince."

Theodora gasped, her hand sweeping to her chest as if her subconscious wanted to ensure it was still beating. Rajveer had been alive when she'd followed Maddox and Valix through the portal here. What happened in such a short amount of time to cause this? Her head swiveled in a slow shake of disbelief as she sat down on the couch, the cushions sagging around her.

Helena grasped Theodora's shoulder with such surety and strength. "Don't worry, little dove."

"What?" The shock was almost entirely washed away and replaced with rage. But why did the nickname sound familiar? She quickly dismissed the atrocious name that Helena had just called her. "You know none of this! You're not really in a position to tell me not to worry!"

Helena pulled her in as if to hug her. Theodora stiffened under the attempt, until she felt Helena's breath close to her ear. "We can't talk now. It isn't safe here." In a louder voice, she continued, "Go ahead and get dressed. A walk outside in the fiedelight, spending Maddox's credit, will do your heart some good."

∴ ∵ ∴

The dress Helena gave Theodora was not at all adequate. The fabric barely brushed the top of her knees, making Theodora wonder how short it must be for Helena. What Theodora lacked in height, she gained with her build, the charcoal fabric tight across her chest and arms, making it difficult to move for fear the seams might rip. But most odd were the shoulders; crafted with some additional padding, they bulged upward, and Theodora glanced through her periphery multiple times, unsure of the shadow sitting precariously there.

She left Maddox's bedroom in search of Helena and found her leaning against a counter in the kitchen, sipping from a steaming mug. Here a similar small galley she'd seen in her room on the previous day was mostly bare save the odd contraption. Nearby were three containers with something inside each: one a pale blue, one a pastel pink with swirls of deep red within, and one a sickly gray like the shade of what Maddox had given her for dinner the night before.

"Where would you wear an outfit like this?" Theodora asked as she fidgeted with the fabric, attempting to pull the length further down her legs. She felt naked and exposed.

"I think I wore it a few weeks ago."

"For what occasion, exactly?"

"I was still alive," Helena proffered with a shrug.

"Well, that's rather morose."

"Did you want sustenance?"

"Is it more of that gray stuff Maddox made me eat last night?"

"Gray?" Helena cocked her head quizzically before she turned and picked up the tube. "You mean this?"

"I don't know. It looks the same color as the stuff that was in my mug last night. It tasted of nothing."

"It's called Paste."

"Paste?" Theodora's brows furrowed.

"Did he not explain the food to you?"

"No? He just brought me a mug filled with that gravy shit and told me to eat it."

Helena laughed. It was weird to see the lines of her face, so like her brother's, carved out into an actual, full-bodied laugh. Theodora's heart ached with the small idea that Maddox could have laughed like that with her, in a lifetime of possibilities that no longer could be.

"You would think Maddox of all people would be aware enough to explain this very distinct difference between Lume and Petram," Helena continued, small chuckles and a big smile still apparent across her face. She was so different from the woman she was around her brother. "Well, I'm sure you've realized some on your own, but our world functions based on efficiency. Instead of, for example, raising cattle to butcher, which requires us to provide a place for them to eat and breed and to be properly cared for, we merely make a liquid of vitamins and minerals necessary for the body to function. We put that liquid in various forms to provide differences in textures, which also helps the body with our teeth and digestive tracts and such, and spices to prevent boredom, but there is no luxury of food. Its sole purpose is to provide the necessary nutrients for our survival." Helena drank deeply from the mug before she said, "Let me guess, you had one of the best sleeps you've ever had last night?"

"I guess that would be accurate. At least of the ones I can remember recently."

"Your body finally received all the vitamins and minerals it has lacked over the last few fiedations eating your limited Lumen meals."

"So, why is it called Paste?"

"Again, it's all the same, so we call each kind by its texture. My personal favorite is Prickly. They add some bergamot to provide additional flavor. You should try it; it's probably one of the milder ones, without being completely bland."

"What are you drinking?"

"Coffee."

"So, the drinks are the same here?"

"Sure." Helena shrugged as if this was all completely normal and given her entire life was from here, it made sense. "We allow the planet to provide our required needs, but we do use a portion of the land to cultivate specific plants such as coffee beans and tea leaves since it requires little work to process them to be used."

"What about vocatus?"

Helena shook her head. "A luxury for Seclus alone."

"Interesting," Theodora mused as she picked up the tube with the pink goo inside. "What's this one?"

"That's the Prickly one."

After Theodora stuck the tube into the top of the device, Helena reached over and pressed the buttons. At least she wouldn't have to try to figure that out again. As she waited for the device to heat up and produce the breakfast she'd be eating, in the mug below it, Theodora faced

Helena. "Do you know why the season is different here? On Lume, it's astrum."

"We don't have seasonal changes," Helena said, taking another sip. "We use weather stations for rain regulation; it rains every day in the early morning and afternoon for a set time. Otherwise, it is always sunny, and always the same barely warm air. Everything necessary to optimally produce our plants appropriately."

"Wow," Theodora's voice slipped out. It was as if the Petrans had answers—solutions—to every possibility.

Helena must have anticipated the onslaught of coming questions because she prompted, "Hurry up with that mug, little dove, and we can go shopping!"

Alive

It had been a few days since Maddox had entered the underground tunnels of Seclus. With the successful coup, he'd spent most of his time portaling between the castle or the capital city directly to Petram, attempting to balance between the two worlds. After fiedations of calling Seclus his home, it was slightly strange to return. The underground city, of course, continued to run properly, keeping the currency systems in place for it to remain operational under disguise on the Lumen planet, but he looked forward to when travel between Lume and Petram would be much more seamless.

The grinding of machines reminded him of his necessity to make it to the workshops for petrik reports, and yet, he also needed to check in with Theodora—mostly he was curious if Theodora or his sister had started a fight with the other. Of course, he wasn't sure who would actually win out.

Following the curving of one of the bridges, he twisted through the paths to locate Mekari's business. Upon opening the door, a piercing jingle announced his arrival. Maddox glanced at the small bell in annoyance, as if it had betrayed him somehow. Footsteps bounded up the stairs set in the back part of the room, and Mekari emerged wiping at his hands with a cloth, speaking before seeing him. "How can I help you?" Glancing up, Mekari halted in his tracks, shoving the cloth deep into an apron pocket. "Sir, I wasn't expecting you. How can I be of service?"

"It was a last-minute decision on my behalf. What are you working on?"

"I just finished setting up some tests to compare dosages for a new antitoxin."

"I wanted to see the prince's hand. Is it still available?"

"Yes, it's on ice right now. I wasn't sure if you would want to see it for yourself, so I started the process to have it preserved, at least for a few days." Mekari gestured for Maddox to follow, turning back to head down the stairs from where he'd come. His shop was one of the few that had space deeper within the ground. No windows could be found, and at the bottom an array of warm jackets hung along the wall across from a glass door, the one which protected the lab from the rest of the shop—or the other way around, depending on how you viewed it.

Maddox had helped install the glass and proofing system along the perimeter walls during its build, making it more adaptable for Mekari's various tests. Maddox declined an additional jacket of his own, broaching the threshold. As soon as Mekari opened the door, they were met with chilled air and a sterile scent. The tunnels were usually slightly cooler on their own anyway, but deeper into the ground with the colder seasons approaching, it was even more brutal.

A handful of tables sat around the room, most bearing various equipment Mekari and his predecessor had built and installed with the help of other Seclusians over the fiedations. Adjusting to Seclus had always been hardest for the older people, the ones who had lived a majority of their lives on Petram with its technology. But the youth who grew up here combined the resources presented to them in their formative years with the knowledge passed down from the minds of their ascendants. Once the portal was functioning, there were long discussions among the Council about how to proceed. Maddox, even in his youth, knew if anyone were to locate a new world, build an establishment, and prepare a plan to take control, he wanted it to be him. After a fiedation of traveling under the protection of Valix's father, Stavros, Maddox had selected the perfect place, a hidden tunnel system. It was agreed, and equipment was logged and requested as Petrans of various ages, families and independents, agreed to take their one-way trip to Lume as Seclusians, prepared to build their new city.

Mekari directed him to one of the tables and proceeded to the freezer closet, a way to slow decomposition and preserve tissue samples. Exiting from the icy prison, Mekari brought over the container, stood opposite Maddox at the table, and presented it to him.

Upon opening, Maddox was quickly able to confirm it was Rajveer's metal hand, the rods previously installed into his forearm still attached. The memories of the Lumen king's request to have it crafted surfaced quickly. The late king always was compulsive, acting quickly and without regard, which rewarded him a son without a hand by his order.

Utilizing the array of tools laid out at the end of the table, Maddox inspected the small skin fragments that remained. Most had been charred or burnt, but with some poking and prodding, Maddox was able to access the same viable tissue Mekari most likely had.

"Did you find anything unusual?"

"With some coaxing and patience, I was able to get a small sample of blood and detected an apparent sedative." Mekari didn't continue, just stared at Maddox.

"Lume hasn't established such a drug yet."

"That's my understanding."

"Is it possible he could've been poisoned?

"The levels aren't high enough to be indicative of poison."

"Is there anything else that might help to show what really happened?"

"I figured you didn't share Valix's quick deduction that the Lumen was dead," Mekari said, "so I spent some time staring at the hand and thinking it through, when I realized the fingers are in a default position." Maddox's attention immediately snapped to where the metallic fingers laid, relaxed and open. "If he burned himself alive, like Valix seems to think, the nerves in his arm would've constricted, forcing the fingers to clench into a different position before it stopped functioning."

"So, he was relaxed during the removal?"

"The sedative I'm sure helped with that."

"Which means someone in Seclus is helping the new king, because there is no other way for him to have access to such a substance otherwise." Mekari merely shrugged his shoulders as if to say, *it's your show, boss,* before Maddox continued. "And if they indeed obtained the sedative, the person probably helped with performing a surgical removal."

Mekari spoke once he realized where Maddox was headed. "For this to be planted."

"And for Rajveer to still be alive!" Maddox slammed his hand down onto the table. His pulse quickened, but he closed his eyes and took a couple deep breaths. Rajveer was far smarter than Maddox originally gave him credit for.

"Speak of this to no one, including Valix and the Gems." Maddox glowered. "Is that clear?"

"Inescapably, sir."

"Check the logs, although I'm sure you won't find any requests for the sedative. Keep your ears to the ground for any murmurings among the Seclusians here and try to learn where he might be hiding. We need to track him down, immediately."

"Not to question you, sir, but do you want me to leave my current testing for this? Typically, these are tasks for the Second."

"They are. And now they are yours." Maddox emphasized the order, intensifying his tone.

"Yes, sir."

"I'll return later this evening. Again, no one, Mekari."

Maddox turned from the table, letting his calculated facade fall back into place. Before Maddox reached the lab door, Mekari called out to him, "Good work, boss."

Maddox combed his hair back out of his face and turned to Mekari. "Save your applause for when I find the rest of the king."

Unspoken

When they left the building, Theodora didn't forget what Helena had said: *We can't talk now. It isn't safe.* The words replayed in her mind while she tried to decipher whether she should, or even could, trust Helena. After all, she was an Umberto. Fates, she was a Petran, which seemed to imply disloyalty almost immediately.

Theodora ignored the urge to tug her dress lower. "I guess you won't divulge why Maddox even still has me here?" Helena appeared to have a knowing smile, one which made Theodora *want* to trust her. "How do I even know if I can trust you?"

"Patience, little dove. It'll be explained soon."

Theodora bit her tongue to not question the nickname, especially with its second time—or was it the third?—being used on her this morning. They approached a long building, short compared to the others around it. It appeared to take the whole dimensions of the block, but never stretched upward, only outward. A portion of the wall was missing, a gaping hole left open where Petrans flowed in and out, bending around each other smoothly like a river. At first, visions of the Lumen market square flashed in her memory; the hum of voices as they mumbled along with one another.

But that was where the similarities ended. Stepping into the building, Theodora found it was one massive room, metallic poles strategically placed to keep the structure standing. There were no decorative fabrics or colorful banners of offered goods. It was all muted shades of blacks, grays, whites, the occasional tan, and the even rarer dotting of color.

Over top of the natural rhythm of people, there was a consistent drone of automated voices, like the one she'd heard in Maddox's room. Pings and tones in underlying harmonies made Theodora's eyes widen in amazement. Following Helena forward as if she were Theodora's puppeteer, her brain couldn't process all the input her eyes and ears were providing, causing her to pause when she realized the lack of smells. At the Lumen market, it was *the* indicator you were almost close to the vendors—spices and scents mingled together, sometimes in peace and other times at war, but they existed. Here, Theodora couldn't even detect a sweet aroma of flowers or perfume, even though people swirled around her, and some spooned the weird Petran goop from bowls and mugs into their mouths.

They approached a tall, metallic box that was unlike anything she'd ever seen. A screen, bigger than ones she had witnessed wrapped onto the forearms of Seclusians, was tucked into the top half of the box, the bottom a clear covering with a gaping hole. Theodora didn't know whether to feel vulnerable from the lack of information she'd been given to attempt to function on Petram or amazed with their advances.

Helena tapped the screen to life and a neutral handprint appeared. Helena placed hers on top automatically and turned to Theodora. "Once you start producing, we can have you registered in the system so that you can make your own necessary purchases. Today, we're using Maddox's since he gave me authority. Everyone here is provided the basic necessities: food, water, shelter, clothes." Helena continued tapping a series of buttons. "You are provided with them based on the expectation of you producing at a bare minimum, doing your necessary requirements at work. For those who do more for the society—whether participating in various committees or offering ideas to help increase our production or providing a greater skill set—they are given additional bonus credits for a handful of luxuries, such as leave off work, participation in local games, or seats for bifiedal entertainment." She stepped back, allowing Theodora to step closer to the screen. "That's Petram in a nutshell. Go ahead and browse for the things you want. I have it filtered to items I assumed you would be more comfortable with: practical tunics and trousers, plus any accessories and gear."

Theodora had never witnessed such an array of clothing. She wasn't entirely sure she'd even owned this number of items in her entire lifetime. Becoming increasingly overwhelmed with the choices, she settled on a couple simplistic tunics and trousers, plus a cross-over bag. She wanted to select a new pair of boots, but without gun rigs, she didn't want to risk losing her weapons.

Satisfied, she looked up to Helena. "The clothing will be tailored to your size and delivered to Maddox's rooms," Helena prompted, continuing to tap away. "Now, to answer your question on trust, it deserves a drink. Would you like one?"

"Sure." Theodora shrugged as she continued to eye the other Petrans, the beeping surrounding her pulling at her attention. Helena tapped other buttons, breezing through screen after screen, making Theodora's head spin, unable to keep up. "How does it know my size?" Theodora asked.

"For the clothing? Cameras, of course. Inside the building are various cameras and recordings. You've been monitored anytime you are within a public area of the building. Simple audio recordings take place in some of the more secluded areas such as hallways and rooms. I'm unsure if audio devices exist in Maddox's quarters though. We have visuals only within the streets, although a camera will start recording in a more private place if certain words are used.

The main computer system can use these recordings of you to take the required measurements it needs. It's also part of what gauges participation in work for those additional luxuries." The machine whirred to life and the plastic piece below lifted, revealing two mugs tucked within. Helena retrieved them and offered one to Theodora.

Theodora glanced into hers and, lifting it up to her nose, confirmed by its scent that tea was inside. She moved to sip the steaming liquid, but Helena stopped her.

"Follow me," she said. Theodora followed her out, though she eagerly continued to witness Petrans in their day-to-day. It was entrancing, like watching the cogs of a machine. Yet Theodora noticed the lack of comradery found on Lume—the shouts for assistance, the bombarding negotiations of trade across the market square, the excited shouts when friends were rejoined once again. It had been a family to Theodora, one she didn't entirely appreciate until now. Subconsciously she began to take another sip of tea and didn't realize it until Helena spoke again. "You're really going to drink that?" Helena tossed the contents of her mug into a shrub positioned just beyond the entrance doors.

Theodora followed her a couple more paces until they were in an alcove, behind tall metallic beams situated within sight of the building, but more secluded. Helena zipped open a pocket on the side of her dress, producing a flask. "Vocatus," Helena answered Theodora's unasked question.

"You've been to Seclus?" Although Maddox had told Theodora of the second pocket watch Helena held, she never got the impression Helena used it.

"Always full of questions, little dove. You're going to make people think I merely get off on withholding." Helena winked as she poured the liquid into her own mug and motioned for Theodora's own. Theodora tossed the tea and held the mug out in anticipation.

"Since Maddox will surely arrive shortly," Helena said, "I'll try to give you as much information as I can." She closed the flask and slipped it back into her pocket. "To answer your question from earlier this morning, yes, Maddox has always been this way—he was raised to be manipulative, calculating, and an all-around arrogant, egotistical, smartass."

"That question was so long ago," Theodora said before taking a sip.

"I like to satisfy. But," Helena indicated with a raised finger, "back to Maddox. I do believe feelings exist; feelings he didn't know were even entirely possible for him to have. Unfortunately, he has lived his entire life between worlds, removing him from all social interactions except for those that would ultimately benefit him."

Theodora heard the portal; a sound she didn't realize she'd ingrained into her memory. It didn't go unnoticed to her how she felt her shoulders tense immediately at the whoosh. She made to turn in the direction it sounded, but Helena grabbed Theodora's chin between the fingers of her open hand, demanding her attention. "Listen carefully, little dove. I've been to Lume for many fiedations. I have been in touch with Alouette and helped her get back to the capital. No matter what you might hear from Maddox right now, Rajveer *is* alive, and I think we can take back the capital and give the power back to the Lumens." The words were low and rushed. Theodora reminded her brain to keep up. *Listen.* Helena glanced to her side, most likely in search of Maddox, slipping her fingers from Theodora's chin and taking another sip. "I'm going back tonight. Can I tell them we can count on you?"

"Why the nickname?" The name stuck in Theodora's brain, and during the rushed explanation from Helena, she realized where she'd first heard it. In those first moments being brought back from the fates' clutches—those were the first pleasant words she'd heard. Ones she hadn't noticed she'd latched onto, the ones she used as a lifeline to bring her back from the brink of death.

"He's approaching. We don't have time for this."

"Why, Helena?"

"Little dove, because you are a symbol of hope."

Helena's face transformed from the soft expression she'd witnessed all day to a harder one, the one Theodora recognized she wore when they first met, one she wore in Maddox's presence. Theodora slipped on a mask of her own before raising her glass to her lips, shifting her body closer to Helena, as they both faced where Maddox approached. She spoke into the glass, blocking her mouth with the mug. "You tell Rajveer I'll do whatever it takes."

Theodora didn't know what that would entail, who she might have to betray and manipulate to help save Lume, or what her endgame would be. But even stranded here on Petram without being able to return home, she knew she had to try something.

They both drained their glasses, an unspoken vow.

Bargain

Rajveer woke with a jolt, staring into the darkened room. The curtains remained drawn, and he was unsure of where he was except in bed. He moved to raise his left arm, his back muscles straining at the newly added weight. A rush of memories crashed into him. He attempted to admire his new extremity until he heard a small inward breath of air and movement next to him. He stiffened for a moment, glancing down at who lay beside him when his breath caught.

Alouette's hair was free of her headwrap, long strands of cascading brown swirling around her head on a pillow. Still asleep, he watched as she turned from the wall to him, tucking her hands beneath her cheek. He leaned onto his right side to allow his new hand to reach for her face, wanting the first thing the foreign nerves sensed to be her. Trailing the tip of his index finger along her skin, he followed her face from her temple to her jawline. Sensory responses sailed up his arm like electricity to his chest.

He slid back down onto the bed, pulling the sheets up around them, and simply stared at her. Small amounts of light peeked around the cracks in the curtain, giving Alouette a hazy aura. He wanted to capture this moment and relive it every morning.

Rajveer didn't know how long he watched her sleep, memorizing the way her eyelids raced through her dreams, the way her chest rose and fell like soft waves on a lake, the serenity of her face without all the worries of the world.

It wasn't until she slowly blinked her eyes open, her smile growing upon recognition that he was watching her, that he realized how much he was still in love with her. He had loved her for fiedations now. Fates, he was sure he had fallen in love the moment he met her, and the reality of their situation weighed heavily against his heart. He didn't want to claim thrones and squash rebellions; he didn't want to alter traditions and force change for the betterment of the citizens on his continent; he didn't want to destroy an advanced underground city and remove an experienced Lawless from his capital.

But, with her, he would do it all. He would face whatever challenges and battles came, knowing she was his. Before she could even whisper a good morning, before she would be forced to think about plans and strategies for the day, he seized the moment.

"Alouette Rayne Martin, will you marry me?"

A whisper. A bargain. A plea.

"Yes, Rajveer Iyer Klauduisz. It's always been yes."

Another

Maddox felt a sense of unease when he left Lume to return to Petram and locate his sister with Theodora, clearly both alive, uninjured, and agreeable toward each other. Although, having them like this was preferable to them being at each other's throats, especially if they were going to have to hunt down the traitor among Seclus.

On his approach, he immediately turned to Theodora. "That's what you're wearing?"

"It would seem so," Theodora quipped.

He stared at her hard for a moment before addressing Helena. "You couldn't find anything else for her to wear?"

"You didn't provide a list of requirements for her attire, Maddox. You simply said to get her clothes so she could shop for her own." She waved in the direction of Theodora. "Her. Dressed. Shopping. I did what was expected."

"Barely."

"The minimum," she grumbled through a diabolical grin. "If that's all that is required of me, Committer" — Helena mocked a dramatic bow— "I shall take my leave. With your permission, of course."

Maddox stared at her, feeling slightly embarrassed by her temperament, one of the only emotions Helena was able to pull out of him. "Leave, then."

Turning on the heel of her boot, her elaborate gown of black swirling around her, she swiftly continued along the streets toward whatever attempt at pretending to help Petram she determined appropriate.

Before Maddox could even release his sigh, Theodora turned away from him, heading back to the communal shops. It was odd to follow her, yet his boots did, if only propelled by his own curiosity. He closed the distance between them quickly and fought the urge to reach out his hand to guide her—but to where, he didn't know.

Theodora slowed and stopped before one of the kiosks. She rested her elbow on top, her mug dangling from her fingertips in front of the screen and turned to him as if her intentions were entirely clear. Maddox forced the question from his facial features, and she raised her other hand to her hip.

"I'm not registered yet. I need to use your hand to make a purchase.

"To buy what, charm?"

"A dagger, of course."

"One, we don't have such antiquated weaponry here. And two, that's not entirely a good idea, Theo."

"It's Theodora, if you've forgotten. Put your hand on the screen, Maddox." After he refused to move, she continued. "Helena told me Rajveer's dead and if I'm going to adjust to the Petran life, then at least allow me to look at what choices I *do* have here."

"You didn't notice?" Maddox watched her face, but it never changed and when she didn't speak, he continued. "Petrans don't use weapons here. None of them have the shineguns or flash crystals that you are so accustomed to seeing in Seclus."

"Cut the bullshit, Maddox. I'll find someone else then." She slid away from the kiosk, turning in the direction of whomever she thought might help. Maddox leaned patiently against the kiosk and watched her. After the fourth person glanced in Maddox's direction for his authority before declining her, she simmered before storming from the building.

He followed her and when she stepped outside, she slammed the mug on the walkway, shattering the peace that hung in the perfectly tempered air. "I told you," Maddox said. "We don't have weapons here. There are no Satelles. We run tests of gear like that for Seclus only and then they're resourced there."

She whirled on him. "You're exactly like Danika. You always have been, haven't you? Always trying to see how I can ultimately be used to your advantage."

"What the fuck, Theodora? You spent half a morning with my sister and now you're back to thinking I'm not on your side?" Maddox's voice never rose to meet hers. "What about our discussion from last night? What more do I have to do?"

Theodora's face flushed, angry imprints scattering across her cheeks and neck. He stepped closer and smelled the vocatus. "Have you been drinking?"

"I had one glass, if you must know. Like it's actually any concern of yours."

"Will you talk to me instead of fighting me?"

"That will depend entirely on whether you will be able to provide me with the full truth."

He let out an exasperated breath, turning away from her toward the building once more. He didn't know what Theodora was stuck on; her explosive tempers were erratic. A headache began to form along his brow. But if Helena had told her about Rajveer, what else had she divulged?

After days of little to no sleep, it seemed to finally be catching up to him. He was becoming drained, spread too thin. He hadn't wanted to argue with Theodora. It was another hurdle in his plans, slowing him down. Yet, here he was, cleaning up after everyone else's mistakes.

If she wanted answers, she'd change her tone because he wasn't going to merely stand here and coddle her.

He began walking away, and Maddox didn't miss the soft thud of her boots following. Maddox greeted fellow Petrans as they passed each other.

"Were you even going to tell me about Rajveer?"

"Theodora, I haven't even seen you yet this morning."

"That doesn't answer the question."

"The answer doesn't matter. But to make you feel better, I hadn't thought of it yet." Theodora picked at her fingernails, something he'd never witnessed her do before, as she walked alongside him. "Let your nails alone, charm."

"You better watch it, Maddox. I'm pretty sure you need me more than I need you."

"Why would you think that? If you've forgotten, I have Lume completely under my control."

"I'm sure I could present my decision to sacrifice myself to the Council and they wouldn't even blink an eye. And if I did that, who'd be left to do all your dirty work for you? Who would you be left to trust with all your secrets? Feels awfully familiar if you ask me."

"I don't keep secrets. And when are you going to stop throwing this back at me?"

"You still haven't provided me with any insight into your motives, this world, or what our entire relationship has been based on. I met you as a child, Maddox. How long have you played me as a fool? And you think by giving me another task, we can just sweep fiedations of betrayal under the rug?"

Maddox stopped walking, causing Theodora to shuffle to a stop. He angled his body in her direction, and she met his gaze. Those eyes seemed to peer beyond his face and into the depths of his soul. "Are you okay to take a walk in that dress?"

"I'll manage."

Exacerbated, he tugged the pocket watch out, but, after glancing at the time, tucked it back within the fabric. He followed the smooth streets, slowing when he didn't hear Theodora follow. "Come on, charm, I can't promise an answer to every question you might have, but I can tell you the beginning."

Spark

It was surreal for Rajveer to realize he was betrothed to Alouette once more, especially when, to the rest of the world, he was considered dead. When he tugged Alouette from the bed to head downstairs for breakfast, he peppered her with small kisses. The grin on his face was a twin to hers. His happiness made him feel weightless. He opened the door and was assaulted by the scent of sausages and potatoes; his mouth began to water, expectant.

"Raj, why don't you slip on a tunic first?" Alouette said brightly. "No sense seeing the wound still healing. Although with Helena's medicine, it shouldn't take too long." She tugged him back to the room, helping to get his metal arm through the hole of his tunic. His skin was a bright pink where it met the black metal. He'd forgotten for a moment—his mind preoccupied by her agreement to marry him.

"I can't believe you didn't try to stop him?" Danika's voice trailed up the stairs to meet Rajveer where he descended.

"What did you want me to do? Tie him down?" Miles responded, a hint of ire in his tone.

"That's exactly what you do when the king—"

Rajveer entered the dining room and his Satelles stopped speaking. "Please don't stop on my account." He settled into a seat while Alouette disappeared into the kitchen, most likely to help Amabel. "You'd tie the king down when what, Danika?" Rajveer asked as he took a chair of his own.

"When you make stupid plans with the likes of Maddox's sister," Amicus interjected. It was only then

Rajveer noticed Kadena sitting in the corner of the room, her chair pulled away from the table.

Amabel entered the room with a plate of the sausages and potatoes he'd smelled, and Alouette followed behind with eggs and bread. They worked in silent tandem around the table as Amicus continued. "This should've been discussed. Even if we could trust Helena, you shouldn't have made such a quick decision. This isn't something you need to figure out alone."

Alouette started to walk away, whispering of her return in a moment, when Rajveer slipped his fingers loosely around her wrist. She stopped in her tracks and smiled down at him. It was enough to make him break. He tugged on her arm lightly, silently asking for a kiss. She leaned forward to oblige and Rajveer whispered a thank you to her before briefly touching his lips to hers.

Amicus cleared his throat. Once Alouette slipped out of the room, Rajveer spoke again. "What's done is done. Let's move on and eat." He shifted forward in his seat, grasping his knife and fork to begin eating.

"Albani wasn't pleased, of course," Amicus spoke, his irritation still apparent in his tone, but he shifted the discussion while the other Satelles moved forward to begin eating as well. "But news of your death has spread quickly across the capital and into Seclus. They've announced the funeral ceremony for both you and your father to take place in two days. Maddox has informed the Lumens he currently holds Theodora in the prison. Some are starting to demand she be hung for the assassination."

"I'm curious how he'll address it, since I've heard nothing more from her since she followed after Valix," Miles offered.

Amicus only shrugged. "We're certain that following the ceremony, Maddox is going to request Lumens allow him to take the throne, and the current word seems to be most will accept it. To them, Maddox captured the assassin, confirmed the fate of their prince, and helped ensure their safety. With those outside of the capital remaining none the wiser." He paused to drink from his mug. Alouette returned from the kitchen to take her own seat at the table before Amicus started again. "Danika thinks we need to come up with a plan to overthrow him before he secures the throne officially, but I just can't agree with that. By making drastic decisions, we run the possibility of sacrificing more Lumens. We've already burned Digere, which I think has deflated a lot of people."

"We need to do *something*." Danika continued her assumed argument from earlier.

"What are we supposed to do? Announce the king isn't dead? Try to get them to rally to get him back on the throne? Seclus will really bury him before he even leaves the capital outskirts."

"So, we let Seclus win?"

"No." Amicus deflated. "But we need time to establish a more elaborate plan. The Lumens' hope is shattered. They were set on Rajveer wedding Theodora, and now they've learned she's a traitor and the throne is vacant."

Rajveer swallowed down a bite of his meal. "I think with a new wedding to announce to the Lumens, we will get them to quickly forget about Theodora."

"Raj." Alouette placed her hand on where Rajveer continued holding his fork, still sifting through his meal. "Don't you think we should wait to say this? You haven't spoken with Albani yet, or with Hakon or Helena for that matter. We don't really have a plan right now."

"No, Ettie." Rajveer looked at her. "We've wasted enough time. And with nothing until my funeral, it's the best opportunity for us." He turned to his Satelles, preparing to place his utensils on the table. "Alouette—" His voice trailed off with her name, the fingers of his left hand unable to open. "Why—" He grabbed his left forearm with his right hand, using every ounce of energy to make his fingers open. "Why isn't this working?" He shook his forearm as he stood from his chair.

"Oh!" Alouette quickly rose from her own. "Helena said last night this might happen. It might need some recalibration until it's figured out properly. Hold on, let me get the thing."

As she raced from the room, Rajveer shouted, "The thing? What thing?!"

"I don't remember what she called it!" Alouette shouted back.

Kadena quietly rose from the corner and collected finished plates and mugs, leaving Rajveer holding his knife hostage. He'd meant to ask why she was here, but Miles had told him to trust, and his confounded arm demanded his attention.

"Here it is." Alouette huffed out a breath. "Helena said to use this tuner thing. I just have to stick it into this corner piece…" Her voice got softer as she focused on the task of shoving the fabric of his tunic out of the way to stick something into his shoulder. A small, black rectangle remained in her hand, and after a few moments and a few beeps, the knife clattered to the table.

Rajveer moved his arm and wiggled his fingers.

"There," Alouette whispered as she placed the tuner thing on the table, returning to her seat and her plate. "Good as new."

Rajveer stared at his arm in disbelief for a moment when Miles spoke., "What were you going to tell us before all that?"

"Oh, yes! Damn arm distracted me. Alouette has agreed to marry me!"

"Again?" Amicus' tone dripped with sarcasm.

Rajveer pointed a finger in his direction and opened his mouth to speak.

"It's okay, Raj," Alouette offered. "He's justified in this opinion. And we know there will be other Lumens who'll think the same way Amicus is right now."

Rajveer ignored her, raising his voice. "She is going to marry me, Amicus, and she will be your queen. You better find some respect."

Amicus huffed out a laugh. "Is your anger only from my question? Or are you using this opportunity to also be mad about what happened at the castle with the shinegun?"

"Oh, so you aren't going to act like you didn't fire a shinegun?"

"Do you want to talk about it now?"

"Say your fucking piece," Rajveer said. "Explain to everyone why *you* had a shinegun. But you'd better hurry up because I'd rather go make wedding plans before Helena returns. Because when she does, we're strategizing to take back the Lumen throne. Danika's right. We aren't going to sit idly by anymore. You're either here to help or hurt, and if you're not helping, you might as well leave now."

"Raj—" The look Rajveer gave Amicus must've made Amicus reconsider how to proceed. "My king." He placed his hand over his heart with a slight bow of his head. "My loyalty has always been to the crown. Being your father's captain for so long, I heard a lot of discussions. Unfortunately, that didn't grant me the chance to learn your father had turned to Seclus to prevent you from accessing the throne. But it did provide me with information about Seclus' tech and the advantages it presented, especially to someone whose sole purpose is to ensure the longevity of another. We were in the process of creating the stelgladios when I went to Seclus and acquired a shinegun of my own. No one knew of it except the one person I had purchased it from in Seclus, and if my memory serves me correctly, they've long since passed away."

Amicus rose from the table and walked the length of it to where Rajveer remained seated. Amicus knelt, his knee thumping on the floor, the other Satelles witnessing. "I promise on my life and honor that my loyalty remains to Lume and her king."

Danika and Miles rose and knelt beside Amicus; their heads bowed to the floor.

"And what of her future queen?" Rajveer asked.

"We pledge our lives," they vowed in unison. His Satelles, decorated in their jackets of gold, their capes cascading down their bodies like rivers of green, still knelt before him while he, their king, sat in loose trousers and a half-buttoned tunic.

Rajveer slid from the seat, dropping to his own knees before Amicus. He placed his hand on Amicus' shoulder, and Amicus met his gaze. "Together, my friend. Together we will bring Lume forth from her ashes, even more beautiful than she was." He dropped his hand away and took a moment to look at each of his Satelles. "Today, I may be king. And tomorrow and the day after and the day after. But one day, when Lume is ready, we will make changes here, ones where friends do not feel obligated to bow." Rajveer stood and made an elaborate wave of his hand. "Rise, my friends. Let us rejoice, for when Helena arrives, it will become a time for action. But for now, let us celebrate my engagement to my beautiful bride."

It wasn't the announcement Rajveer ever expected to have. Well, he never would've anticipated he would've shared his own news of his planned wedding. When he and Alouette had agreed to marry before, it was a task his father ensured was taken care of. Banners and gossip spread through the capital like wildfire, and he merely soaked up the congratulations and bright smiles of his citizens.

He glanced around the room and felt a spark of happiness. A small spark, yet still there. His Satelles, his friends, were understandably worried. They were all short-tempered and on edge. Everything was chaos around them, but here, in this small home, Rajveer was surrounded by people whom he trusted and appreciated in his life.

Undermined

Theodora followed obediently behind Maddox. In those brief moments of silence though, her brain wouldn't stop overturning everything she'd learned, and it would have been a lie if she didn't acknowledge that everything was turning into absolute shit. Maddox, Rajveer, Helena. Theodora struggled to find peace now. After a short time of thinking she would be able to live in her cottage, away from Seclus and Lume, avoiding technology and politics, she now felt drowned by it.

But as much as she wanted a distraction, or even answers, Theodora said nothing, tired of feeling like she was merely nagging Maddox to empty his secrets, remedy his betrayals. Now with her agreement to help Rajveer and Lume once more, she just didn't care. She felt if she continued to do so, when all of this was over, she would be entirely broken, discarded and abandoned.

And that didn't include what would happen with Maddox. Her heart and mind were still completely at war with how to proceed with him.

"Why are we walking, Maddox? I would've assumed with how busy you are you wouldn't have time for such things."

"Do you want to hear the story or not?"

Theodora said nothing more, remaining silent.

"When I was a young boy, I was sent to shadow in the workshops. My father would say it was to help boost my skills in hopes I could take over as Chancellor, but my mother would tell you it was because I needed something to work on.

My mind was restless with the stillness of day-to-day education and the mundaneness of daily life. It wasn't long before I'd helped my fellow Petrans, using a resource we'd secured and hoarded. We'd used it to help establish and create our weather control, but not first without eliminating a good bit of it. We knew we'd eventually need to find more and began testing out recreating portals. Unfortunately, the number of failed tests left us with only two. We—"

"What do you mean recreate?"

"That's how we got here in the first place."

"Got where?"

"To Petram."

"Maddox, wh—what are you saying?"

"Petrans are from Lume. It was fiedations ago, longer ago than the Klauduisz royal line. Using Lumen resources, those who sought to find a new world figured out how to portal and chose to leave the world in hopes to abandon the king's rule, to start a new, and hopefully better, world."

"Then why didn't you have that portal?"

"After they'd established the Council and secured our resources, they decided there was no need for us to be able to return. They had it destroyed. That kind of power in the wrong hands…"

Theodora's mouth fell open in disbelief. "But we-we have…" She couldn't form words. "Why doesn't Lume know of this? Why do we have no record of it?"

Maddox shrugged. "If the stories aren't shared, they'll only be lost to time."

Theodora, unable to find words, shook her head. There was nothing that would've prepared her for this.

Maddox spoke again. "We reported the issue and the Council agreed to convert the Second Committee's task to locating an additional resource."

"What resource?"

"Aximum."

Theodora's brow furrowed. She'd never heard of it—was it within the ground of the underground city?

"The Chancellor assigned the Second Committer, my supervisor, and granted me the tempat—the pocket watch. With the limited supply and their ultimate power, the Chancellor refused for them to be given to anyone outside of his family. Hence, my sister and I have them."

Theodora crossed her arms over her chest when he seemed to be done with his monologue. "Go on," she demanded.

"The Council agreed to not only sneak into the world to obtain the resource, but also to establish a location on Lume in case we needed to infiltrate it. We didn't know how much aximum existed or how difficult it would be to obtain. While Seclus was built, we sent out scouts who ultimately found the aximum in the bottom of the Syrenic Lake." Maddox continued his slow meandering, and Theodora felt as if these were hidden secrets no one knew of, glancing around as if someone might eavesdrop and sweep them away. "We quickly secured a group who'd start incorporating our tech into the existing world of Lume, and when the Committer felt we'd proven our worth, he transferred responsibility to me while he returned to Petram to continue his initial role as leader."

"Okay…" Theodora trailed off hesitantly. "But why involve the Lumen king to begin with? Why rope me into this whole assassination with Rajveer anyway."

Maddox chuckled. "The assassination was never our plan. Our intention was to establish Seclus first and gather the aximum to create more tempats. Eventually, we'd figure out if we needed to gain control, or if we could find a way to live in mutual exchange. But the assassination itself was entirely the king's idea."

"King Richard Klauduisz? Rajveer's father? He is the one behind all of this?"

"Yes–"

"Bullshit. I don't believe you. That just can't be possible." Theodora's mind plunged back to when she'd stood before the Lumen king. Had he not said a similar thing? Hadn't everything King Klauduisz granted her before his death been truth? *I needed my son out of the way. Lume could never survive under his rule…I reached out to the Seclusions. And with a little patience, my name will continue in infamy in the storybooks, and Lume will triumph.* Theodora said nothing, speechless.

"I'm sorry, charm. It's always been him. A few fiedations after establishing the city, we started working with Lumens within the capital. We bartered secrets and exchanged goods hoping to establish a type of trade system."

"And that's how my parents got involved in this?"

"Unfortunately, yes. They'd started catching onto what Seclus was trying to do and creating too much noise, gathering too much attention. We were given no other choice, attempting to keep our mission secure." Maddox paused. "But the king wasn't an idiot, at least not then, and started to learn of what we were doing. I later found out he remained cagey afterwards in order to gather intel, so when he summoned me the night before Rajveer and Alouette's wedding, I would be forced into a difficult predicament."

Theodora said nothing. Her mind felt as if it'd run around the market square a handful of times and she didn't know where to begin her focus. She glanced at Maddox, his hands tucked so casually into his pockets, and all she could feel was rage. "So, now that you've spilled all of this, I'm expected to forgive you? Act like none of this ever happened?"

"What you decide to do is your choice, entirely on your own. But don't act like my lack of emotions means I don't care."

Silence fell around them as Theodora continued to trail Maddox in the direction of another building. Regardless of what she wanted, there was something else amiss between these two worlds. At one point, she may have loved Maddox; fates, she most likely still did, but she needed to brush the past aside and move forward with Maddox as her weapon.

She swallowed her pride and forced her feet to stop, Maddox observant enough to follow suit. He seemed to be patient in waiting for her to gather what she hoped appeared as courage. She dropped her eyes to where her fingers knotted in front of her. Returning her gaze ahead, she released a breath, holding onto hope, the same hope the Lumens saw in her, the one Helena saw.

"The past is behind us for a reason, right?" A lopsided grin fell across her lips, and she looked at Maddox again, searching his eyes, and she was shocked to see a glimmer of hope sitting there, too.

Surprise

Why is she here?" Rajveer inclined his head closer to Danika, throwing a thumb over his shoulder to point as Kadena slipped out of the room, toting their finished dinner plates. Fates be damned about keeping his mouth shut.

"You weren't the only one hurt by Theodora's actions."

"What do you mean?"

"Theodora was one of the few in the capital who used Kadena's stables. Otherwise, Kadena depended mostly on travelers from Conlis, and we know how far and few those were. Plus, the gossip has stirred. Even Amabel is struggling with her business now." Danika drained the water from her mug. "It's why she was late last night."

"You weren't here. How'd you know?"

"I might not've been in the house, but I was still working."

"If you don't mind me asking, where'd you go in the middle of the night?"

"The king prefacing with that?" She chuckled, but her cheeks flamed with an unmistakable blush. "You're really going to have to work on that if you're dealing with Satelles more often. I can promise you they are not all as straightforward as I am."

Rajveer grinned because he figured Danika didn't realize how much she gave away with her facial expressions, how he witnessed her track Kadena's movements from across the room. Danika was so different from Theodora—it was no wonder they'd never worked out. "For what my lowly opinion might mean to you—"

"We might butt heads, Your Majesty, but I always listen to you, even when you're wrong."

"I think Kadena is a far better person for you than Theodora."

Danika's gaze drifted back to where Kadena spoke with Alouette and Miles. "I think so, too."

Rajveer leaned back in the chair, reaching for one of the wine bottles Cora had stolen from the castle. While he was opening it, Alouette called him from the corner. "Raj, can you help in the kitchen a moment?"

"What in the fates could I possibly help with?" he mumbled to Danika, who hummed her agreement as he rose from the chair.

"Yes, love?" he questioned in the dimly lit room. Pans and pots Amabel had used to cook with earlier were washed and stacked on the center butcher block.

"Please don't take this the wrong way…" Alouette started, and Rajveer's heart plummeted into his gut. "But please don't drink. You don't need it."

"I—I don't know how to function without it. Ettie, you were gone for so long. I don't think I'll ever be the man you remember sober."

"Of course you aren't the same. We've both had to deal with a lot of shit. That doesn't change my love for you. And you'll never be that man drinking either. I can't follow you into your drunken worlds, but you can stay in this one, in this reality, here with me."

She loved him.

She *loved* him.

That's all his mind was able to initially focus on. He knew from anyone else this would've felt like an ultimatum. But from her?

He caught her eyes, staring into their warm depths. He leaned forward, dragged in by her orbit, brushing his lips along hers. "You still love me?" he whispered into their shared breaths. She licked her lips. Rajveer watched as she took a hard swallow before she nodded. He leaned forward. "Say it," he mumbled along her jawline.

"I love you."

His heart thundered in his chest as he barely touched his lips to her face, moving toward her mouth. When he made it there, he gave the softest kiss—a silent oath before he spoke. "Okay," he whispered.

Quick as lightning, she grabbed him behind his neck and pulled him into her, forcing his mouth open for her to deepen the kiss. As their breathing started to quicken, the taste of her in his mouth borderline addictive, he pulled away slightly, slowing the kiss. "You know, Ettie," he said, his voice rough, "I would show up on my worst day for you."

He felt her smile. "I know."

"And my best day. And every day in between."

"This is only the beginning, Raj."

He wanted to keep kissing her. He wanted to continue showing her how much he loved her, how much he'd missed her, how much she made him feel safe. He wanted his lips swollen and his body tired from relief, knowing tomorrow he could do it all again.

Instead, he gave her another peck. He didn't know if he'd be able to hold onto his restraint if they continued kissing like that, and he didn't want their first time after so many fiedations to be on the counter of someone else's kitchen. She seemed to understand his desire to wait—of course she did—and fixed the headscarf around her hair.

"We always have tomorrow," he promised.

∴ ∵ ∴

Rajveer regretted his decision to stop sneaking kisses when Helena arrived from Petram with only difficult news. It took a large amount of mental focus to stop himself from slouching.

"Theodora has agreed to help. I don't know what your plans are, but I'm sure she is contemplating how to deal with Maddox. Of course, Maddox will have his own plans, which will be hard for me to learn. I'm hoping I can persuade Theodora to act a little more forgiving, so he thinks she's on his side."

"I'll want to meet with Theodora myself," Rajveer said. "I'm glad she has agreed, but with how things ended, I have some words for her."

"That appears to be the running theme," Amicus quipped, earning him a glare from everyone else.

"In any event," Rajveer continued, "she believes we set out to kill her parents. I need to make sure she knows the truth and that clearly, my father was far busier than he ever let on."

"How do we know Theodora isn't actually a traitor, saying she is working with us but going to be working for Maddox instead?" Amicus questioned.

"She wouldn't go against her word," Danika said, quick to defend her.

Rajveer raised both hands, calming the room. "We aren't going to make accusations," he directed to Amicus, "or defend," he said to Danika, "without Theodora present. All of this will be discussed, and our issues resolved, before we agree to work with her. Helena, I'm going to trust you aren't going to share what we discuss with Theodora until I allow it."

"How can you be so sure you can even trust her?" Amicus pointed a finger at Helena.

"She has worked with and helped Alouette over the past fiedations. To me, that is proof enough that I can put faith in her. But, for those who need a little more evidence, I think there is more that Helena is not telling us." Rajveer lifted a brow in her direction, a silent request to expand.

"You don't get to demand such things from me, Prince."

"King," Rajveer grunted.

Helena's grin didn't fall as she sipped from her glass. "I think you have more important matters to discuss than my past, *Prince*."

"You and Theodora must've really hit it off. She was always adamant on that nickname, too."

"Trust me, by the end, both worlds will fear us."

Rajveer chuckled and sipped from his mug, the water doing nothing to ease his tension. "I think we need to remove Seclus' hold over the capital, which means destroying the city. Are you going to be okay with that, Helena?"

"Although I was born on Petram, it does not mean my loyalty remains with them. However, a lot of Seclusians are distant from the decisions being made by your Lawless. On Petram, they work to maintain their quotas, but here, they merely work for klaud just like Lumens do. Most who have been here have forgotten the Petran lifestyle. Do you really want to murder so many innocents?"

"What would you suggest? We can't extract the Lawless from the innocent."

"It's clearly something we'll need to discuss further with Theodora since she's lived a balanced life between Seclus and Lume. But didn't you say you'd get another Seclusian involved?"

"Yes, Hakon," Amicus said, playing with the ends of his locks. "He isn't Seclusian per se, more a Lumen earning easy klaud with a side business in Seclus. He helped secure Theodora for the assassination, through Maddox. Do you think we can continue to trust him?"

"Oh, Hakon." Helena stopped Rajveer from speaking. "He's always been about money from Maddox's reports. As long as you can provide him with enough, he'll go along with anything. I say we allow Hakon to listen to the overall impressions from the Seclusians about Maddox becoming king regent. Although most probably didn't cause a ruckus with Maddox taking control, you might find they prefer their prior prince in charge instead of reverting back to their ancestors Petran lifestyle."

"Is it really that different there?"

"Yes. It has its advantages, but I think Seclusians, save for the handful of dedicated Lawless, would rather see both their city and their tech incorporated into Lume instead of it completely falling under Maddox and the Chancellor's rule."

"So where should we focus our attack?"

"At the head. Cut off the head of the snake, prince." Helena's grin returned and Rajveer had to actively avoid rolling his eyes.

"Oh, magnificent Helena, how would we ever survive here with your unending guidance?"

Helena looked at Alouette. "He's growing on me, Ettie. I think we can keep him."

Alouette only offered a small smile before picking up a cube of cheese. Rajveer turned to his Satelles sitting along the length of the table. Cora, Danika, and Miles were grazing through the snacks Amabel had placed before their discussion, while Amicus focused entirely on the conversation. Rajveer knew they'd eventually return to the castle but appreciated the casualness and closeness the group had grown accustomed to. He hoped it'd continue.

"We need to get someone into the castle to see how many Lawless we are talking about having to overtake."

"What if we just go in with a surprise?" Helena offered. "I'm wondering if I could portal Theodora in and you could ambush them from the outside?"

"No," Rajveer said. "I want Theodora at the end. She provides us with more benefit by staying close to Maddox and keeping him less focused on what's going on here. Helena, you talk to Theodora and see if she can get Maddox to take her out, show her around, or something."

"He is showing her around now, but I'm sure she can come up with something else."

"We need Hakon to persuade Seclusians to stay away from the capital. When he is off doing that, we will round up the Satelles we have scattered around the capital, plus whoever we think can help swing a blade, and raid the castle. We focus on finding Valix and those twins. I think without them, most would yield. Without Maddox, they will be unable to portal. We can kill any who stand in our way or hold hostage those who are willing to surrender the throne back to me."

"Do you think we should attempt to recruit some Seclusians so we can get their tech?" Danika asked.

"I can get you the tech," Helana said. "What do you want?"

"All of it." Danika didn't hesitate. "I think getting us shineguns and flash crystals will help, of course, and give us the element of surprise."

Rajveer spoke before Helena could retort. "I think the portal gives us the element of surprise. Shineguns might just add confusion, especially since most of our Satelles don't know how to use them."

"It will take some time, but I can get them, if that's what you want. But be warned, once you use Seclusian tech, the Petrans in the castle will realize someone is helping you. Maddox's attention will shift to finding the traitor."

"Hopefully, he won't think to look too closely."

"We can only hope. When do you want this all done?"

"Do you think you can get Theodora here tonight to discuss? Alouette and I get married tomorrow and then there's the funeral ceremony; it must happen then."

"I'll see what I can do."

Loyalty

Helena started to exit Amabel's home when she heard someone behind her. She stopped short when she felt Miles tug the door from her hand to hold it open as she stepped outside. He followed her, softly shutting the door in the quiet of the night.

"I don't need an escort, young Satelle." Helena turned away from him and followed the cobbled walkway in the direction of the market square. "I'm far more equipped to protect myself than you are."

"I'm sure you are, but unfortunately, I can't let a beautiful woman walk the streets at night, even if she's fully sober and decorated to the teeth with weapons. Even an alpha wolf is never alone."

"I…" She stopped walking and glanced over her shoulder to gaze at him. "You're an odd one." Helena waited another moment merely staring him down before she turned away and continued onward.

She debated going to one of the taverns merely to see if he would follow her there—if he would stay and dine with her, but as much as she was drawn to the young man, she needed to return to Petram. Although it snagged in her mind, knowing she was pressing her luck by staying another moment, she couldn't help but slow her steps and face him.

"You are loyal to your king." It came out more as a statement than a question.

"I am." Silence before she watched his shoulders bounce in a small chuckle.

"Why do you think that's funny?"

Miles let out a sigh, glancing around for a moment, his smile still hanging on his face. "It's something that isn't usually appreciated. It's typically a joking point among most of the Satelles."

"I mean, I know that isn't something that's unlearned, but if you don't mind me asking, why *are* you so loyal? Why not harden your heart and turn out the world like Theodora? We know she'd trade anything to never feel again."

"If I'm being honest?"

"Please." Helena stepped closer, lowering her gaze slightly to meet his, but he kept staring off across the darkened street. She could tell that he wasn't looking at anything on Lume; he was looking back through memories when he spoke again.

"My parents died when I was young. I actually don't know the details because of my age. Through the mercy of the prior Lumen king, he secured me a new family. They raised me, taught me to appreciate the more important things in life, like family and love." Miles let out a sad laugh. "I'd give anything to have one more moment with my birth parents just to know their names, to see if I looked more like my mother or my father, to ask if they'd be proud of me."

"I think they would be very proud of you."

His smile remained and Helena couldn't stop herself from thinking how handsome he was in that moment—a nearby lamppost drew a sliver a light across his face. "You've known me for such a short amount of time. Don't take it the wrong way if I don't entirely believe you."

Helena cocked her head as if to analyze his statement. "With whom my family is, I think that's a strong argument that I'm probably right." Miles' gaze fell and she didn't want to see him burdened with such dark thoughts. She changed tactics. "Plus, if you haven't learned by now, I'm usually never wrong."

He glanced back up at her and she winked.

"It's true." Miles' smile now wider, his teeth glinting in the light. "I think if you didn't have the Petran crap to deal with, you'd be very easy to be around."

"Crap?" Helena's laugh was full-bodied. "My little Miles, do you not curse?"

"Not all of us have a dirty mouth like yours." And damnit, if he didn't smile up at her and flash that one-sided dimple.

"You have no idea." She leaned closer, glancing at the fullness of his lips. She wondered if his hands were rough from training with a stelgladio or still baby smooth with his youth.

"What about you?" he whispered in the shared space between them. "You have this built-up façade. When it's you and Alouette, you're kinder. Or even now. Why your defenses?"

He still hadn't balked from her intense stare. Helena had had her fair share of affairs, but nothing felt as genuine as the way he looked at her. She searched his eyes for some hidden meaning, some dark secret he must be unwilling to part with, when she noticed him glance down at her cleavage. No, she was falling into this far too quickly—so she did what she always did best. She jerked her hand down into her dress, pulling the tempat free. "Until next time," Helena whispered as the portal crashed open behind her and she swept herself away.

Trust

The austere building was similar to the other ones Theodora had entered within the last few days of being on Petram, harsh metal softened by the leaves and tangles of nature. When she first followed into their world, they seemed impressive, but now they seemed merely lackluster in comparison to those on Lume. Petram felt stagnant. Even Seclus adapted to the world, but Petram seemed to never evolve out of its current state. The interior walls were slate gray with the occasional sign to advise people where to go. She and Maddox walked past, stripping Theodora of the chance to read them.

Following Maddox, she entered a transport, unsettlement easing into her stomach as she felt the floor move downward.

"What's below?" Theodora hoped to distract herself, focusing on facts and details.

"This is where the testing I oversee is conducted. With all that has been happening on both Lume and Petram, I haven't been able to confer with my team to see how creating another portal is coming along."

"If you've been able to find this aximum on Lume, why hasn't a third portal already been made?"

"Although we found the aximum, I haven't had much opportunity to facilitate the portal testing. We may be able to make another portal, but with two already working, there wasn't a rush. I wanted to make changes to the portal's current design to suit our needs. Plus, with the unease on Lume, my focus was there. Once we learned of the king's assassination plan, the Council agreed to let us take over Lume fully. It wasn't until recently that I've been able to spend a great deal of time back here."

"Your parents must've been so happy to see you again." Theodora only noticed her tone once the words left her mouth. Could she be jealous—possibly?

"I'm sorry," she said. "I didn't mean to belabor the subject; I only meant they must've been glad."

"I'll not pretend Petran families are similar to those on Lume."

The transport doors opened, and Theodora was greeted with a wide room, spanning the depth of the building itself. In Seclus, being underground, the tunnels and rooms had a dimness that never left, no matter how many lamps were illuminated. But here, there were rows and rows *and rows* of bulbs, a blinding white light shoving every shadow into the corners.

Tables ran the width of the room, long sheets of metal aglow under the sterile lighting. People were stationed nearby, working with various gadgets and screens before them.

"Are all these people working on the portals?" Theodora asked in amazement at the mere number of workers.

"No, I have a lot more ideas in testing right now. But a few of them are working on limiting the necessary charge time, and others are attempting to get the aximum from Lume equipped with our tech so we can have additional portal units."

They descended a set of stairs, bringing her to the floor among additional workers. Beeps and automated voices floated down the runway of tech. It was overwhelming, the chaos in a world of structure, so different from the mere mumblings of Lumens crammed inside a tavern. And yet,

Theodora felt a sense of peace in the idea of being entirely absorbed with solving a problem.

"What do you want from me?" she asked before they reached the first table containing a local Petran.

"I don't know who to trust anymore." He looked out across the room like a captain of the sea, only his domain was metals and screens, wires and tools. "Rajveer isn't dead."

"What?" Theodora's whispered question wasn't forced. She'd only just learned this from Helena, but how did he already assume this? When she glanced at him, she saw it wasn't even a thought to him; he firmly believed it. "How do you know?"

"We found his metal hand and did some testing on the tissue that remained. He was given a sedative, one that Lumens don't know exists."

"So, you think what?"

"Someone in Seclus is helping them, and I can only believe it's Valix."

"What makes you think it's him? You have a number of Seclusians who could've had access to it, right?"

"Ever since I failed to follow through with our initial plan, he is questioning every decision I've made. He's undermined my authority in front of the Council and continues to be lax in the directives he's been given."

"And what of the Gems?"

"I've given them some time with their families; they earned enough credits for leave, and I couldn't deny their request."

"Hmm." She turned away from him, looking along the tables to peek at what the others were doing. They'd barely even glanced in their direction since their arrival, their work far more demanding of their attention.

"What? No questions?"

Theodora shrugged and looked back at him. "I have so many, but if I'm supposed to be here for a while, I'm sure I'll figure it all out in time."

Maddox rubbed his chin for a moment, and Theodora sensed there was more. His gaze was intense, and she couldn't help feeling he was studying her, or even testing her.

"What is it?" she asked.

"How'd you survive the shinegun blast, Theodora?"

"Wait—wait… you think I'm the traitor from Seclus helping?" She refused to look away from him.

"Why are you deflecting?"

"Seriously, Maddox? How would I have helped Rajveer? I got shot by Valix and found you all on Petram. How would I have left here to help him get a sedative to remove his arm?"

"But you healed."

"Who said I healed? I stitched my stomach up, found spare clothes, and immediately went in search of Valix. A corset does wonders for keeping stitches in place, and you know damn well I wasn't going to sit and die when revenge was left on the table."

What if he asked her to lift her shirt to see the wound? He stayed in quiet calculation, so Theodora threw him another distraction. "I've been here for a couple days and now you're asking. Not, you know, when you first saw me?"

"There were more important issues at the time."

"I asked on the rooftop in Lume, during the flares for the Astrum Festival, whether you trusted me." Theodora's voice sounded cold in her ears. "What did you say?"

"Of course."

"Does that still hold true?"

"Yes, charm."

"Good, then trust me. Now give me a damn tour."

Restless

Although giving Theodora a small tour of one of the workstations provided a distraction from the unending list of tasks Maddox needed to address, it didn't resolve any of them. He was giving Theodora space to think through all the information he'd provided, with the intention of making her more receptive to a life here rather than resorting to flight mode and fleeing.

The committee meeting he'd attended earlier after giving Theodora her tour had been pointless, merely informing the Chancellor of where they stood with the funeral ceremony and their expected changes to begin. They would be slow, gradual ones to not cause Lumens to stir a rebellion, but ones that would start to mimic Petram's culture.

After dropping Theodora off at her own quarters, Maddox paced the length of his own for—he could only imagine it was—the tenth time. His mind wanted to focus on discovering who this Seclus traitor was or how to deal with Valix's unending insubordination. Although it wasn't a blatant punishment, Maddox leaving Valix on Lume for so long would undoubtedly earn him an earful of questions from his second when he finally returned. Maddox needed someone overseeing Valix, or at least keeping an eye on him, but he was limited in options.

He'd instructed Mekari to keep the information about Rajveer's hand to himself, but he couldn't be sure of Mekari's loyalty either. He knew the Gems had earned their time away; he couldn't deny their request simply because he'd never had family to escape with. But when their time away ended, he'd need to push down harder on them, to help alleviate his unending need to be at multiple places at a time.

With another pace, Maddox slipped his hand into his pocket. It should be easy to relax on Petram; there were families spending days away from the community, grand adventures in the trees as children called them, and moving art displays. But Maddox felt restless, craving the organized chaos of Seclus.

He moved from one world to the other, opening the portal in the tunnel directly in front of Ludi Votivi. He hoped by entering the den, where Gustavo was still positioned at his place behind the bar, would ease some tension in his shoulders, but it did nothing. Walking through the tables, smoke twirling around him, he noticed Mekari and Renz seated together. Maddox contemplated interrupting, to further discuss what he and Mekari found, but they had no new information, and seeing the happiness on their faces as they whispered back and forth animatedly and sipped their glasses stopped him.

With a sigh, he fell into his preferred winged chair in the back of the room. The young lad Maddox saw win his first game barely even a petrik ago rushed a glass from Gustavo over to him. He nodded to the boy, taking the glass, and sipped the liquid, the cinnamon liquor racing down his throat and igniting his stomach. With his ankle propped up on his other knee, he attempted to settle into the cushion of the chair.

He'd check on how the funeral arrangements were coming along shortly, to see exactly how well Valix would follow instructions. But for now, he would watch the cards as they folded onto the tables and slid across the wood, focusing entirely on the intricacies of the various games, contemplating his next move.

Nothing

The night sky was darker than Theodora expected, an inky mix of bluish-black, so stark and faded against the blinding lights of the community buildings. Theodora tucked herself under a blanket, another hot mug of tea in her hands, and stared out through the wall of glass, attempting to locate the stars she'd seen in the Lumen skies before.

"All the lights from the buildings prevent you from finding them." Helena's voice should have startled Theodora, but the soft whisper of the portal opening was becoming a familiar sound in her ear.

"Finding what?" Theodora asked, taking another sip from her mug.

"The stars. Unfortunately, here you only see Fiedel and Lume."

"You say that as if you've actually sat and watched Lumen's night sky."

"I have. It was absolutely breathtaking to see other worlds blinking back at us. I always found it extremely humbling—a reminder we are but one small piece in a vastly significant universe." Helena walked around the couch and took a seat at the end of it. "Although my brother doesn't have time to notice such things. As much as he thinks he was cursed with growing up on Lume, I loved being there."

"Your brother is already getting insight." Theodora raised an eyebrow to help emphasize the word. If she couldn't speak openly when they were in Maddox's rooms, she also didn't feel comfortable in the space they provided for her. She mouthed to Helena: *Where can we speak?*

Helena mouthed back: *Follow my lead.* "Are you planning on staying here again tonight?"

"I'm not entirely sure." Although they were merely covering their tracks for the audio feed, Theodora couldn't help but spill the truth to Maddox's sister. "I don't really know where our relationship currently stands, and I know he had some business to attend with his committee."

"Look at you already sounding like a Petran. Well, come on. You can at least spend part of the evening with me. No sense in being cooped up alone." Theodora rose from the confines of her warm blanket. "Oh, look, you've changed your outfit!"

"I did," Theodora said. "Some of the pieces I chose were delivered here."

"It looks amazing!"

Theodora took a long glance down at herself, but there was nothing spectacular about it: black sleek trousers tucked into wool socks, with a cream tunic. The outfit was plain, matching the neutral tones of Petram, and generic in shape compared to Helena's own outfit. Her dress was skin-tight and of a different, shinier material, dipping low in the front displaying her cleavage, with long sleeves of black lace.

The two women began their route to exit the building, chattering away like the ones Theodora witnessed numerous times on the cobbled streets of Lume, as if they were old friends, gossiping about local business. By the time they left the main doors, they were cackling as they practically fell out into the night air, earning them a good glare from a handful of passersby.

"You seriously haven't seen them yet?" Helena inquired, holding her ribs as she gasped between her laughs.

"No! Maddox said the same thing. Why are you both obsessed with Rajveer's shoes?"

"They are the most outlandish thing I've seen." Theodora wiped away the tears that dotted the corners of her eyes, her mouth hurt from the strain of smiling for so long, as Helena continued. "He still wears them—those damn things. They're still hideous, too. Although I think Alouette bought him a new pair and is trying to persuade him to dispose of them."

As their laughter began to calm, the occasional chuckle bursting forth, they tucked into one of the shadows of the building. With the outside air, they quickly transformed to the task at hand, ducking behind a shrub near the building. Helena plunged her hand into her cleavage, and after a quick shimmy, produced a pocket watch similar to Maddox's.

"That doesn't seem easily accessible."

"Isn't it? It took me no time to reach it."

"Well, I—"

"And I distracted you, too. Never forget the assets that you were born with," she proffered with a wink of her shadowed lid.

The portal opened within the shrub, showing the innards of a house. As Theodora followed Helena through, she found that a deep breath confirmed their whereabouts quickly, the scent of Amabel's sweets unmatched. The sitting room was exactly how Theodora remembered: exposed wooden beams were above her, and the fireplace raged in the corner of the room with brown couches arranged before it, eager for hosts. Various voices could be heard down the hall, and her gut heaved in anticipation.

"I figured you might need a minute." Helena walked around her to the archway, which no doubt led to her fellow Lumens. "Take your time, I'll let them know you've arrived." She turned away and Theodora's courage slunk with her.

The last time she'd seen most of these people, they'd been in the castle dining room allied to remove their king. Instead, Seclusians had ambushed them, ripping apart their plan as if it were flimsy as paper. She'd thought Rajveer betrayed her, having assassinated her parents, only to learn she'd abandoned him without regard—her now king.

But if Theodora ever allowed her fears to overcome her, to make her their prisoner, she wouldn't have enjoyed this life she had, and most likely, wouldn't have survived it. Now, when facing the possibility of change, to help correct the mistakes she'd made and save the Lumens whose lives she threatened, she would not yield to them.

She wrapped herself in strength as if it were her abandoned blanket in Petram and headed to face the new Lumen king and his Satelles.

∴ ∵ ∴

Theodora stayed tucked in the small space of shadow the archway into the dining room provided. She watched as Alouette and Helena spoke, their long friendship apparent. Rajveer and his Satelles were talking, and Amabel and Albani, alive and well, ate quietly. It was like a family reunion, and she didn't know if she'd be welcome anymore.

Helena saw her hesitation and walked forward, grabbing her hand in hers. "Come on in, my fellow Petran." She forced Theodora's feet forward. "Before we begin, I imagine there are certain transgressions that need to be addressed. Since it's your world and your people, Prince, why don't you take the floor?"

As Theodora finally left the hallway, she was assaulted by the number of eyes staring in her direction from around the dining room table. Amicus and Miles had claimed seats, with

Danika leaning against a serving table directly behind them. Rajveer stood in the corner and cleared his throat, gesturing to the table. "Everyone, let's take a seat."

Danika shifted around and took a seat next to Miles. With Rajveer standing at the head of the table, Alouette moved to his immediate right. Helena stayed nearby as Theodora took the seat directly across from Rajveer. Amabel and Albani quickly gathered their places and excused themselves, but not before Amabel placed a reassuring hand on Theodora's shoulder.

"We have a lot to discuss, Theodora, but first, let's make one thing very clear." Rajveer was quick to speak. "This is my world, and I will not see it fall under my rule like my father before me. If your plan here is to trick or manipulate the Lumens any further than they already have been, this is your opportunity to leave."

"Rajveer—"

"One, I'm not done speaking. Two, until I know you can be trusted, you are to call me king." Rajveer didn't raise his voice or throw down his hand in annoyance. The person before her was no longer the one who'd desperately begged her to kill his father. "Now the real issue at hand: we need to discuss what happened during the assassination. I told you during the dinner that I didn't know where those masks came from, and I was being truthful. I've never done or said anything deceitful. Instead, you chose to side with Seclus and, unfortunately, learned the hard way. Although my Satelles would like more details of what happened, and they'd love more than anything to watch you beg for forgiveness, it will do Lume little to keep attention on what *has* happened."

"My king—" Amicus attempted to interrupt, but Rajveer silenced him with a look.

"I've said my piece on it. If you have qualms with one another, that's for you to figure out. I'm not here to babysit anyone. I've lost fiedations being a prisoner to my own father. I'm not going to spend the rest in a constant state of worry."

"You're sober for a day and already spouting wisdom like a prophet?" Helena murmured, causing Miles to choke on his drink.

"Helena," Alouette warned.

"Sorry, Ettie. It's just so easy."

Theodora had to force the smile off her face as she turned back to Rajveer. With a questioning look, she gestured to herself, silently asking if she could speak. After his brief nod, she started. "I'm unsure if I'll be able to answer everyone's questions. I'll begin by saying I've wanted what was best for Lume, but I've always wanted the best for me, too. I've wanted to see changes happen and I think King Rajveer is the best person to help Lume and Seclus learn to peacefully live amongst one another. I know everyone probably feels betrayed by me, but you must realize the people who were most like family to me as a child and taught me almost everything I knew have also betrayed me. I followed Maddox to Petram with the full intention of killing both him and Valix. It may not have happened yet, but that was because I learned they were holding Lume hostage, and I wanted to help free her." Theodora took a moment to look at every Lumen before her. "You may not trust me, but believe me when I say I'll do everything I can to save Lume from Petram's grasp."

"Even betraying Maddox?" Rajveer questioned.

"I feel that is the only way."

Helena didn't waste a beat to speak again. "So, what's your plan, Prince?"

"Initially, we'd planned to flood the underground city, but Helena mentioned most Seclusians know nothing of this long-drawn plan of Petram. Helena suggested prepping for an ambush at the castle during the funeral ceremony, but was unwilling to discuss more of the details until Theodora was present. It is my understanding that Helena is at least in the process of getting Seclus weaponry for us to use."

"I agree with leaving innocent Seclusians out of this," Theodora offered. "You don't want their blood on your hands, and it won't help with your goal of uniting the two cities."

"That was a dream before all of this went down."

"You might want that to be true, but I know you still have high hopes to make this world a better place. That doesn't happen with genocide," Theodora said as Rajveer attempted to shrug it away. "Maddox will be forced to be at the funeral, and I'd imagine Valix and the Gems will be with him for his protection, leaving the castle mostly unarmed."

"And what of this Hakon?" Helena intervened.

"He's alive?" Theodora looked to the Lumens eagerly.

"He is. We were going to use him in Seclus though."

Theodora released her breath and fought to keep control. "Not Seclus. I have a better idea."

∴ ⠧ ∴

It wasn't entirely easy to come up with a plan that ultimately betrayed Maddox; at least, it wasn't easy for her conscience. With Helena's insight into her brother, it proved less difficult than Theodora had anticipated.

Using Maddox's desire for Theodora to forgive him and to 'fix' whatever little relationship he felt they still had would be their best advantage.

"If no one has any other thoughts, I think we're in general agreement," Rajveer said. "My Satelles will start by informing Lume and getting weapons out to the people. Amicus, I'll leave that to you to delegate as you deem appropriate. I'm assuming Theodora needs to get back to Petram?"

Helena nodded.

"Perfect, because I have some wedding arrangements to finalize." Rajveer rose and left the dining room, Amicus and Miles quickly following him out.

"Wedding?" Theodora asked the room.

"Oh, I forgot you didn't know that one, little dove," Helena said. "Ettie and the prince are getting married before all this goes down."

"Cutting it a little close, aren't you?" Theodora looked at Alouette, who in turn, looked to Helena instead.

"Helena," Alouette said, "a word in the kitchen, please?"

"Certainly." Helena followed but turned back to Theodora before she left the room. "I'll be back to get you in a moment."

With the room now empty except for Danika and Theodora, Danika moved from her seat. Her boots made a soft thud on the carpet as she neared Theodora. "So, the hero returns."

"Come off it, Danika." Theodora stood, adjusting her position to face her fully. "I just explained to everyone why. Maddox used me. He. Used. *Me*."

"Yes, Maddox manipulated and betrayed you, but is it so different from what you did to me? You're not the only one who's been hurt, Theodora. I loved you." Tears brimmed in Danika's eyes, and Theodora felt as if she'd been punched in the chest. Were these not the same words Theodora had pleaded to Maddox? "So, don't act as if you're the only one. We've all lost people, especially with this stupid assassination shit that's been going on for almost a petrik now and a coup planned for almost just as long. Lumens' lives are being toyed with, by Seclusians, by people just like you."

"I'm sorry, Danika." Wasn't she about to manipulate Maddox the same way he'd done to her, the same way Theodora had done to Danika fiedations ago? "You're right. I—"

"I don't need to be told I'm right. I don't need excuses. It would do you well to remember everything isn't about you." Danika turned, her cape trailing to keep up with her pace, but she suddenly whirled, the green falling around her like a storm-churned sea. "Did you ever care?"

"I've always cared about Maddox."

"Not for that Petran bastard. *Me*, Theodora. But I guess that answers the question anyway."

"Danika, I did. But you scared me with all the talk of taking me away from Seclus."

"I never wanted to take you away. I wanted to save you from it, to save you from this—from him!"

Danika stormed out of the room, not turning back this time, and Theodora slumped into her chair, fearful that when this was over, she'd have nothing left.

Promises

The ebony ceremonial jacket Rajveer chose for the late afternoon was thicker than his usual rich green. It kept the typical Satelle stitching, a swatch of Lumen green fabric across his right breast bordered with ribbon stitched of gold. It should've felt heavy due to the added fabric, and yet Rajveer's emotions were far lighter: anticipation and excitement and a small amount of relief.

The words of his father shouldn't have mattered before such a ceremony, but they stalked his mind like a shadow, its presence becoming more and more intense as Fiedel descended from the sky.

"All you needed was to find a wife… if Lume does fall, it will be because of you. You will shoulder that burden."

Rajveer had told his father he would regret it: his decisions and his inability to listen to him, only to learn his father had been playing a much grander game. The thought that Alouette could possibly be involved in another scheme wouldn't leave him, no matter how small the idea, especially with Helena having been involved through the fiedations as well.

No, their wants could align in this one action. His marrying Alouette didn't mean he was choosing his father. Her agreeing didn't mean she was helping Seclus, or Petram. Rajveer hadn't known all those fiedations before, but upon seeing Alouette arrive back in the capital, abandoning Freta to save him, and still harboring feelings for him, he knew now how much he loved her.

The door announced its opening with a jolt of the wood frame, and Rajveer turned to see Amicus' head peering in. "Are you almost ready, sir?"

Rajveer cleared his throat, but was unable to voice any response as he reached for his stelgladio where it rested on Kadena's kitchen table, having been polished earlier by his Satelles. They'd spent most of the day slowly traversing the tunnel system from Amabel's to Kadena's farmhouse. Danika remained adamant it was a terrible idea, but Rajveer wanted to give Alouette *something*—their wedding was already nothing like what he wanted for her.

He followed Amicus through the hallways to a door leading to the pasture beyond the house, stepping outside where he spotted pots of flowers decorating the dead grass fields. Rajveer forced himself to stay diligently behind Amicus, allowing him to lead the way to his bride, jitters of excitement moving up from his stomach and falling into his limbs. His Satelles had erected a structure: a pole stood unblocked by Kadena's home, decorated with flowers and greenery, but once he stepped beyond the building wall, Rajveer's eyes found nothing and no one except Alouette.

She was beautiful, and somehow the word felt unfilled in describing her. She wore a laced veil of green and gold, a pendant pulled over the center and rested on her forehead. Her hair had been pulled back but her dark waves complimented the matched jewelry. Alouette's attention hadn't shifted to him yet, focusing on the far-off horizon, and Rajveer savored the moment, appreciating all the details of his soon-to-be wife.

The top of her dress was ivory with contrasting arms of deep green, both covered with gold embroidery that grew heavier down her arms. The dress continued with similar embellishments to bold fuchsia accents along the bottom representing tradition and hope, a strong reflection of them.

Alouette turned in his direction, and he immediately placed his hand over his heart to ensure it was indeed still beating. Rajveer tried everything in his power to force himself to memorize this moment, to have it forever seared into his mind's eye. He wanted to look upon it at least once a day, a reminder to himself of the hardship they'd gone through to somehow make it here to this moment.

They had a plan. They would figure this out and take control of the throne. Him and her, his queen. Lume's queen.

Amicus nudged him forward with an elbow, remaining on the outskirts of the floral structure with Miles, Cora, Danika, and Kadena.

Rajveer approached Alouette. When he got closer, her scent floated to him in the light breeze. Noble Zyair gestured for them to move forward before following them. They'd agreed, their vows would be exchanged in private, away from the ears of their comrades. Rajveer had apologized to Alouette more times than he cared to admit for not being able to provide her an elaborate wedding ceremony, one before the entire capital, one where they could return to Nemaaer and celebrate with her family, but she'd dismissed them.

They pushed through a curtain of flowers into a smaller structure featuring four walls created with hanging greenery. Amaranthus interrupted the vines to gather around them as the only other witnesses aside from Noble Zyair.

"Rajveer." Alouette's voice was smooth, unhindered by anything like the nerves coursing through him now. "Some people dream of meeting the Lumen king; I get to marry him. No matter what hard decisions lay ahead of us, choosing to be your wife will always be the easiest. I vow to risk everything for you—to give over my life for you and to Lume—and, to the best of my ability, be the greatest partner for you to love."

"Ettie," Rajveer choked out. He paused, swallowing down his nerves, and began again. "Ettie, it matters not where our story began, but rather where it ends. Our beginning was nothing like what is left to come. You are the best parts of me—my wife, my love, my Ettie—and I give you everything I have and everything I am."

Before the Noble could grant him the chance to kiss his bride, Rajveer realized the vows he'd spoken were not mere promises to her. They were a privilege granted to him, one he never thought he would receive. He wasn't forced to spend the rest of his life with her; he didn't have to honor or cherish her, he *yearned* to. She was the happily ever after he thankfully received.

∴ ∵ ∴

After Rajveer's and Alouette's vows were finished, the Satelles left the newlyweds for the capital to busy themselves with food and company, knowing Rajveer demanded time alone with his new wife before tomorrow's chaos.

Rajveer tugged Alouette up the stairs to the guest room of Kadena's stable house. The stairwell darkened with the failing fiedelight. He pushed the door open and peeked inside: Kadena had lined the windowsills and filled every flat surface with candles, casting the room in an orange glow. Rajveer turned back, releasing Alouette's hand to sweep her into his arms.

"Raj!" His name turned from a giggle to a laugh.

"Queen Alouette Rayne Martin Klauduisz, please let me show you to your room." He pretended to bow with her still in his arms. After crossing the threshold, he let her down carefully, her arms remaining steadfast around his neck.

He hesitated. Alouette was here, here and his, and it felt like a dream. But if Alouette held any reservation, she didn't let it show, immediately grabbing his face and pulling him to her. Flares filled his gut as he grabbed her hips before he dragged his hands up the curves of her body, around her back, and into her hair.

Their kisses turned urgent as if to make up for the fiedations before; their tongues explored, remembered, memorized.

He pushed her forward until her back pressed against the wall. A soft gasp escaped from her lips and Rajveer shifted himself to kiss along her jawline, down her neck. The taste of her skin was an addiction he never wanted sated.

She reached out to undo his jacket, and Rajveer lightly tugged her hands, pinning them above her head, trapping them beneath his against the wall. "Not yet," he whispered as he kissed her mouth once more.

They'd have a lifetime together, but he wanted to relish this moment. Take his time with her, commit her body to his own's memory. And when the stresses of future days would force this memory to fade, when night fell, he could do this all over again, never to be forgotten.

His hands trembled as they fell to the back of her dress, loosening every button down her spine—he didn't even know how many there were, he'd lost count stumbling over them—his attention focused on how she kissed him. She was confident and fervent, and it formed an ache deep within himself.

He finally found her tender skin beneath the layers of fabric, and it was fire beneath his hand. He slid his hand upward, gripping the shoulders of her dress to free her arms before he dragged it down her body to the floor. He slowed their kiss, eager to see her. He kept his gaze on the crumpled dress and took a pace back before he slowly raised his eyes, taking in every inch of her.

Ornate in black lace, Alouette's bare skin peeked through, and Rajveer realized his breath was frantic, like he'd swam the entire Syrenic Lake in a single breath. "By the fates, you're beautiful."

She smiled at him. "Come here," she whispered, and within one quick stride, he returned, pressed up against her body, and claimed her mouth all over again.

She reached forward, unbuckling the clasp around his throat, before moving to his jacket's buttons. When her fingers faltered, he playfully shoved her hands away to take care of it himself. Alouette giggled against his mouth, and he was drunk on the sound.

As he removed his jacket, Alouette reached for his trousers, but he leaned forward, hoisting her up off the ground. She giggled again, and he drowned the sound with another kiss while he carried her over to the bed, lowering her carefully onto it. He leaned up on a hand, his other walking slowly up the bare skin of her stomach.

He looked down at her, her hair cascading to frame her face. *Fates, he'd never stop loving her.*

"My wife." He leaned forward and kissed her forehead. "My wife." He kissed her temple. "My wife." He kissed her cheek. Each time he spoke, his voice became softer and gruffer; each time his lips got closer to her mouth. "My love." His lips finally met her mouth, a quick, chaste kiss before he pulled away. "My Ettie." The final time, he pushed her lips apart for his tongue to mingle with hers. He didn't speak again, letting him show her, fill her, so she'd always remember they were forever.

Ambush

After a long and much needed shower, Theodora tugged her trousers on in the confines of Maddox's bedroom. She hoped Maddox was still out in the main space, eager for the beginnings of a new plan. She swept her damp hair over her shoulder, where it quickly began to darken her tunic, before she opened the door.

She lifted her gaze and there he was. Still here.

Theodora was mildly shocked, but at least it was easier than trying to track him down, especially since once he started portaling, it would be far more difficult.

"I wasn't expecting to see you." She stepped out from the bedroom, her bare feet padding across the room to a corner, where she folded her arms across her chest.

"I always like to remain unpredictable." He offered the smirk she knew that *he knew* infuriated her.

She scoffed and rolled her eyes. "Why are you still here, Maddox?"

"I enjoy beginning my day with you." He shrugged, as if he could do the same with whatever feeling he was attempting to mask. "Maybe with you being on Petram, and staying in my home, I've gotten used to the idea."

Her opportunity. "Take me with you."

"Charm…"

"Come on, Maddox. I want to see it again. I didn't realize when I followed you, I'd never be able to see it, feel *weather* again, say goodbye to friends or even Down River."

"I don't know if you could do any of that anyway if I took you. You're Petran now; we can't allow you to mingle with Lumens. I reported to the Council you aren't a threat to us—letting you do that makes you a liability."

"Okay." She looked down at her feet. *Think, think.* "What if I stay with you? Let me go, feel the astrum breeze one more time. See the Lumens as they mourn their king and prince…"

"Only King. We might be holding a ceremony for the alleged dead prince, but I still don't believe he's dead."

"Are you expecting an attack then?"

"I don't know."

Theodora dropped her hands, palms outward as she took a step forward. "I can help."

"And how do I know you won't run off as soon as an attack began?"

"You said you still trusted me, Maddox. You're just going to have to let go and see if I fail."

∴ ∵ ∴

Maddox walked briskly from his room through the portal into the hallway of the Council Building, which led him to the door of one of the conference rooms. He shouldn't have agreed to let Theodora go with him. It was an impulsive response and it felt odd and new and different, but also somehow right.

Fuck. Now he'd have to figure out how to address this with everyone else. He brushed his fingers through his hair before he opened the door and was immediately greeted by an argument between the Gems and Valix, whom Maddox had returned to Petram the night before.

"Maddox needs to be in the square. We can't have him gallivanting all over Lume," Valix imposed, hand gesturing across the table, which glowed with an iridescent blue dimensional image of the capital and the surrounding areas.

"I don't gallivant anywhere," Maddox stated by way of greeting. He turned to the Gems. "Fully immersed back in work, I see."

"As always. We know where our expertise lies." Gemmie's voice was haughty as she stared down Valix. "We've told him having you in the capital is ludicrous. We shouldn't be making irrational decisions based on the possible impressions made on Lumens. The Second Committer's longevity remains the important piece to this."

"And since it's two to one," Jemma offered with a shrug as if to say, *point made*.

"This isn't up for a vote, Gems." Maddox intervened before Valix could offer a retort. "We will follow Valix's directive. He's spent the most time on Lume over the past few days, and whatever can help provide an advantage over their citizens and get us the throne with the least resistance possible, that's the path we shall take." Maddox saw a brief look of concern from both twins, but he turned his attention to the city replica. "Valix, show me where you are placing the stage and pyres."

Valix pointed, his hand going through the various digital renditions of the buildings that floated above the table. "Along this perimeter is a taller building, some antiquated shop of books and baubles. I'll request the fourth-floor room looking out over the square be vacated to provide an unobstructed view for the Gems."

"And what's the general timeline?"

"We're to parade in from the castle, flanked by a handful of Seclusians for protection. We'll head into the market square and have the pyres unveiled. I'll say a few words, you can say a few words as Regent, and then we'll light them. We'll let them burn through the night with someone on watch to ensure there's no desecration."

"And the throne?"

"It took some digging, but we learned Lumen tradition dictates a petrik must pass before a regent is to accept the crown and fully inherit the throne."

Maddox didn't trust Valix, not anymore, yet Maddox needed him for the time being. He needed to give Valix the opportunity to falter and show his betrayal, enough evidence Maddox could use to have him removed by the Council. "Suit up, Gems, so I can deliver you to the capital. I'll return for Valix once we're charged again."

∴ ∵ ∴

If Rajveer wasn't considered dead, he would've married Alouette in the throne room before the grand windows overlooking the lake, then they would have had the luxury of a petrik-long celebration, visiting the other cities on the continent so all Lumens could meet their queen. Yet today, the capital citizens, and those Lumens willing to travel, would be attending a different ceremony.

Earlier, Rajveer and Alouette had returned to Amabel's house, knowing it would provide a faster route back to the castle as the ceremony preparations began. They busied themselves with their own requirements in anticipation of their ambush on the castle. While Rajveer remained in their same guest room, Amabel had tugged Alouette into her room, determined to find her something suitable to wear, against Rajveer's adamant wishes she remain behind. But with her now a queen, how could he deny her when she wanted to protect and save her people?

Rajveer tucked the ends of his loose shirt into his uniform pants before walking down the hall in the direction of the room Miles was in, entering while slipping his arm into the sleeves of his jacket. Helena leaned over Miles, her hands cupping his cheeks, as Miles' hands roamed over Helena's body. For a moment, Rajveer stood speechless as they continued their kiss, Helena's dark hair draping their faces in mock privacy. The shock wearing off, he cleared his throat, and Miles slipped out quickly, tripping over the rug and collapsing onto the bed, his eyes wide like an animal caught in a trap. Helena simply wiped a long finger along her lips, her eyes wonton, as she smirked at Rajveer.

Rajveer turned his attention back to Miles. "If this is what I think it is, I don't want to know."

"Oh, come on, *Prince*, now that you and Ettie are wed, the four of us could have a wonderful time." She straightened her dress and jerked her head to force her hair from her face. She strode forward, inching her mouth close to his ear. "After so many lonely nights, I'm sure we could make your most wild fantasies come true."

Rajveer turned to meet her gaze, and Helena's eyes lit up in playfulness before she winked and swept out of the room.

Miles finally found his voice from wherever it was buried in his body. "Sir, I can explain."

"I said I don't want to know." Rajveer began to button his jacket. "Are you at least ready to go?"

"Yes, sir."

"Fix your collar and let's move."

Miles could only offer another note of compliance, dropping his head in what Rajveer assumed was disappointment over being caught. Rajveer tried to erase the image from his mind's eye as they walked down the stairs, but he couldn't deny he was happy for the boy.

∴ ∵ ∴

The vantage from the fourth story of the bookshop offered Maddox an extended view of the Lumens pouring into the market square toward the stage. Dressed in their robes of green, under the setting Fiedel, they looked like a dark river flowing straight to the heart of the capital. The Gems stood facing out over the crowd at the nearby window to his left, most likely doing the same as him, attempting to locate any possible weapons or anything out of the ordinary.

"Does it feel too calm to you?" Jemma asked. "Like it's almost too easy."

"Well, Lumens have spent a good deal of time remaining mostly compliant." Maddox's breath fogged the window in front of him. "You know they'd follow each other off a cliff if the first was brave enough."

"Sir." Gemmie's voice dripped in disdain at Maddox's sarcasm, and he knew the look she was most likely giving him.

"I know, Gemmie. They aren't very compliant most of the time; that's why we're here, isn't it?"

"I feel like we should be somewhere else and not here."

"And not here?" her twin asked.

"It just doesn't feel right."

Gemmie grunted. "And leave the Second Committer alone with this crowd?"

"He could easily portal away as a last resort."

"You know perfectly well he has no sense of self-preservation. Remember what happened in the alley, trying to be all mighty."

"I guess you're right. Or the time he was trying to impress Theodora in front of Earleen."

"That wasn't to impress," Maddox interrupted, "and you two can stop squabbling as if I'm not right here."

"You're not required to listen, sir."

"If I ever listened to either of you, I'd guarantee we'd be at the bottom of the Bethnec Sea."

∴ ∵ ∴

Theodora stood behind Maddox at the Council building as he spoke with Valix, all three fully decked in their weapons. Maddox was prepared to take the two of them to the castle grounds, the Gems having been delivered to the shop to keep watch as Maddox and Valix would parade through the capital to the market square.

"What is she doing here?" Valix huffed as he approached. Maddox looked back at her, and she merely shrugged her shoulders. She'd done her part, persuading him to take her; now she only needed Maddox to do his: deal with this obstacle. "Why are you looking back at her? She doesn't get to make these decisions...she doesn't speak for you," Valix spat.

"I find your temper exhausting, Second." Maddox rubbed at his brows. "Theodora is going with us. She'll be by my side until we reach the capital and then I'm putting her in the Gems' protection until the ceremony is done."

Bullshit, Theodora thought. She'd never make it to the twins.

"This is stupid! She has no reason to go."

"Your opinion on the matter isn't of significance," Maddox said calmly. "But if you must know, she is a Lumen and should have an opportunity to watch."

"No, after the Council decision, she's a Petran." Valix pointed a finger in her direction. Theodora didn't let her face morph with her feelings. Valix wasn't entirely wrong, but it didn't matter; she only needed Maddox to let her go and she knew he'd see this as an opportunity to *fix* whatever their relationship was after his betrayal. She wished people would stop trying to remedy her like she was some type of problem, but if they were going to continue, why not take advantage of it?

"She's going, Valix. End of discussion."

Valix groaned and punched at the air.

"Such a temper," Theodora mocked.

"Charm…" Maddox warned.

"You shut up!" Valix pointed again at her.

"Point that finger in my direction again, and I'll cut it off and shove it down your throat," she hissed out. Valix flashed his middle finger at her instead. "Such a child." She crossed her arms and rocked back on her heels, knowing she'd won by ruffling him up.

"And what happens when people recognize her?"

Maddox shrugged this time. "Doesn't really matter, does it?" He turned to Theodora. "You suited, charm?"

Already having changed earlier into her all-black attire to match Maddox and Valix, she replied, "I have my dumgun and shinegun, what more do I need?"

Rushed

Each Satelle decorated in their cape followed Rajveer, with Alouette alongside him, her hand warm in his, as they navigated through the tunnels from Amabel's house. While they headed for the castle underground, Amicus lead his own group of Satelles on the topside. It felt odd to return to the castle but was even more so to be removed from his home to begin with.

Though Alouette was without a cape, they all carried stelgladios, daggers, and tampered shineguns. It was a small requirement Rajveer almost forgot during all the commotion, but luckily Helena thought of it and ensured it was taken care of.

Their march was mostly quiet, with only the occasional whisper among the press of boots to the dirt-covered tunnels and the slight hums of their blades. Rajveer previously hadn't noticed the soft noise of their weapons until Theodora had brought it to their attention days ago, or maybe even an entire lifetime ago with how time seemed to move at present.

Alouette squeezed his hand, grabbing for his attention as he slowed to a stop. "Yes?"

"Are you sure this is a good idea? What's a throne without a king to take it?"

"I'd rather die trying to get my capital back than live to see it in the hands of Lawless scum." He brought her hand upward, kissing her knuckles. "I still don't like the idea of you joining us."

"Raj, we made vows to one another." Her eyes appeared darker in the dimmed lighting. "Together."

He leaned forward, brushing her lips with a kiss. "Together," he whispered back before turning and continuing their silent march forward.

Approaching the Klauduisz tomb, Rajveer slowed his group to listen beyond. They had no way to communicate with each other and only held onto hope the others were doing as instructed: Theodora with Maddox, Hakon with the Lumens, and Amicus with the other Satelles, who should have been approaching from the outside of the castle soon. He reluctantly released Alouette's hand, signaling for them to stop their progression. The group gathered along the walls, extreme focus on every step and every breath taken.

Rajveer crept down the long hallway to the stairs that led to the castle above, his wife and soldiers continuing in their silent obedience. His ears felt as if they were ringing in the pure absence of sound. He climbed the stone stairs, stopping a breath away from the wooden door, listening for any noises beyond. They all waited, breaths held, bodies tense in anticipation. It felt like an eternity passed in their frozen state, as if the fates forgot to keep time moving onward.

With a jolt, a flash crystal exploded in the direction of the castle entrance, and they followed the cue, tugging shineguns from their holsters and stelgladios free of their sheaths, riding the wings of hope.

∴ ∵ ∴

A mare whinnied beside Theodora, bringing her out of her trance as she stared at the Seclusian mask in her hands. When they had portaled to Lume, it was the first thing she was handed. It was black metal adorned with gears she'd never learned the purpose for, and now she was expected to wear one at any moment, becoming one of the very people who'd murdered, razed fields, and created orphans.

She focused on the dumgun and shinegun tucked in her worn and weathered boots—*they* were comfort. She only needed to follow the other Seclusians to the market square; then, hoping Hakon and Rajveer took care of their parts, she'd be able to rip the awful thing off. She also hoped it would happen before Valix began his terrible speech—she'd heard him practice bits of it, and it was atrocious. She needed to reevaluate the intelligence of her fellow Lumens for them to even entertain the idea of listening to the likes of him.

In her peripheral, Theodora noticed Valix approach the group of Seclusians, Maddox mounting his horse nearby.

"We head for the market," Valix's commanding voice began. Theodora forced her face to show indifference. "We want to keep the Lumens in the dark about Petram's secret. Therefore, we will be entering the market square on good ol' horseback. We've secured a handful from the Satelle's stables. Find one, partner up if necessary, and get to the market square. There should already be Seclusians on guard there from the setup. We've erected a stage and the pyre near the fountain since we'll be breaking Lumen tradition. Your job is to maintain control of the citizens. Understood?"

Agreement flowed from the crowd of masks. People began making their way into formations. Theodora recalled when the queen had been laid to rest. The priests didn't use a pyre, but rather laid her body into her stone sarcophagus. Blessings and prayers and flowers were thrown as it was loaded into a carriage and returned to the deep belly of the castle. Although she'd hated the man, she couldn't help but wonder what the late king would think of all this. He'd demanded power and forced the underground city to fall to his bidding and for what? His beloved traditions were thrown to the wind and his body would be burned, never to return to his wife again.

"Maddox may trust you, but I don't." Valix's voice broke into her thoughts, sneering in her direction. "There will always be someone watching, so you better not make a fool of yourself, or I will personally see to your execution."

"Don't make promises you're unable to keep." She kept her voice light as she turned to join the formation herself.

When she was fully out of Valix's vision, she braced herself, placing the mask over her face. She felt her hands begin to tremble at the claustrophobia within the mask that immediately consumed her. She followed the Seclusian soldiers in front of her, but with their uniforms and masks, she couldn't locate Valix anymore as they began their parade to the market square.

∴ ∵ ∴

Valix had told the truth. More masked individuals stood guard around the perimeter as well as along the front of the wooden stage. Wood was strategically placed in a pile, covered by a drape of cloth, where another wall of masked guards divided the ceremony from the Lumens who stood waiting in their mourning robes.

As Theodora stood next to Maddox off-stage, she watched Valix ascend the stage stairs and begin speaking to the crowd. *Damnit, where was Rajveer's distraction?* She'd hoped to get out of hearing this. She tried to look at the Lumens through the small slits in the mask, searching their faces, eager to find one in particular.

"When I approach the stage, I want you to go into the building behind me," Maddox whispered. "It has a navy door.

After the ceremony, I'll come find you and we'll see if we can get a moment for you to collect your things from your home."

She nodded her head slightly, letting him know she'd heard him.

"From ground they rose and as ash they will become one with Lume once more." Valix's voice continued to project over the crowd. "We ask our king regent to address our people before we light the pyres."

Maddox began forward, and when he reached the steps, he glanced back at her, jerking his head in the direction of the building before taking the stage. "My Lumens," he began, his voice sending goosebumps skittering across Theodora's skin.

But before he could continue, the Lumens collectively moved, tugging stelgladios from their robes. *Finally.* Theodora ripped the mask from her face and realized the Lumens were not wearing mourning clothes, but rather had wrapped Satelle capes around them, now pushed back to their shoulders. They provided the distraction she needed as she tugged a blade from the waistline of her trousers and searched for Hakon.

Lumens raced in all directions and Theodora tensed to protect herself, but she had no desire to murder these people. She noticed Rabb as he barreled in her direction, his stocky build like a battering ram. Theodora twisted lithely out of the way, swinging her body out of reach of his thick arms. When she turned, he already had the blade raised over his head, preparing to drop. Theodora propelled her legs forward, rotating in the air until she was positioned to the side of him as he swung the blade. She brought her shinegun up, letting the metal of the barrel block the attack.

"Rabb! It's me!" she yelled.

"I know exactly who you are, king killer!" He swung again, enraged. Another swipe and she leaned back, the metal barely missing her neck. She charged forward this time, but when he brought his sword upward, she pressed the barrel of the shinegun to his knee, firing a small blast. She knew he'd survive it and hoped it wouldn't be severe enough to force an amputation, or he'd be treated fast enough—but she didn't have time to find out. He fell in a wail and Theodora turned back, searching the crowd, hoping to avoid another Lumen catastrophe at her hands.

Almost immediately, another Lumen was upon her with a punch to her face, jerking her around. She realized it was Hakon. "Fuck," she grunted. "You don't have to hit *that* hard." The fighting around them almost drowned out her words. When she shook off the dizziness, he swung again, grazing her jaw.

"It's not every day you get an opportunity to hit *the* Theodora," he huffed, bouncing on his toes, eager to continue.

She raised the shinegun when he charged forward. He smacked the gun away before punching her shoulder joint. Pain seared down her arm. He moved to punch again. Theodora attempted to block, but her right arm refused to move. He struck true, the pain ripping further into her back.

Her vision blurred, stars peeking on the edges, and she tried to breathe through the agonizing pain.

"Hakon…" The word was breathless. He shifted to swing again, and Theodora raced to throw her left arm up to stop the blow. "Hakon, it's supposed to be a ruse."

"I'm tired," he said, and he pushed her backward, "of all these"—he pushed again—"little games between"—again—"you, and the king and Seclus."

With his final push, she stumbled, landing hard. She swiped a dagger from the ground and glanced upward as

Hakon strode closer, pulling his stelgladio over his head. *Definitely not part of the plan*, Theodora thought as she scrambled to throw up her only good arm to protect herself. But the blow never landed. She peered upward. Hakon stopped mid-swing before he collapsed in a heap before her. Behind him, Maddox stood, shinegun raised.

∴ ∵ ∴

She's safe, Maddox told himself as he closed the distance to Theodora. He leaned forward to offer her a hand, and she appeared a little too eager to take it. She stumbled for a moment, and he wrapped his arm around her waist, letting her drape her left arm over his shoulder. They started walking, but her shorter stature was making his back stretch in discomfort from awkwardly bending over for so long.

"Fuck it," he whispered before he dropped down to pick her up. Her right arm hung loosely as she grasped at his neck with her fingers. "What's wrong?"

She threw her head back in pain when a missed cobblestone made him jostle her slightly. "Pretty sure it's dislocated." She spoke through gritted teeth.

He got her into an alley and placed her as gently as he could against the wall. Almost immediately, two Lumens charged him.

Slipping out of the grasp of one, Maddox pushed him away when the second rushed. The man attempted a punch, which Maddox slapped away, but not before they used his free hand to bury a blade into Maddox's thigh. Maddox struck the man's forearm, and the blade dragged out, dropping Maddox briefly to his knee. Maddox stared down the man when the first jumped onto his back. A gnarled yell escaped from Maddox, as his knee wanted to buckle beneath him, but he was yanked upward to his feet, the man's arms wrapped tightly around his neck.

Maddox watched the second lunge for Theodora where she attempted to rise. The Lumen reeled his arm backward and Maddox threw his body forward. He launched the attacker on his back forward, knocking him into the other and out of the way. Maddox rose quickly, swinging his fist at their faces, waiting for their heads to loll.

With both Lumens unconscious, Maddox reached his hand outward in Theodora's direction. "You're a worthless fighter if we don't get that fixed immediately." When she grabbed his fingers, he pulled her in front of him and reached for his pocketwatch. The portal opened to meet them, and with a quick glance to ensure no one followed, he pushed her through.

∴ ⁖ ∴

The blade of Rajveer's stelgladio sliced into one of the Lawless in the castle. Once he and his group had exited the stairwell, they'd found disorder from the explosion. Debris and dust filtered into the entryway from the first flash crystal. He raced into the heart of the castle, knowing a second crystal was sure to follow soon.

Rajveer entered the entryway hall with the full intention of finding Alouette's hand and not letting go, but they were separated in mere seconds. The clouded air and tangles of green capes and black apparel covering every person, Lawless and Satelle alike, meant he'd lost her quickly. And with Lawless using their stelgladios and Satelles armed with their shineguns? Chaos was the only word for what was before him.

A Lawless charged him, arms raised overhead with a blade, a guttural war cry roared from his mouth. Rajveer kept his shinegun in his dominant hand as he reared his metallic arm backward with the stelgladio, letting their blades clash together in a fizzle of magnetism before he pushed forward with all the strength the arm offered him. The Lawless quickly fell backward, and Rajveer raised the shinegun, aiming a blast into his chest.

Gathering his confidence, Rajveer continued pushing forward toward the throne room. Another explosion expelled bits of stone and dust to his left. Rajveer ducked to shield his head before looking in that direction. He spotted Amicus amid the tussle of black and green. "Stop blowing holes in the castle. There isn't going to be anything left!" Rajveer shouted to Amicus as he shot two short bursts at a group of Lawless.

"Why do you think that's my fault?" Amicus shouted back, low grunts breaking up the question.

Somehow the path before him cleared, and Rajveer took the advantage, holstering both his stelgladio and shinegun to help garner speed. Before he reached the expansive archway dividing the entryway to the throne room, a Lawless stepped from around the wall, shinegun raised in his direction. Rajveer reached his arm back, grabbing the fabric of his cape to pull in front of him, shielding his body. With the blasts absorbed, Rajveer twirled his arm forward, arching it upward, spinning the cape around the attacker's arm. He grabbed the Lawless' elbow and pulled their body forward, kneeing the Lawless in the groin. He slid his shinegun out and fired a blast into their head, barely seeing the body slip to the ground before he was moving again.

Rajveer strode forward through the threshold and a shadow appeared from his right. He twisted his body, bringing the shinegun upward, but stopped the pull of the trigger when he recognized Helena.

She didn't bat an eye or even flinch, merely picked at a nail before speaking. "I checked and Maddox isn't in the capital—thought you'd want to know everything went as planned. Valix and the Gems are stranded here until, hopefully, the morning, giving you ample time to secure the capital."

"Where did you get a cape like that?"

Helena looked at him in amused puzzlement. "My closet."

"That didn't sound like sarcasm," Amicus offered, out of breath at the archway.

"That's because it isn't. *I* designed the capes."

"Impossible. We have those capes here."

"That's correct. I designed them, and had the plans inserted into an old text that happened to be positioned haphazardly open for your father to see."

"Do you care nothing of family?"

"You should know as well as I, Prince, that sometimes family is merely a shared name."

Another rumble of a flash crystal and Danika stumbled into the room. "Are you all going to stand here talking or are you actually trying to help?" She turned to head back into the attack.

"Wait!" Rajveer called. "Find my wife."

Captured

Curiosity wrangled Helena from Petram to portal into the castle. She'd watched the Satelles in action for the past few minutes, entertained by the way their disgustingly bright gold jackets caught every sparkle of light, but always entranced with how their capes whipped about with their movements, like added shadows.

Maybe it was her pride that dragged her back to see them in their heightened glory. The capes had become not only a useful tool for the Satelles but also an iconic accessory. She'd designed it in her youth, around the time Maddox was born and before he stole her future, reducing her to the Twelfth Committee and *healing* people.

She scoffed out loud from where she remained tucked against an alcove, her arms crossed over her chest, as she watched the continued fight. Helena refused to join in. It was already a dangerous game with her appearing here amidst this coup—the fact that she was a traitor would become obvious, and she didn't need anyone to start assuming she was involved.

A succession of shinegun blasts burst into the room, instantly killing the other three Satelles who helped Rajveer. On instinct, she took a step forward to assist before she remembered she couldn't. She tucked herself deeper into what little shadows the towering pole and stacked ceiling offered.

The Gem twins marched into the room, their braids swishing against their low backs. Rajveer lifted his arm with the shinegun, but the Gems moved too quickly. One lowered herself, sweeping her feet out, arms raised. The other ran to her, linking their hands together, before she swung her lower body upward, using her sister to support her upper half, as her feet collided with Rajveer's face.

He staggered back, but not before the twin who'd kicked him, flipped herself backward, landing next to where Rajveer dabbed at his face, checking for hints of blood.

In a swift movement, she hit Rajveer on the back of the head with her shinegun. His eyes rolled back, and he collapsed forward.

The Gems did not speak out loud to one another, using whatever sibling-twin telepathy they had until they secured ropes around the king's hands and feet. They picked him up and carried him out of the throne room—where the other Lawless no doubt would help them get Rajveer to Seclus.

"Fuck," Helena whispered, and she tugged the tempat free, her fingers quick to move the turners into position. "Leave it to the silly prince to get himself captured."

Falling

They stumbled a room stonework peeking along the edges of the building which Theodora recognized as the underground city. Maddox must've taken them to his room in Seclus. Theodora immediately collapsed onto the bed. The room was small, and with Maddox towering over her, it felt even smaller.

"Will you sit down so I can look at your wound?" she grounded out.

"Shut up, charm. You aren't going to help with shit until we get that shoulder back in place."

"You don't have to do that."

"I think I do." He scrutinized the joint before he spoke again. "I hate seeing you in pain, Theodora." She rolled her eyes and turned away from him. He reached out to lightly grasp her chin, forcing her to look back at him. "I still won't lie to you. I hate seeing you in any pain. I hate it even more when *I'm* the one who caused it." He released her chin, but he didn't drop his gaze for a minute.

When he turned back to her shoulder, he said, "This is something I can fix." And in one swift motion, he pulled, rotated, and popped her shoulder into place. Theodora couldn't stop herself from crying out, tears burning at the corners of her eyes.

"Breathe," he whispered as he rubbed her back, careful not to jostle her shoulder again. "Like I said, *that's* fixable. I don't know what to do about us—what I can do to help."

"Maddox..." She couldn't stop the warning in her voice.

She blinked slowly, letting go of all her questions and regrets, the past slipping away from her mind, and fully embraced what they could've been.

"Let me look at your thigh." She shifted, aware of her shoulder, not eager to put any additional strain on it, at least for a few minutes. The blood was bright against the black of his trousers. "I can't get a good look at it."

"Charm, if you want my pants off, you only need ask."

Theodora shook her head—not even allowing herself to glance up to see that stupid, shit-eating grin she knew was plastered on his face. "I don't want your pants off."

"Sure."

"I need to look at the wound."

"I don't need it looked at; I just need it mended."

"You are *sooooo* incredibly difficult."

"Not as much as you, charm." He raised an arm, pointing at the dresser across the room. "Top drawer on the left. There will be a long, cylindrical tube."

She went over as instructed and glanced around. The room was meticulous. She didn't know the last time he'd been here, but there didn't even appear to be a speck of dust. Not only was it entirely clean, but also there were no signs of it having been lived in either. No décor, no color, nothing. An empty shell of a home.

She found the tube and handed it to Maddox. He made quick work of removing a piece from one end, exposing a large needle. As he sucked in a breath, he jammed it into his thigh, near the wound. Seconds went by, Maddox slowing exhaling, before he withdrew the needle and covered it once more.

"Now in the washroom, get a towel, so I can wipe up the blood."

"So bossy," Theodora said as she went in search of his demands.

"You love it."

She returned and knelt to carefully dab the wound. Maddox trapped her hand beneath his. "You don't have to be gentle. It's healed now." He moved the towel across the wound, and he spoke the truth.

Theodora knelt, touching the small patch of pinkish skin. Pink, but healed. No open wound, no blood, no scab.

"It's a miracle," she whispered.

"No. Just science, charm." His voice was far gruffer than she expected—than it needed to be.

She looked up at him and realization dawned on her that in her eagerness, she'd dropped herself between his legs. Theodora licked her lips, reminding herself this was part of the plan—distract him, let him take his time so she could keep him here, away from whatever chaos was enveloping Lume now. Sure, Hakon might've been a little more zealous than she'd expected, but they'd succeeded in getting Maddox away from the capital.

She swallowed heavily. She moved her hands, letting them rest on his knees for a moment before she rose, his attention wholly on hers, lifting his chin to keep her trapped in his gaze. Not letting herself overthink what she had to do, she closed the distance, gripping his face between her hands and leaning down to kiss him.

As she tried to deepen the kiss, his fingers trailed up her thighs, leaving paths of fire behind. She leaned forward, their tongues eager to remember what had happened barely even a petrik ago. Maddox squeezed her backside with both hands before they slipped further down her thighs, pulling them forward, forcing her to straddle him.

Theodora's fingers tangled in his hair as she savored that cinnamon flavor that never left his mouth. She wanted more of him but was unwilling to break the kiss.

She felt his fingertips dig into her before he lifted her up in his arms. In two strides, they were across the room, Theodora's back pressed up against the wall. Maddox grinded himself against her, his lips kissing softly down her jaw, down her neck.

She was dizzy with desire. But her shoulder began to ache, protesting the position and drastic movement.

"I'm falling," she mumbled against his mouth.

She felt him smile against that sensitive spot near her ear. He whispered back, his breath hot along her skin. "Don't worry, Theo, I won't let you."

Maddox laid in the bed staring at the barely-lit ceiling from washroom lamps. Night would start taking over Seclus now. Although the tunnel sounds started to quiet, Maddox's thoughts only became louder as he let his mind wander through everything that had happened today, unable to move from the warmth of Theodora's body next to his.

It was then that he realized Theodora didn't have a scar on her stomach.

She. Didn't. Have. A. Fucking. Scar.

He didn't wholly realize it until he'd been left to sit here in silence while she laid peacefully, her limbs intertwined with his. But when he thought back, initially blinded by his excitement, he realized she bore no scar. No markings of stitches, no raised texture from any other way Satelles would've patched her back together. She had perfectly smooth skin where Valix had shot her. He was certain of it because he'd kissed her there, determined to try to erase their past, an indirect apology.

And yet, he still struggled to move. He wanted to tell his brain to erase the memory, to alter it somehow, so he could ignore it, act as if it had never happened.

But the conclusion shouted at him within his mind: Theodora was working with someone in Seclus.

Maddox slipped his legs out from hers, tugging the bedsheet back up to cover her. He moved around the room, quietly gathering his things to get dressed. Was this throe of passion all part of whatever scheme Theodora was working on? She was supposed to be helping him deal with Valix, not conspiring with the enemy. Just the thought of Valix's name was enough to snap him out of this deprecating self-pity. For all he knew, Valix could be dead on Lume, which would be far easier than the bullshit he'd need to deal with to have him removed from the committee.

That was the first question he needed answering, then he could focus on Theodora.

Of course, Maddox didn't know where to begin with locating Valix. He buttoned the top of his shirt and withdrew the portal, choosing to settle on the Lumen market square. It would offer the chance of listening to Lumen gossip, an easy source when he needed information quickly. He walked purposefully in the direction of the collapsed stage and eavesdropped on the few who'd chosen to venture nearby.

"I still can't believe King Rajveer survived."

"It's a miracle, that's for certain."

"Can't believe they've actually overtaken the Lawless."

"I heard they ransacked the castle, too. Good day to be Lumen, isn't it?"

The whispering told him enough to know that if any of the three from his committee were alive—and odds said at least one would be—they would've returned to Seclus to guarantee some type of report back to him.

Knowing enough time hadn't passed yet, he succumbed to walking. He strode away from the uncommon ruckus of the capital when he realized another thing was out of place—there were no guards, neither Satelles nor Seclusian. Maddox's brows pushed together inquisitively. If Rajveer had taken back control of the capital, where were his Satelles? And if Valix still had control, why'd Seclusians withdraw from their posts? Unless Valix had directed them to.

Following the stone pathway out of the market, Maddox approached the location of Kadena's stable house, where he knew Theodora typically allowed Down River to stay, choosing her over the stables within the capital's limits. He didn't know what Theodora had done with the mare recently. Cutting through the memories, another oddity surfaced. The would-be, white-washed building remained unlit. It wasn't late enough in the evening that one could assume Kadena was asleep, and even if she was, he remembered the building had a lamppost nearby to illuminate the trek to the stables. Maddox slowed his pace, scratching along his jawline as he stared at the area, as if the answer would appear before him.

He debated following the hill up past the gates surrounding the property to investigate further, but his hand involuntarily twitched, reminding him the charge was complete. In a spin of the dial, he left the questions here for the answers he'd find in the recesses of the underground.

Taking the steps two at a time, he entered Ludi Votivi, looking over the patrons. He spotted the Gems at the bar, both seated and relatively calm.

"Report?" Maddox didn't hesitate.

They both shook their heads as they slunk out of the high-top chairs. Without another glance from him, he proceeded past them to a door at the back of the den leading to Gustavo's office. As soon as the door shut behind them, both twins spoke simultaneously.

"There was an attack at the castle."

"Rajveer is alive!"

"What?" Maddox questioned, trying to listen to both. They repeated their comments, separately this time.

"What do you mean an attack?"

"When the Lumens started fighting," Gemmie began, "we initially thought it was anger toward the ceremony. But we felt something was amiss; it seemed too organized and convenient, so we returned to the castle. There was a group of Satelles attempting to take back control of the throne. They'd used our flash crystals to blow open the front entrance and we learned they'd gotten shineguns."

"Shineguns? More evidence we have a traitor in Seclus helping." Maddox paused. *What the fuck was Theodora doing?*

"What do you mean?" Gemmie asked.

"Wait, why aren't you surprised about Rajveer?" Jemma questioned.

"I was already having Mekari investigate Rajveer's death from the start since the Digere was burned down. I think we have a traitor among us."

"Do you have any additional information to tell us who?"

"Nothing concrete." He didn't need someone else looking into Theodora yet. She'd sniff it out immediately. "But this helps to support the thought that Rajveer clearly has someone working with him."

"There's more, sir. We found tunnels within the Klauduisz tomb, connecting various shops and Kadena's stable house to the castle. We think it's how they were able to move the king unnoticed. We have a handful of Seclusians mapping out the various connections as we speak."

"Come on, Gemmie, you're not telling him the best part." There was excitement in Jemma's voice, which he wasn't used to hearing. "We were able to capture Rajveer." Jemma clapped with excitement, as if she'd won an award.

"Is he being detained here?"

"Yes. Although we were able to remove him from the castle, the throne remains in possession of the Satelles and the other Lumens. When we saw him by himself near the throne room, we took the opportunity to grab him, as we didn't have enough force to take back total control. We left Valix in the capital, but he returned a few moments ago. He's down with Rajveer now, most likely preparing him for questioning."

Maddox moved around the twins to open the door, to track down Valix, when Jemma stepped in front of him. "We couldn't find you after the Lumens began their attack. Where'd you go?"

"Don't worry about it."

"As you wish, Committer."

∴ ∵ ∴

It didn't take long for the three of them to make their way to the detention cubes. Valix dropped his hand from rubbing his face and strode forward. "And where have you been?"

"My whereabouts are of no concern to you." Maddox closed the distance between them, side-eying a fellow Seclusian. He dropped his voice, looking down at Valix. "You will also learn to mind your place, Second. Defy me with witnesses present again and I'll have your rank stripped from this committee. Am I understood?"

Valix huffed out a breath, biting his lip in apparent compliance.

"I asked you a question."

"Understood, sir."

Maddox maintained eye contact with Valix a moment longer, ensuring his words held the vindication of a promise as opposed to an empty threat. Satisfied, they turned in the direction of where Rajveer was detained.

Imprisoned

He knew he hadn't been imprisoned for long, but the darkness already infiltrated Rajveer's mind. His eyes played tricks on him with the way the shadows shifted in the smallest way, making him question what was real and what was his imagination.

He'd dropped his head into his hands where he squatted within the intricate field detaining him; the cube gave off barely a faint glow and the buzz along his skin felt familiar, like that of the stelgladios, offering the slightest indication he was close to the perimeter. The Gems had stripped him of his weapons, naturally, as well as his cape and jacket.

He rubbed his fingers along his brow and down the bridge of his nose, feeling somewhat defeated but not entirely surprised given his luck from the fates. Rajveer wasn't concerned about what would become of him. No, the issue his mind warred with was what would happen to Alouette and his people. At least he'd given Lume a queen. With Helena's help and the use of his Satelles, Alouette was smart enough to continue the control they'd gained. They only needed to find a way to get rid of this arrogant prick.

"I could take a drink now!" Rajveer shouted into the vast dark, knowing perfectly well if anyone brought him anything, it would only be water. Maybe he could make wine his final request before he died.

He stared at the cube, letting his eyes focus and unfocus, blurring the glow before blinking it back to shape once more. He didn't know how long he did it, with the faint whooshes and clinks from the belly of the world as his only companions before a thought alighted in his brain.

But what of his metallic arm? It'd been constructed by a Petran, but he'd never seen anyone in Seclus, or Lume for that matter, with other similar limbs. Images flashed through his mind of Maddox's possible home world filled with metallic people and humans armored in metal. Was it possible? Fates, it could be, but he needed to take the gamble.

Tentatively, Rajveer reached his left arm outward in the direction of the cube, the buzzing intensifying as he shoved his pinky closest to the invisible wall. He stopped his progress when he felt a steep pressure on his finger, yet he merely gritted his teeth and pushed forward. It felt like a ripping sensation, but he noticed nothing physically along the metal of his arm. He continued forward, shoving his tunic sleeve past his elbow, and yet he could see no physical markings. If he did any actual damage to the arm itself, he was sure Helena could fabricate him a new one, which was much better than the alternative.

He finally pushed through far enough to grasp the cube, the light making shadows dance along the cavern walls around him. He picked up the little box but was only able to bring it in slightly, the intensity of whatever weird tech radiated around it and making the rest of his body itch with a burning sensation. He twirled the cube between his fingers, trying to determine a way to deactivate whatever the irritant was.

Rajveer sighed to himself, finding only smooth surfaces emitting its mocking glow. "Well," he said to whatever creatures may have lurked in the darkness with him, "if I'm gonna die, it's going to be after I enjoy my last drink. Or at least damn it all to try."

With his fingers still firmly grasped around the cube, he rose from his squat, his arm outstretched away from him as he tentatively took a step forward. The electric current around him pulsed through his skin but slowed again. His metallic arm remained intact, so he proceeded to the nearby archway. With a few more steps forward, he crossed the threshold, or the stack of boulders, which seemed to act as some type of division before entering a tunnel. It was more lit than where he'd been, yet still visibly within the ground.

Rajveer made an educated assumption they were in Seclus. Although his kidnappers had put a hood over his head, he believed if a portal had been used, he'd be able to tell. He was curious about what the highly advanced underground city looked like. With another step, all ideas of what Seclus would've been remained in his imagination as he was stopped by a Seclusian on guard in his cavern of solitude.

"What are you doing?" The guard's voice was gruff, but it seemed to be his actual timbre as opposed to an attempt at intimidation.

"Oh, I'm sorry." Rajveer awkwardly turned, the cube still limiting his movements. "I've somehow found myself trapped in this thing. Seems to be some kind of mistake, though."

"Nice try, Lumen."

"Well, there's certainly no sense in going down without a fight."

"You call this a fight?" he grunted, looping his fingers through the weapon belt slung along his hips.

"Obviously. Can't you see it? It's a fight for a small favor." Rajveer indicated the smallest amount with two fingers of his free hand.

"What do you want?" Although the man appeared skeptical, he was offering an opening, which was more than Rajveer expected.

"Just a glass of some wine, or…" he paused after trailing off. "'What's the stuff around here? Vocatus?"

The man wasn't allowed the chance to decide before Maddox, Valix, and the twins turned into view from around a boulder. Without hesitation, Valix questioned the Seclusian.

"He walked out of the hold like that," the one guarding Rajveer's underground hole spoke. "Clearly his metal arm gave some protection against the holding field."

"Clearly," Valix deadpanned.

"He requested a glass of vocatus." The guard's voice was accusatory.

"You're just going to give me away like that?" Rajveer acted baffled. "I thought we were becoming friends."

"And what do you think?" Valix proffered, but immediately denied the guard's response with a dismissive wave. "Actually, you shouldn't even be thinking, should you? You should be doing as ordered."

Maddox interrupted. "Go ahead, Brannon, get the Lumen king a glass. I doubt anyone present at Petram's committee will debate much, and soon Rajveer will be joining his father. Grant him his last request."

Rajveer was grateful for the decency but didn't miss the unspoken exchange between Maddox and Valix–something was amiss, something that hadn't been present mere days before. It was odd to see, but it might be an advantage, at least one for Alouette and his Satelles.

Maddox turned to leave, and Rajveer caught his attention. "Maddox? What am I to do with the cube?"

"Give it a roll and see if your odds improve."

∴ ∵ ∴

The portal itself was not a new phenomenon to see in front of him, but knowing the one before him led Rajveer to a new world was a slightly out of body experience, even if the gracious amount of vocatus he'd consumed helped numb his nerves and prevented him from fully thinking clearly. His hands were bound in front of him, one metallic ring firmly locked around his metal wrist separately before connecting to his other. He proceeded forward, an energy forming around him as he passed through the lighted ring of orangish-yellow. Rajveer glanced upward, where he toed the line between the two worlds, a rip in the landscapes around him, dark underground tunnels blending into bright blue. Rajveer's gaze followed the cloudless sky down to a tall structure covered in vines like a sleeping green giant.

Although Rajveer followed the ones who had been his allies a few days before through a small courtyard, he wasn't entirely disappointed to see Petram appeared to be a real-life paradise. If he'd woken up here, he would've thought he'd died and gone to the Land of the Fates.

They entered the sleek building, the doors opening automatically for them. "Anyone want to let me know where we're headed?"

"Why does that matter to you?" Valix asked, anger lancing the words.

Rajveer glanced to the side and noticed one of the twins had a sly grin on her face.

"Mere curiosity," Rajveer said as he offered his own smile to the twin. "And with this portal ability, why don't we arrive precisely where we need to? Why do I have to walk into the building?"

"You know, Maddox," said the other twin, "I don't think I like this one. He talks too much."

"I mean *I* personally love myself," said Rajveer as he brought his hands to his chest, "so I would prefer living, if I have any vote in the matter."

"Oh! Are we voting again?" the first twin asked, sarcasm clear in her tone.

"No." Valix's response was short and terse.

"Someone must've been riding him hard recently," Rajveer mumbled under his breath.

"You mean, he hasn't been ridden," the first twin began. "Your jokes are lacking, handsome king."

"One, I wasn't entirely prepared to have company. And two, I really didn't want to let anyone down in my final moments."

"Do any of you shut up? The Gems aren't allowed to take leave again; it makes them too likable." Maddox turned to face them all, stopping them in a hallway before another set of double doors. The doors beyond him opened on their own accord as if to beckon them forward. Rajveer swallowed down his fears, his regrets like an added chaser.

Fates, how he would change everything if given the chance, or he at least liked to think he would've, deep down knowing this was the only path for him.

Rajveer followed his escorts, the doors unceremoniously dumping them into a vast room filled with people. They appeared no different than the mash of people he'd seen within the capital city, but their clothing marked them as other. Most here wore sharp lines along their fabric's edges, sleek metal accessories of gold and silver, as well as shades of rose and ebony that were new to him, accenting their attempts at soft fabric. Some wore several layers, folds upon folds, to give their outfits an entirely new dimension and shape. But no matter the fabric choices, the people still felt sterile and stiff, like the temple workers he'd witnessed performing ceremonies when he was a boy with his parents.

His vision jumped over the crowds of people and immediately snagged on the massive wall beyond, illuminated with some type of lighting from the rear, showing images of various pictures and text as if conjured by someone's thoughts.

Rajveer forced his mouth to remain closed, refusing to give any of these Petrans the satisfaction of seeing him impressed. He clenched his teeth as he continued following the group along the center aisle of tables leading to the front of the room. His eyes caught on where Helena stood behind one of the arched tables in the middle of the room, her face remaining stoic, refusing to give their acquaintanceship away. But he was unable to suppress his surprise when his eyes found Theodora.

Friend

How in the fates was Rajveer here? Theodora couldn't stop her jaw dropping from surprise, but she quickly regained composure. Why did every plan involving the Satelles and Seclusians turn into actual shit? She wasn't sure which were the culprits, but she needed to become uninvolved with these two sides.

Although his wrists were bound, Rajveer appeared to have a calm grace about him; looks were always deceiving though, because she knew his emotions must be waging a war inside him.

Jemma tugged him forward to stand in front of the committee tables, and it wasn't lost on Theodora that a few days prior she'd been where he stood now. She forced herself not to meet Helena's eyes, at least not yet. Luckily, all the Council discussions were open assembly, otherwise someone might question her attendance.

Theodora shifted and she felt the weight of the dumgum in the hem of her trousers move slightly. Although she assumed she'd need the weapon to protect herself from Valix, not to defend a friend's life.

Friend. Was that what Rajveer was? That's what he'd been before she'd feloniously accused him. Friends were rare to find, yet maybe when both were hurt by something out of their control, they could find the trauma as common ground to befriend another once more. Friend, yet... In this chaotic madness of two worlds poised against one another, she would not choose one over the other. It would not be Lume versus Petram.

She would choose those who cared for the betterment of people, of life; favor those who appreciated what she could offer, no matter how little.

The Chancellor's voice calmly commanded the room. "Second Committer, you have the floor for the emergency meeting to discuss the life of the detained. Present and proceed with your accusations."

"Thank you, Chancellor, and those committee members for convening on such short notice." Maddox clasped his hands behind his back and started at a slow, leisurely pace. Theodora risked a quick glance in Helena's direction, finding her gaze was unmet, Helena's focus firmly on where she picked her nails. "As the Council knows, the Second Committee went to Lume yesterday with the intention of holding the funeral ceremony for the last remaining vestiges of the Klauduisz line. However, during that time, we were ambushed, and later learned the Lumen king remains alive. We've taken him, detained, for actions against the common peace of Petram, and he now stands before you for judgment."

Maddox paused, and Theodora wasn't sure if he had wished to speak more, or if this was a planned pause.

"And the Second Committee's recommendation?" A woman spoke, her bald head glistening under a beaded veil. Theodora swallowed, turning back to Maddox, but the voice filling the room next was not his but Valix's.

"I'm certain my Committer will be willing to give Rajveer an opportunity to defend himself, yet I must intervene to give my dissent on the continuation of this meeting."

"On what grounds?" the bald woman asked.

"Are we really going to entertain this?" Maddox stepped forward, throwing a hand back in the direction of Valix. "This is yet another occasion now in which my second has stepped out of his required duties. I'm going to request that the Council, immediately, discuss stripping his rank and having him removed from the Second Committee. He undermines my decisions and continues to question the authority granted to me."

"Authority that must be questioned. You continue to make decisions out of selfishness—"

"That is quite enough." The Chancellor's voice interrupted the debate, silencing the small murmurs, which had begun to circulate among those present. "This is not the time nor the place. You two are bickering like children, and not Petran children either, I'll admit that. Maddox, present your recommendation. Valix, you are to keep your mouth shut. One more word from you and you'll be removed from this room personally by Stavros."

Theodora knew little of the political dynamics of the Council but had learned Stavros was Valix's father. It must be some significant threat, as Valix hung his head.

"Given Petram's ultimate goal with Lume, we have no choice but to have Rajveer executed," Maddox continued his argument. Almost all members of the Council nodded slowly, deliberately, in agreement. "We need to secure Lume under our control, and as long as he lives, he remains a symbol of hope to his citizens."

"Are there any in disagreement?" the Chancellor asked, looking carefully at each member.

"Do I have a vote in the matter?" Rajveer asked, raising a hand, the other one bound with it.

Theodora's gaze shifted between the Chancellor and Maddox, to Helena; to anyone who might intervene.

"Rajveer Klauduisz, Lumen king, it is deemed under our scrutiny you are a dangerous man against those of Petram and therefore will be executed. Maddox, with your shinegun, you administer the lethal shot. Any final words?"

"All I'm gonna say is you'll miss me." He pushed his shoulders back and faced fully in the direction of where Maddox stood. Theodora didn't understand how in a matter of moments a decision regarding someone's *life* was so easily found. As Maddox raised his arm, preparing to take aim, Theodora vaulted over the tables in front of Rajveer, arms outstretched to attempt to block the aim with her body.

"Wait! Please!" Theodora's body remained fixed across Rajveer.

"What is it you wish to say, Theodora? Although your time to indicate you disagreed was mere moments ago. I'm only allowing the delay since you are recently becoming accustomed to our ways," the Chancellor said. Theodora didn't know how much sway she had with Maddox's father; probably significantly less than she could hope for.

"Please." Her voice seemed too small in the grand room. She kept her attention on Maddox though, instead of everyone else or even the Chancellor. He'd be the one to persuade the room to prevent this from happening. "Please," she tried again, "let him live. You only need resources from Lume, and he can be your ally. We can work together in harmony, or even with minor agreement, but let the Lumens keep their hope."

"For what?" Maddox asked, lowering the weapon.

"For me." Tears rimmed her eyes. She'd do this. She'd save Rajveer and help Lume. "Didn't you always say I was meant to save Lume? Well, here I am. Don't let me fail in that."

"We're to just let him go?" Maddox asked. "Let him know of this world and expect no repercussions?"

"Maddox, we can find a way to make this work. Seclus didn't get a chance with Rajveer's father; let your people find a way to live on Lume peacefully with Rajveer."

"What are you going to do? Stay on Lume? Be a part of his court?"

"No." Her voice cracked slightly. "I'll be here, with you. Helping Petrans here with managing Seclus so this alliance can turn into a benefit for everyone."

"No retirement?"

Retirement. No, Theodora didn't give herself a moment to think about that. "Petram seems like a pretty good place to spend my life, free of being Lawless."

Maddox turned to the Chancellor, some unspoken words clearly passing through their expressions, although she couldn't translate them properly.

The Chancellor faced the assembly then turned to the Council. "I'm in agreement with our new Petran, Theodora. We need resources and with her oversight and relationship with the new Lumen king, we can still obtain those and proceed to move forward with the exploration plan.

"Theodora," the Chancellor continued, "you are bound to never return to Lume. Your feet are to never touch Lumen soil again, or it will be considered a traitorous act against Petram. Rajveer, you are bound to never return to Petram. Your feet are to never touch Petran soil again, or it will be considered a traitorous act against Petram. You both will communicate through Maddox and Maddox alone. He and the Second Committee will remain the only ones free to portal between the worlds." She didn't look at Helena. Theodora kept her attention solely on the Chancellor as her fate was sealed.

This hadn't been part of their plan. She'd never see Down River again; nor Amabel or Kadena, nor Rabb or

Hakon, nor the Lumen children whom she'd loved to watch racing through the streets. The cottage would remain abandoned forevermore.

"All in agreement?"

The Council mumbled amongst their tables, angled their faces, and spoke in hurried whispers, until one by one they waved their hands in agreement.

"Unanimous, it seems. Always a good result for an emergency meeting. Maddox, secure those resources immediately. This project is already on the verge of being delayed and I don't want to see it happen. Dismissed."

The citizens were eager to leave, heading for whatever necessary jobs were required of them. The committee members, not eager to stay behind either, rose and grouped up with others before exiting down the center aisle as well. Theodora wasn't blind to the fact Valix and the Gems stayed eerily still as if movement might bring additional attention to them. She was surprised by Valix's composure, certain he'd break the demand from Maddox.

"Little dove?" Helena caught her attention, and Theodora eyed her warily before angling her body slightly. "I'm not sure how much I can help with your adjustment to Petram, but I'm at your disposal."

"I'm going to take care of my adjustments tonight; just prepare yourself."

"Sorry, for the interruption," a man with a patch over one eye said, Theodora recognizing him from the committee table. "The Second has always been a reactive sort, sometimes causing the committee to turn from what would be an easier path. I think you are a wonderful addition to them, hopefully you can bring some added balance." Theodora assumed her face must have questioned his approach. "You see, we've been monitoring Lume for some time and therefore have learned a lot about you. It's a shame we couldn't have met under better circumstances. The name's Whittaker, and I work with the Sixth Committee on agriculture projects."

"Did you help with the Paste idea?"

"My committee did, yes, although it was my ancestors who helped to see the project through to completion."

"Well, it's very nice to meet you, Whittaker." Acknowledging she must have come off as terse, she forced a smile on her face, imagining one of the Lumen shopkeepers in his place. "You'll have to excuse my manners, but I'd like to say goodbye to my king."

"Certainly." He left her with a small bow.

Theodora opened her mouth to speak again to Helena, but with an almost imperceptible shake of her head, Helena turned in the other direction to mingle with other committers, Theodora could only assume.

Theodora shifted her body in the direction of where Rajveer was currently being detained, Petran guards in their full black encircling him until he was sent back to Lume. She wouldn't allow herself the chance to think about the consequences of what'd just happened, focusing only on the present situation. If only to keep her sanity, but also to keep her attention on the large number of Petrans surrounding her, few she would even remotely begin to trust.

Only taking a few steps, Maddox entered her path, forcing her to slow. "I guess you are to thank for listening to me." She tried to push genuine gratitude into her voice, but it sounded forced in her own ears.

"You better know what you're doing. This won't end well for either of you. This isn't a game."

"Isn't that what it's always been? I didn't force your hand Maddox; this won't be on me."

"Bullshit." Maddox closed the distance between them. "I know you've betrayed me, working with some Seclusian traitor. In case you didn't know before, Petram is your home now. You need to get your priorities in line by the time he's portaled back to Lume, because the three of us will be working closely together to ensure these resources are secured and more portals can be manufactured."

How did he know? The question echoed in her brain, but she schooled her facial features, focusing on the rest of his demands. "I'm well aware of what the Chancellor ordered and what I agreed to in order to save Rajveer's life." Theodora stepped around him toward Rajveer.

"What was it for?" Maddox's hand wrapped around her upper arm. Tight enough to grab her attention, but not firm enough that she couldn't slip away if she wanted to.

"What do you mean?"

"Why save him? Why does *he* matter?"

"He'd do the same for me."

"Would he? With such a short time you've known each other, you think he'd risk everything for you?"

"Who said I risked anything for him?" Theodora jerked her arm away. She wanted to remind Maddox that he'd ensured she had nothing left to lose by bringing her here. Instead, she chose to swallow the words down as she produced another sentence in its place. "Sometimes the path with the most resistance turns out to be the easiest in the end."

Vengeance

Rajveer watched as Theodora spoke with Helena, some unknown Petran, and Maddox. It felt like an eternity until she finally approached, although he wasn't entirely sure why he'd expected her to say anything before he was portaled off world.

Though she was dressed in her usual style, which was unique to Lume, here in the presence of other tinkerers, she looked at ease. The small smile she'd given to the unknown man appeared sincere. Rajveer sifted through the small memories in his head, trying to determine if he'd ever witnessed anything even remotely similar on Lume.

Unfortunately, the answer was he hadn't.

In a short amount of time, he'd begun to trust Theodora. Obviously to a fault, or to a believed falsehood merely days afterward, and yet he couldn't fully hate her. He harbored some ill-feelings, sure, given he thought she'd betrayed not only him but also Lume. But even in this moment, surrounded by others who'd not yet gained her trust, she sacrificed again for his people.

"Consider your debt paid," Rajveer said by way of introduction once Theodora was close enough. The Petran guards stayed firmly nearby.

"What debt is that?"

"We've both betrayed each other under the wrong assumptions. I won't go back to Lume with the possibility of unreturned favors. We've both sacrificed and bled for our own over the last few days. I wanted it clear we owe nothing further to each other outside of our general agreement to work with one another as leaders of our respective worlds."

Theodora glanced down, and Rajveer was certain she almost saw a flash of disappointment in her face. "That's it? That's your goodbye?"

"In the presence of your new citizens, yes." Rajveer offered his hands to hers, and she clasped them. He pulled her forward, kissing her cheek, but when he moved to kiss the other cheek, she spoke quickly and quietly.

"When Fiedel sets, the rocks of Undost River. *Only you.*"

Rajveer jerked his eyes in her direction, meeting her gaze. He was certain his mouth hung open as words raced through his brain, but by the time he was prepared to speak, she'd already turned and disappeared.

∴ ∵ ∴

Theodora was slightly surprised by how the Petrans failed to interrogate their new citizen. Did Maddox report so much that most weren't even remotely curious about her, especially with her life now bound here?

It didn't matter though now. There were plans to set into motion, the first being leaving the high community building so Maddox could push Valix to his breaking point. She knew Valix would follow her, especially with how the decision of the Council had fallen. Valix had become predictable, which was the easiest beginning of a trap.

∴ ∵ ∴

Maddox watched Theodora as she approached Rajveer. He figured she'd offer one final word before they departed, but there was something amiss he couldn't place. It wasn't the kingly gesture that felt awry, rather the tensing of Theodora's muscles when it occurred.

Shaking his head, he brought his attention back to the conversation at hand. He stood in discussion with the Chancellor and his mother as well as Valix's parents. Valix's father made his displeasure known.

"You can provide them with all the information, Stavros," the Chancellor said, "but without any regard to make the right decisions, it becomes fruitless."

"I don't understand where he faltered. You would think being a son of a committer, being second to a committer of his own…"

"You cannot compare your son to mine. Trust me, Maddox has made mistakes of his own. Haven't you?" The Chancellor looked in his direction, but continued before Maddox could acknowledge him. "Give them time. They've spent a far deal of time off world, away from our directions and from universal knowledge. They'll adapt as they always do."

"Yes, I guess you're right, Chancellor. I never expected such outright disagreement toward authority from him." Stavros rubbed at the thick beard growing along his jaw.

"If I can make a recommendation?" Maddox asked as he clasped his hands behind his back. On Lume he needed to exert command and authority; here, he'd need to show obedience of his own if he was going to get the Chancellor to agree.

"Go ahead, Second Committer," the Chancellor granted.

"I think it would be to everyone's benefit for Valix to be put on leave. After the number of fiedations he's served on Lume, he should be more than qualified to earn it."

"Yes," Stavros asked, "but for how many days are you recommending?"

For once Maddox stumbled over his words. "Permanently, sir."

"What would he participate in if not securing resources from Lume?"

"Valix could do well in one of the local mining projects."

"Mining projects?" Valix strode into their circle of conversation. "Seriously? After a lifetime together, that's what you're going to try to succumb me to?"

"Valix, you know you're out of control. The Chancellor and your father agree."

"You mean our fathers. They don't know what actual control or power is. They've become blinded with false ideologies."

"Maybe you're a little too close to Lume. Clearly, you've spent too much time with these other Lumens." Stravros attempted to soothe his son's temper.

"No, Father, he's the one" —Valix jutted an arm in Maddox's direction—"getting too close to Lumens. My loyalty is to Petram. I know what my duties are—"

"Do you? Given your recent outbursts and your inability to obey commands, it's hard to believe." Stavros inclined.

"Am I required to obey commands of someone who is no longer adequate to fulfill their role?"

Maddox didn't respond; it wasn't necessary for him to. Valix was making the argument for him, providing more and more evidence of why he needed to be removed from Lume.

With a new second in position, Maddox could focus more on whatever was happening between Theodora and Rajveer to ensure a smooth transition and success in crafting more portals. The portals remained his highest priority, as they would produce technology for the other committees to begin their colonization protocols. He knew the Chancellor would be making the same conclusion, one Stavros already feared.

"Valix," the Chancellor began, and immediately Valix's face deflated before the order even left his mouth. "You will switch to the mining project. Due to the Tenth Committee' having already being established, you'll have no role or title there. You are to report directly to Mien."

"Not only am I being switched protocols, but also you're demoting me? Where's my chance before the Council to make any sort of argument?"

"As always, there are chances to move up rank. You'll have to show you can obey orders first though. And no. With two Committers presenting arguments in favor of your dismissal in your current position, as well as evidence I've witnessed myself, this won't be required to be presented before the Council. If they find ill intentions, a member can request a meeting themselves. Any requests by you to have one will immediately be vetoed."

Valix lifted his head, tugging the lapels of his jacket. "If there is nothing else, sirs."

"No, you're dismissed."

Without an acknowledgment, he turned away from them. Stavros and the Chancellor continued their discussion, but Maddox's gaze followed Valix. He'd kept a cool appearance in the room, but once Valix neared the doorway, his face darkened with revenge. Maddox needed to get Rajveer back to Lume, so he could ensure Valix didn't turn to vengeance instead of obedience.

Future

In a short time, Rajveer felt a wide range of emotions. He felt guilt and despair and acceptance of the possibility his life would be ending. Even with the vocatus allowing him a small moment of peace, he'd been scared knowing Alouette would be left fighting for Lume in an interplanetary war. His Satelles would've helped see her safe and ensure her position as queen, but that knowledge 'didn't stop the emotions. With the alcohol wearing off, he craved another glass even more than before.

But now he was going back home. He couldn't fully appreciate what that meant though, because of what Theodora had mentioned to him before he departed. *The rocks of Undost River.*

He knew the place. Having earned no special title other than "the rocks," they were positioned near the abandoned town of Perdit, where the Undost River and the Bethnec Sea met. Large boulders of reddish rock staggered into a crude circle, they were a demarcation of something ancient. The stories scribed into their old text never indicated what they meant or why the town had been forsaken. Of course, there were myths and lore that occasionally sprouted throughout the fiedations, a gentle reminder the place still existed.

Some, especially those educated by the Reme Temple, spun tales of the fates. One involved a fate, angered by the actions of the Lumens, who pounded a fist on their continent, rocks sprouting from his rage, his fury destroying Perdit. Others told outlandish lore of sea demons attacking klaud raiders hidden in the town, a cascade of turbulent waves raining down on the area from both the coast and the sky.

Most perplexing though wasn't which fantastical myth might ring most closely to the truth, but why Theodora wanted to meet there and within a short time, too. There were no windows in the committee room where he impatiently waited for Maddox to open a portal for him to return. The walls were concealed by screens. He'd have to make it back to the castle, unless Maddox would be ever-so-gracious as to take him there, to find Alouette and his Satelles, and to secure the capital as well as a team to go with him. Even if Theodora's voice had hinted at a warning for only him to be present, Alouette would never allow it. Never mind what Amicus would say at the possibility; he'd most likely laugh.

Maddox left whatever discussion he was participating in and finally approached. With Theodora's comment, Rajveer felt a boost of confidence. He was almost sure Maddox knew nothing of what Theodora had planned. Oh, how the tables had turned. Then again, Rajveer was none the wiser. Did she have hopes to destroy them both?

Maddox said nothing as he tugged the pocket watch from his jacket, playing with whatever turners and pieces would open the portal.

"Why a pocket watch?" Rajveer's curiosity couldn't be smothered.

"You never think twice about looking at such an object. It's a timeless piece. It fits into your outdated world of technology and yet isn't at odds with our efficient one."

"You know…" Rajveer moved closer to the portal, the odd energy making him twitch slightly. The feeling was like what he'd experienced when he'd forced his metal arm through the detention cube and the sensation that wrapped about stelgladio blades. "With how you view the world, you could do far more good."

"Good is subjective, Lumen King. Who is to say what I'm doing isn't for the greater good? Maybe what's best for most people doesn't include what's best for you?"

"Where are you taking me?" Rajveer asked, changing the subject. He wasn't sure he wanted to attempt to process the implication within Maddox's comment. Maddox always made him think far more than he ever wanted to.

"Home."

Rajveer stepped through the portal and realized he was in his old bedroom. He almost wanted to pass out in relief at the sight. "Why here? You could've portaled me to the northernmost point of Lume."

Maddox shrugged. "For your good," he said with a smirk. "Besides, we have a long future of working together, best not to start off in the wrong direction."

Plan

As soon as Theodora left the Council building, she ran as hard as she could in the direction of the workshops Maddox had previously shown her. After the few days being on Petram and being portaled around by Maddox everywhere, she realized how dependent she'd already become on such transportation.

If any of the Petrans found her outburst odd, no one tried to stop her. Occasionally someone's gaze would follow as she streaked past, but they immediately returned to whatever had their attention before.

When Maddox gave her a tour, she'd paid attention to every piece of information he proffered. He thought she was eager for her future here, not realizing she'd never be a pawn in someone else's game again; she was a queen.

Theodora slowed outside of the building, and Helena appeared from the shadows. "Doing a lot of work in a short amount of time, little dove."

"We have to. Maddox's too smart. He already thinks I'm involved in something. He just assumes it's with someone in Seclus right now. He'll start to realize something is wrong if we don't act on our plan immediately. Right now, he's focused on me imploring him to save Rajveer and getting Valix off his committee. If we give him time, he'll figure this out."

"The best plan is no plan?"

"Oh, it's a plan," Theodora said. "Just not detailed and fully thought out."

"Here's what you asked for. I'll see you inside."

∴ ∵ ∴

Helena struggled with leaving Theodora to take care of everything, but she'd been right when she warned Helena that she was their best option. Helena's involvement remaining a secret would ensure that if the plan failed, there was still hope.

Hope. The one thing Theodora always brought back to Lume time and time again.

∴ ∵ ∴

Once the portal closed and Maddox was off Lume, Rajveer raced to the windows to push the curtains aside. Fiedel skimmed along the horizon. Fates above, Theodora was trying to kill him. He grabbed a spare stelgladio from the corner, slipping it into his empty sheath, and left in search of Alouette and his Satelles. Time was against them.

∴ ∵ ∴

After Helena gave Theodora a case of detonators, they entered the building, a sense of foreboding filling Theodora's lungs as if she needed it to survive instead of air. Initially Theodora had requested flash crystals, but Helena told her of something better. The detonators were small, barely longer than the screens Seclusians wore along their arms.

The case was tucked into the belt of her trousers as she toed quietly into the main hall of the building. As she passed alcoves and small crevices, she planted detonators like a trail to the workshop. She expected there to be a handful of workers, but many of them must've gone to the Council building to witness the Lumen king's fate. Helena was to use the portal immediately after Theodora separated and hid inside the workshop since keeping Helena's identity hidden was key.

Theodora approached the top of the workshop stairs, and the few workers inside barely glanced at them. She made it down, checking to make sure no one witnessed her continued placement of the detonators. The table she'd seen portal plans depicted on had a Petran sitting at it, perched on a high stool, pencil-like pieces stuck behind both ears. She almost didn't notice them around the full beard covering his face. It was rare for those on Lume to wear facial hair, and when she'd seen it occasionally in the other cities, it had been unwieldy, like her own thick knots. But this Petran's beard was slick and shaped with harsh lines following his face, all neatly trimmed.

She looked down at the table, so at odds with her own at home covered with papers and books. Here massive screens stacked neatly along its surface, with a couple larger screens held above it.

The Petran peered up at her for a moment before turning back to the screen along the table, one of the pencil-like pieces in his hand. She peered over his shoulder and saw he was sketching out an elaborate design. She couldn't entirely tell what it was supposed to be, but it looked like a small shape cut open to reveal a cylindrical tube as well as some wiring and gears. Although Theodora was here for a very specific purpose, she couldn't help but ask. She felt as though she were a child again, witnessing her parents with their tinkering.

"Why don't you use paper?"

He lifted his head and turned in her direction. "Paper?"

"Yeah, paper. You're using some type of pencil-y thing and no paper."

"This"—he lifted the object—"is a stylus. And these"—lifting one of the screens—"are NoteScreens. You can sketch or make notes on them, and they become integrated into the computer. I'm not sure what this paper is you speak of."

"You don't have any? Do you not use trees?"

"You're Theodora, right?" She nodded. "I thought I recognized you from when you came down before with Maddox. No, we don't use trees for that. Wait a second." He held up a finger, tucking the stylus next to the others behind his ear. How he kept two there was about as much of a mystery as this paper conversation. He swiped his hand upward, and a rectangle with letters all over it appeared. He quickly moved his fingers over the letters, making them show up on the table screen. He typed 'paper,' and with a blink another screen showed a series of pieces of information, but Theodora couldn't absorb any of the words in front of her. Wonder escaped her mouth in a breath.

"It says here," the man continued, scanning over the screen, "on Lume you have paper." He mumbled the words as he read, his finger following along. "Oh, you use paper to write and create books. Wow, you use trees to create them. Interesting. I mean, the idea is unique, and given the lack of other materials, I guess it makes sense. But it looks like a lot of work and ultimately damaging for something that takes up so much space in your world."

"You don't have books?"

"Why would we? They're a waste of space. Our main system houses every bit of knowledge, information, or fantastical story you could imagine, and it's completely compact. Plus, never mind the savings on resources and efficiency for people."

"And what of the portal information?"

"What do you mean?"

"Is that stored in this main system house or whatever?"

He smirked at Theodora. "You're a smart one, aren't you? I guess it's a good thing you'll be working with Maddox." Leaning back onto his stool, he continued. "To answer your question, yes. But that remains strictly under my supervision. So, yes, the main system does store copies, but no one is allowed access to the plans except Maddox and me. Under the Chancellor's authority, of course."

"Of course. But why is that? Why limit it?"

"Power is not something that should be shared. It's better to keep secrets close."

"Hmm," she mused. It was so similar to what Maddox had said. "Can you show me?"

"Testing my allegiance so quickly?" He let out a chuckle.

"What's your name?" Theodora asked as she leaned a hip against the table.

"Jarven."

"Okay, Jarven. Well, I'm sure you've learned I'm to help Maddox with obtaining these *special* resources from Lume. Why not show me how 'they're used to make a portal?"

"What a surprise to see you here." Valix's voice drew their attention to where he entered at the top of the workshop steps. "First, you weasel your way into Seclus, you ruin our attempt to seize control of Lume, and then you persuade Maddox to have me removed from the committee. And now you're here, in the recesses of our even more advanced tempats, trying to bribe one of our own."

"You clearly think highly of me. But I can assure you, your beliefs are misplaced." Theodora placed a hand on the desk, tugging her dumgun from where she'd tucked it into her trousers, turning to face Valix.

"They're not beliefs when I know they are facts." Valix descended the stairs. "I won't allow you to continue to poison Petram anymore."

Jarven raised both arms in submission. "We don't want that type of aggression here, and I definitely don't want any fighting in my lab."

"Then get out." Valix sneered at him before quickly putting his attention back on Theodora.

"Now, Valix"—he rose from the stool—"you know Maddox's orders here. I won't allow this in my lab."

"Get the fuck out and report it then, Jarven."

Jarven opened his mouth as if to speak, but no words came out. His audible gulp interrupted the silence. Theodora looked in his direction and gave him a reassuring nod. She could only imagine he saw it as her agreement for him to go find Maddox. She removed her hand from the table, taking a few steps away from it to fully face Valix.

"You shouldn't even be here," Valix spat as he closed the distance between them. "You should already be dead, and we wouldn't have to continue to deal with your bullshit."

"That's the difference between you and me, Valix. I make sure when I want someone dead, they find themselves dead." She didn't fire a blast into people's guts, or their shoulders. She slid metal across throats; she ensured blades found themselves twisted deeply into her victims' bellies. And she'd do it again now. She kicked the table, the dumgun sliding off it, distracting Valix's attention long enough for her to pull her blade from the sheath at her hip and throw it, letting it sail into the bottom of his neck. Theodora could've settled for an easy death, putting a bullet into his brain and ending him quickly. But she wanted to make sure Valix's final moments of life were full of knowing she didn't fail. Valix grappled for the handle, choking on the blood draining quickly from his body. She strode forward, close enough to whisper.

"I didn't hesitate. *Sir.*"

Hope

Maddox felt his body lurch forward as Theodora let her dagger fly across the workshop, his chest aching with an unfamiliar tightness.

"What did you do?" Maddox's question flew from his mouth.

Theodora looked at him from where he stood at the top of the steps. "What we talked about only a few days ago. You discussed wanting to have him killed."

"That was only *one* time. You made no plans with me. That was all before the assault by the Lumens, before having him demoted, and before creating a contingency to work with Rajveer."

"Are you regretting your decision to mention killing Valix?"

"No one should be that reactive. There was a possibility of being able to use him in the mining projects."

"Do you regret it? Want me to go back in time and change my decision?"

Maddox paused. "No," he sighed. "It's done."

"I'm sorry, Maddox. I didn't know you'd care this much."

"I've spent a lifetime with him. We grew up together. It was hard to see him fall to his own insecurities. I only wanted to help him."

"And we didn't grow up together?" He could tell Theodora tried to hide her anger, but it still sat there, an ember in her eyes waiting to be ignited once more.

Maddox sighed again, as if all the problems of the world could be blown out like a candle. "You could—" But his words were cut off. A sound like thunder rumbled outside in the distance. Maddox turned in the direction of the sound, but another rumbled. He turned back to Theodora, adrenaline already pounding in his ears at his desire to keep her safe. But his fear was washed away when a portal was opened, and Theodora ran through it.

∴ ∵ ∴

Theodora attempted to catch her breath as she stood on the cliff rocks of Lume. Snow had started to sprinkle from the sky, Fiedel falling to the horizon in a fiery ball of orange. It felt odd to return to this world again; every time the situation became more and more dire. She glanced over her shoulder, noticing a horse racing up the pathway in her direction, and sighed out a breath of relief that everything was going to plan as she turned to face the portal again.

Maddox toed the edge of the portal. He appeared skeptical, as if he'd be able to see Helena's imprint intertwined with the edges of the portal to confirm its making. Theodora met Maddox's intense gaze, staring down his anger. It seemed palpable beneath her skin.

"What are you doing, charm?"

Theodora shrugged nonchalantly, knowing the portal wouldn't stay open forever. She heard the horse's hooves slow to a stop behind her, and a thump of feet informed her Rajveer had arrived like she asked, but there was another set of feet that followed. She tried not to focus on Rajveer's inability to follow simple instructions, because she needed her attention entirely on Maddox. "Did you really think I'd be able to just move forward on Petram like this? As if Lume was nothing?"

"Theodora." Maddox paused, sighing his frustration, rolling his shoulders as if he could shed it as easily as a jacket. "We're changing the world–two worlds, for the better."

"I can't follow you in this." A hard knot formed in her throat, and she attempted to swallow it down as she crossed back through the portal to him. She felt it snap closed behind her as she reached her hands for his, their fingers intertwined. She glanced at them, feeling the chasm in her heart begin to crack.

Her eyes slowly worked up his arms and chest, over his crisp jacket to where his damn cravat perched around his neck, perfectly placed as always, to his face. Rumbles still groaned in the distance from the detonators Helena had placed throughout the city as she took in every inch of him, attempting to memorize the way the corner of his mouth hitched up slightly on the left. She never wanted to forget the way his eyes seemed to brighten for her, or the funny way his one strand of hair fell differently than all the others no matter how he tried to tame it.

As if reading her mind, Maddox whispered, "Please don't do this, Theo."

When she leaned forward to kiss him, she let everything fall away. She filled every part of the kiss with the pieces of her that cared and adored this man before her; she thought not only of their arguments and betrayals, but also of the small smiles and stolen moments, because they'd both known this was never meant to last.

Maddox's hands let go of hers and moved to her hips as their kiss deepened. Theodora prayed to the fates she'd never forget the way he tasted. She tugged on his shirt, pressing his body close to hers, when Theodora detected a small taste of saltiness and realized her cheeks were wet with her tears. She'd been unable to keep them from falling. Maddox slowed the kiss and moved to offer soft pecks to her cheeks, her face burning under the movements. When he stopped to look into her eyes, her vision of him was blurred by the tears that remained. After this was over, would she ever learn to stop crying? She took the moment to pull away from him, stepping back and out of his reach.

The betrayal could be seen on his face, turning more vicious than any anger she'd witnessed before. The explosions grew closer, rising to meet his fury. "Where do you plan to go?" His voice was borderline hysteric. Pure rage. "There is nothing else for you to do but to go back to Petram, to my people."

"I'm going home," she whispered.

At first, she wasn't sure if she had spoken loudly enough for him to even hear because he said nothing, but she let her hand unfold, showing the pocket watch she now held.

Theodora watched as his pupils widened in recognition, and she noticed how his hand twitched. Theodora refused to look anywhere else besides him.

As she opened the pocket watch, the face stared at her as intently as Maddox. She began spinning the turners how Helena instructed her, a special technique to open the portal behind her. She felt before she heard the portal open, an orange glow from Lume now cast upon Maddox's face. Theodora walked slowly backward, knowing the detonators nearby would go off soon, until she felt her feet move from the tiles of the workshop to the solid ground of Lume. She heard Rajveer's boots crunch nearby, and she stopped along the edge of the portal.

"So, you're running away? Running away with him? To do what, Theodora? I spared his life because you begged me to. Was this what it was for, some random moment of bliss?"

Theodora gathered her courage, wrapping her heart with it, as she took another step backward from the portal. She felt Rajveer's hand grip the fabric of her sleeve, and she glanced in his direction. Alouette, and a whole fucking entourage of Satelles, had come with him. She shook her head and returned her attention back to Maddox. In a moment, he glanced down, but Theodora anticipated it—pulling out her shinegun before he could.

"Don't," she whispered, keeping her aim honed entirely on him. He raised his hands, palms outward, in surrender. She secured her footing and waited for the portal to close—willing the fates to let it happen quickly.

He yelled toward them, the explosions gaining intensity. "You know I can't let you do this."

"I know," she yelled back. The last time she stood before him, her heart had been shattered, and yet he hadn't shot. She had to hope it would be the same this time.

She waited for the portal to close, feeling the charge crackle with energy, the edges starting to flicker. Just as the portal soared to close, Maddox moved, quick as death. A shinegun blasted, and three more shots followed immediately after as the portal zipped closed. The image of Maddox's face floated in her vision before she realized he was gone.

She had lost him, and all hope with him.

∴ ∵ ∴

Rajveer heard the shinegun blasts and was certain they would have Petram entering their world before the portal closed. He saw both Alouette and Theodora in the corners of his vision, and neither of them moved or shifted. No one even appeared to breathe. Everything had seemingly stopped, causing Rajveer to look down at himself to ensure it hadn't been him who'd been hit.

His hands fell against his chest and stomach—nothing. He couldn't assume the charge had missed; it was Maddox, after all. It seemed more logical to assume they didn't know the intended target than to believe he'd missed entirely. He began searching around, thinking maybe there was something else he'd shot nearby…

Alouette crumpled, slipping to the ground on her knees, and Rajveer's world tilted.

No.

No, no, no, no.

Maddox wouldn't have shot her. Couldn't have shot her. Why would he have shot her? Not his Ettie.

He lunged for her, his arms catching her around her shoulders. He wasn't sure what Theodora was doing nearby, or any of the Satelles either, for that matter. Every ounce of his being was focused on her, his wife.

The front of Alouette's dress was drenched in blood, the red color deepening through the fabric. Keeping a hand wrapped around her, he reached down with the other, holding her chest where the wound bloomed.

"Ettie." It was a question, an answer, a plea. His heart broke further as each syllable fell from his lips. A wavering breath racked her body, and Rajveer shifted her, carefully lowering her to his lap. "Ettie, you can't leave me." And he couldn't stop the tears from streaming uncontrollably down his face. "No, Ettie, not like this. I can fix this. We can fix this."

He wanted to call out to Helena, to ask anyone to help, but he already knew. No matter how much he wanted to fight it, he didn't want to miss this moment to memorize every line of her face.

She lifted a bloody hand to his cheek, her eyes matching his with their own streams of tears. He searched her eyes for anything—everything. Her mouth opened slowly as if to speak. Nothing, until she tried again.

"Raj." The word left her lips in a whisper with her last breath. Her unsaid words clung to him in waves of guilt. She was his. His wife who was to be with him for a lifetime, to see changes in Lume, to witness him become a better man. His possible hope to start a family.

Gone, lost, in a heartbeat.

He heard the mumbling of Theodora's voice, or it could have been Cora's. He couldn't be sure when grief raged too loudly in his head.

Cold

The portal snapped to a close in front of him, and Maddox couldn't stop the pent-up rage that filled him from his gut to his chest, begging for release. He'd been blindsided by Theodora, and then—another rumble. An explosion, he figured, getting closer. Helena stepped into view.

"You!"

"Me," she said, but the grin lacked the spite it typically held.

"What did you do?"

"You mean today? Or over the past few fiedations?" She pretended to look at a watch on her wrist, one that didn't exist. "I actually don't have time to run through the entire history right now since shit's going down." She glanced around her, the explosions getting nearer. "But to quickly answer your question, I helped Theodora escape."

"Where's the other portal?"

"The what?"

He was tired, furious at her continued fake ass attempts to pretend stupidity. He grabbed her by the shoulders, shaking them as if it would knock some sense into her. "Where is it?"

"Oh, this?" She pulled a fist from her cleavage and brought it between them. With heavy breaths, he glared at her. When she opened her hand, the smirk across her face was almost enough for him to strike her. He glanced at her palm, and there lay the tempat.

Maddox moved to lunge, but Helena brought her shinegun upward, shooting him in the lower leg. Maddox collapsed from the blast. He whipped his face upward, and Helena opened the portal behind her.

"Aw…" Her voice grated over his nerves. "Baby brother. It's okay." She blew him a kiss. "Better luck next time."

Helena turned from him, stepping through the portal, leaving him stranded there, without even a backward glance.

It was enough for Maddox's emotions to boil over. He could no longer control them. He slumped onto his knees and banged his fists onto the hard floor, and then released a guttural roar as if it would terrorize the world for him.

∴ ⁙ ∴

"You did this!" Rajveer screamed at Theodora as his Satelles scrambled into view.

"Sir?!" Amicus bellowed. "Are you injured?" He tugged at Rajveer's face, pulling it away from Theodora's. "Were you shot?"

"No! It wasn't me." He looked down at Alouette again and saw Miles' hand as he weaved his through her hair to her neck. It didn't matter though; Rajveer knew she was already gone. Condolences were whispered, but they barely met his ears. He didn't care for their half-attempts to soothe the situation. He wanted, for once, to be angry. For once to be mad and not fear consequences. He wanted to be irrational and make everyone suffer with him.

"Let me watch her," Miles offered. Rajveer realized in that moment he could be like his father and yell at them, return to the capital and ignore his citizens while drinking himself to oblivion. No, Rajveer would be so much worse.

Rajveer didn't feel himself nod, but he must've provided some acknowledgement since Miles shifted to remove his cape, draping it over Alouette's body, protecting her from the snow, which continued to fall.

Rajveer rose and brushed off his other Satelle's attempts to help him up. He'd barely stood before he spoke, his voice dark and laced with threat. "Give me the portal." Rajveer thrusted out his hand in Theodora's direction.

"Raj, you're not thinking rationally right now."

"Don't tell me what I'm doing!"

"The portal." He paused, waiting for her to move. "Now, Theodora."

A hand leaned heavily on his shoulder, and he looked to see Amicus. "My king." Rajveer knew the words were meant to show respect, but they were like salt in an open wound, burning the raw skin with an intensity that would not die. "I know you're about to walk down a very difficult road, but try to not make reactive decisions right now. Let's get Alouette home."

Rajveer scoffed at the word. *Home*. The capital was never her home; they were going to create a new one to live in, one they would both be proud to call theirs. He sighed out a tense breath before turning back.

"It must've been a mistake." Theodora's words were barely coherent over the unending images of Alouette crumpling in Rajveer's minds. "The portal must've made—"

"You owe me!" He pointed his finger at Theodora. "For everything you've done and failed to do. For every lie and terrible convocation of a plan. For ever knowing that horrible man and choosing to love him instead of killing him—You. Owe. Me."

"Rajveer, I'm–"

"Don't you dare. Don't you dare say those words to me." He stared her down as if it would burn her up and return Alouette to him instead.

"What do you want me to do?" She offered her palms outward.

"GIVE ME THE PORTAL!" he screamed at her.

"No." The sentence was a whisper, as cold and deadly as the approaching heim air.

"You will do—"

"I will do nothing of the sort. You want the damn thing?" She showed it to everyone, outstretched on her palm, before she tilted her hand. The pocket watch seemed to fall in slow motion as Rajveer's brain tried to reconcile what was happening when the heel of Theodora's boot slammed down on top of it—shattering it into pieces.

Rajveer froze in place. His anger burned molten under his skin, but he merely narrowed his gaze at her. *She wanted to play Lawless, fine.* "Theodora, you're under Satelle supervision from this moment forward. Cora, strip her of her weapons and bind her hands."

After she was secured, Rajveer directed the other nearby Satelles. "We're headed back to the castle."

Amicus ordered them to carefully lift Alouette's body from the ground. The cape billowed about her as they began moving her to one of the horses. The snow continued to fall, quickly gaining intensity. He looked up at where Petram hung from the sky, and then at Fiedel's last rays as it stained the clouds an inky violet.

∴ ∵ ∴

It was a stupid idea. There was no other word for it, and yet Helena couldn't help herself. When she opened the portal, eager and filled with a small amount of glee from her brother's failure, she hadn't consciously decided where she'd go. She only knew staying on Petram wasn't an option.

And returning to Lume, to live a lonely life, wouldn't work either.

Without entirely thinking, she'd opened the portal to the tree line near the Undost River. She walked onto Lume, and immediately, life seemed to have been sucked out of the world. As she watched, she learned the harsh truth… One she didn't expect to have to face for a long time.

Alouette was dead.

In all her fiedations, she never believed in true love. But perhaps seeing how happy Alouette and Rajveer had been, how much in love they were with each other after five grueling fiedations, how distraught he now was to live an entire lifetime without her, sparked something new and foreign in Helena.

∴ ∵ ∴

The horse hooves crunched loudly in the thick snow. They'd slowed down the pace of the horses when they'd made it on the main pathway to the castle. Theodora rode Alouette's mare, following behind Rajveer. Amicus was nearby with Alouette's body secured with him. In the few days 'Theodora had been on Petram, Amicus seemed to have aged significantly. Cora and the remainder of the Satelles brought up the rear.

Theodora wanted to be angry for Rajveer's backlash; it was indeed impulsive to demand the portal, presumably to go after Maddox. He'd barely last a few minutes before he'd find a way to kill himself, assuming he could figure out how to open a portal to Petram.

It didn't matter now; she didn't regret destroying it. Maybe she'd been reactive too, ruining plans and removing the few people who knew how it worked. She only hoped

Helena was safe, and that the remaining one would never find its way here again.

If she hadn't destroyed it, she could have tried to barter for a life in Seclus, instead of the dungeons she was guaranteed for.

Seclus.

Theodora urged the horse forward with a small kick to catch up to Rajveer's steed, interrupting whatever conversation he was having with Amicus. "What of Seclus?"

He looked over his shoulder to glower at her. Given the circumstances, she let it slide. "What of it?"

"What's your plan for the city? Is it going to be destroyed?"

"Do you want it to be?"

"No, I think what Helena said before is true. They're mostly innocent of the situation."

"I'll think about it, and it'll be addressed tomorrow."

"Raj."

"You don't get to call me that anymore. It's king or sir!"

"How about prince, you nit-witted buffoon!?"

This caused Rajveer to halt his horse, pausing their entire march. "How dare you!"

"You're being stupid. You aren't the only one who lost someone they loved."

"You think whatever tango you and Maddox had was love?"

Theodora took a moment to find words, but they evaporated from her brain. This wasn't the same person who'd been stripped bare at the lake, who feared companionship and sought nothing more from her than to be her friend. "What happened to the boy I watched the flares with?"

"He died." He crumpled his hands through his hair. "He died when Alouette took her last breath. Now get back in line and let's move. I'd rather not spend the entire night out in the cold."

∴ ∵ ∴

The wall of the castle could be seen through the trees, but he felt none of the weight he bore lifted from the site. It appeared formal and uncaring. Rajveer had no family to fill these expansive halls and empty rooms.

He tried to focus on his Satelles—they'd help him.

"Miles?" He pulled the reigns, tugging the horse to turn. Amicus, still nearby, did the same as well. His eyes found Theodora and Cora quickly. He pushed his horse forward, looking through the handful of other Satelles.

"Miles?" *Why wasn't he up here with them?* Rajveer became frantic, directing his horse back in the direction they'd come. He searched the trees, circling the horse about.

"Miles?!"

"Sir!" another Satelle called, and Rajveer found him pointing. Rajveer turned to see Miles' horse galloping forward, riderless.

One Petrik Later

Sitting in the Council building, Maddox was vacant to the continued discussions around them. They'd learn the multiple lower floors of the workshops were destroyed; the portal plans wiped from existence.

Although both himself and Jarven were still alive, only portions of the information lived within them. The thought of having an additional copy would backfire and they were wrong; Theodora had found the weakness and fucking infiltrated it.

She knew as soon as she opened up to him again, he'd be so focused on her—on being with her, making her happy, on pleasing her—he wouldn't be paying attention to the smaller clues that would reveal an elaborate plan of betrayal.

"Second Committer?"

"Yes, Chancellor?" Maddox glanced away from the patch of wall he'd been staring at the entire meeting.

"Please rise, so we may discuss the future of the Second Committee." Maddox pushed out of his chair and proceeded to the center of the room—the Council in front of him, the assembly behind him.

"We know this must be difficult following your second's death." The Tenth Committer addressed him. "But what is the status of the rest of your committee?"

"Um…" Maddox's confidence splintered; he fidgeted with his cravat as he attempted to stretch out his neck. "The Gems are assisting the rebuilding developments with the help of those assigned to other advanced projects, except Jarven, who is on the select task of reinventing the tempat to return to Lume. The others on the committee were stationed in Seclus, 'their status unknown."

"And can you advise us on"—the Tenth Committer glanced at the screen strapped to his forearm—"the possible whereabouts of Helena, who abandoned her duties and her post?"

"I do not know."

"The evidence presented to the Council is that she is off world. Is it possible?"

"I guess—" Maddox fumbled for the words. "I guess it's possible."

"You do not know where she went when she opened the portal before you in the workstations?"

"I thought—I assumed it was outside the building. To leave the explosions."

"Is it possible she left Petram?" the Tenth Committer continued.

"I guess so…" Maddox's voice trailed off.

"We would request the Council issue an emergent directive to have the committees prepare efforts for a possible attack. If she left the world with the portal, then she has a way to return here, too." Maddox's mind spun at the possibility. Did his sister abandon him here to return to Lume? "Based on Maddox's current testimony," the Tenth Committer continued, there is no change to our prior recommendation as to the Second Committee."

"We've reviewed the recommendation," the Chancellor began, "and at this time, I would agree with it and urge the Council to disband the Second Committee's progress on any tempat or project of similar design. We need to focus on rebuilding and putting the community back into efficiency.

Theodora didn't only destroy sections of the building; the flood of smoke and added chemicals entered parts of the rain system. Now the entire thing is compromised, ultimately affecting our ecosystems and growth."

"But what about the resources? What of more tempats? What of those we've left in Seclus?" Maddox pleaded but stopped himself from continuing. She'd broken him—utterly and irrevocably shattered everything he'd worked so hard for.

"Council?" the Chancellor asked, ignoring his outburst. They didn't turn to speak with one another, and Maddox knew. Slowly, one by one, they waved their agreement. "By order of the Council, the Second Committee will be disbanded from their exploration mission, including Lume, as well as the development and testing of tempats or other projects in nature. They will be tasked, under the continued direction of Second Committer Maddox Umberto, with rebuilding and restoration of the ruins caused by the destroyer." Unspoken was the fact that he'd lost any potential of taking the chancellor title.

The Fourteenth Committer rose, addressing the room, "This session is adjourned for recess. Return at the top of the clock."

"Maddox?" The Chancellor said his name, and a hush fell over the room. "You lost today; you don't have to like it."

Goodbye

They never found Miles' body. Rajveer sent different groups of Satelles out continuously over the last petrik, but there was no sign. Nothing. It was as if he'd vanished entirely. Rajveer had never felt more alone; even when he'd been bribing citizens into lies and abused by his father, he had been happier and sociable.

He'd sent Amicus with a handful of Satelles to return Alouette's body back to her true home in Nemaaer. Amicus didn't want to go, and Rajveer 'hadn't blamed him, yet Alouette's home was never here. He couldn't bury her in the belly of the castle. She needed to be returned to her family, where they'd hold a funeral ceremony.

Now he was about to lose more.

He debated whether he'd made the right decision in announcing to his Satelles that he would be taking Theodora as Lume's new queen. He'd even tried to clear her name to his Lumen citizens, but even though some must have accepted Rajveer's longwinded explanation, some had buried their resentment—not that he blamed them. His decision to marry her was one he'd thought of every night before he went to sleep, and every morning when he woke up. They both knew, and hopefully eventually his citizens would understand, that it was never for love, or even a broken friendship, but rather for Rajveer's own plans.

Theodora was both a tool and a solution for him, and Lume. By making her queen, he had a better chance of showing Seclus of his desire to unite the capital with its rebellious underground city. But also, for much for ruthless reasons, keeping her nearby, as queen, meant Theodora was never granted the chance of slinking into anonymity.

And after many nights awake contemplating why Maddox had chosen Alouette to be his target that day, he'd figured it out—even if Theodora continued to ramble about a missed shot meant for *her* and the portal affecting the blasts, Rajveer knew it was intentional. Maddox had forced Rajveer to live his life widowed and with the unending grief that he'd be alone forever. So, Rajveer bought revenge the only way he knew.

When Danika learned of his arranged marriage with Theodora, she requested that he accept her resignation from her position almost immediately, stating she could not see Theodora as queen—could not adjust to seeing the woman daily, not anymore.

"Your skills will be missed." Rajveer said now as he clapped a hand over Danika's shoulder, no longer the golden jacket of Lume but a heavy cloak in the simplest shade of brown. "I know we didn't always agree; however, I think you made the Satelles a stronger group with your presence."

"With Amicus gone for now, I feel I'm abandoning you, but I know you'll be in good hands with Cora." Danika smiled in the direction of where Cora stood guard at the throne room entrance.

Rajveer glanced over his shoulder to look at his new captain. "I think she will, too. If this means anything to you, I think you're making the right decision. I wish you and Kadena the best of luck in Conlis and I hope to see you again soon— maybe with a far better partner than I now have." He didn't mean to criticize Theodora so openly, especially with their wedding ceremony happening tomorrow—because that's all it was. It wasn't a marriage to his wife; it was a bond to the new

Lumen queen—but Rajveer felt he could be honest with Danika. "Would you like to speak with her before you go?"

"I—I think I would. I think have some things she needs to hear."

Rajveer flashed a sad smile. "I'll send her in. Goodbye, Danika."

"Goodbye, my king." Danika placed her hand over her heart and bowed to him one last time.

Alone

Theodora walked into the throne room at Rajveer's instruction, which had been passed through another Satelle, one she hadn't learned the name of yet. He still didn't choose to actively speak to her, mostly giving instructions by way of others.

It felt weird to be here, in the throne room. Not only because of what transpired almost two petriks ago, but also after spending almost the entire last one locked away in a cell. Her body was weak and frail from lack of food, and even though they'd let her shower the night before, she didn't know how long it would take for the grime to wash away.

She didn't expect to see Danika there, especially not wrapped in a Satelle uniform. For a moment, Danika didn't hear her entry, and Theodora stopped walking forward, slowing her stride to watch as Danika stared through the grand windows, another early snow swirling across the lake.

How different her life would be if she'd stayed with Danika. They'd probably have moved in together at this point; maybe they could've gotten a place closer to the market square so she wouldn't have to pull a vendor cart of her own inventions as far. Or maybe they would've chosen a place on the outskirts, away from the hustle and bustle of the market, to have a wonderous view of Fiedel rising and setting beyond the vast fields. She could've ridden Down River to her own shop, maybe taking up Earleen's tailoring—although her stitching was barely passable.

Danika glanced behind her, doing a double take when she realized Theodora was in the room. "How long have you been standing there?"

"Long enough to realize I regret never taking your offer." Danika strode closer, her hand tucked in the belt of her trousers, a flash from the past when she'd walk with her hand atop the hilt of her stelgladio. "Do we still have a chance?"

Danika looked to the ceiling, and Theodora didn't miss the tears that filled her eyes. "Theo."

"I can go now. We don't even have to stay here." Theodora's voice was urgent. "I'm sure if you asked Rajveer, he'd let you take me."

"You don't get to ask me this now."

"But we—"

"Shut up, Theodora! Just stop thinking you can talk your way out of this. *This*"—Danika waved her hand around her—"is your punishment. You fucked up. You made bad decisions and now you have to live with them—whether you accept that or not."

"I love you, Danika." Theodora blurted the words.

"That—" Tears fell from Danika's eyes, but there wasn't happiness in them. She pointed a finger at Theodora. "That's not fair."

"But what if it's true?"

Danika chuckled and turned away from her, shaking her head as she looked out the window. She let out a few shaky breaths before she turned to face Theodora again. "I don't think it is. I don't think you know what *love* really is. I think you're afraid of being alone, as much as you tell everyone it's exactly what you want. You hate that you are so dependent on *needing* someone, you tell yourself these small lies to justify your feelings, making you actually think you're in love. Trust me, when you find love, you'll never think of yourself again; it'll always be them or the two of you together.

"But you already knew that. It's why you've accepted all this so easily. Because being forced to marry Rajveer means you'll never be alone again, and you'll pray to the fates that he'll return your love." Danika stepped forward, placing a hand on her shoulder. "I hope by the end of your time, you can find a way to love yourself, Theodora."

Seclus

The bitter wind whipped Rajveer's cape around his body as his steed trotted carefreely along the barren path. The boring and stiff ceremony to Theodora occurred quickly yesterday amidst his discussions with Mekari, the new Seclus representative.

It had taken place in the castle with as many Lumen citizens as they could cram into the throne room. It had been hurried and efficient. But once over, Rajveer had been eager to return to making the changes he always wanted to see.

Changes he was supposed to make with Alouette. His body involuntarily shivered with the thought of her name. He forced himself to ignore it, the way it made him feel. He needed to focus on this next task, securing a different Seclus as the seventh city of Lume. Fates, what he wouldn't give for a drink.

Cora, Brandt, and Maude followed him as they headed to the underground city. Although the Heim Festival was not set for another petrik, the fates threatened to unleash another snowy mixture from the south at any moment.

"We couldn't have waited for a warmer day for this?" Brandt yelled through another gust of wind.

"What're you complaining about? You have more than enough body hair to keep you warm," Maude teased.

Rajveer glanced over to the burly Satelle. Maude spoke truthfully. Brandt had thick, grayed hair that was pulled into a braid descending the length of his back, with a matching braided beard on his face. Rajveer let out a huff of a laugh. He was glad to see the banter continue among his new Satelles—he didn't think he'd survive without it.

When the Seclus rocks came into view, two individuals approached from the tunnel beyond. As their horses got closer, Rajveer realized the people were Hakon and Mekari, exactly as expected.

"King Rajveer." Hakon limped forward.

"Are we okay to proceed?" Rajveer asked, as he dismounted his steed, eager to enter the tunnel and get out of the snow.

"Absolutely," Mekari responded. "Did you want to do a final walkthrough?"

Rajveer shrugged. "Just show me what's about to be done. Such a shame though since I haven't seen it before."

"Really?" Mekari turned, directing him to follow, as Rajveer's Satelles stayed within arm's reach.

"My father wanted to act as if it didn't exist. He'd always send Satelles in his stead." Rajveer followed into the darkened tunnel, where it opened outward, showcasing buildings tucked into the cavern walls. Chandeliers of light blue glowed from where they hung, reminding him of the screen techs he'd seen on Petram. "Wow, it's impressive."

"It was cleared out and started when Maddox was a child. When they decided to search for more aximum here, they'd started constructing the buildings as Maddox investigated the bellies of the ground. We'd hoped we would find aximum in the cavern pools, but quickly learned we weren't that lucky." Mekari stopped in the center of a market square, the similarities to the one in the capital topside not lost on Rajveer. "By the time Maddox was approaching adulthood, the city was established, and we prospered in our technology. I'm sure it wasn't long after that, he was crafting his plans with the king." Mekari released a sigh. "We never wanted this. We hoped aximum would be something we could get easily and then live out our lives happily, but it seems some are tempted too much by the possibility of more."

Rajveer merely looked around at the buildings, turning in a slow circle. What would Alouette have thought of this place? The memory of her was immediate and apparent, and almost as quickly, a knot in his throat formed. He swallowed hard, but Cora must've realized his hesitation because she intervened.

"Did you get everyone safely relocated?"

"Yes. We've spent the last few days packing what we could and transporting them. We didn't choose to fully move to Perdit's location, but to kind of a mid-way point between there and here, as it seemed the best area to rebuild."

"We're glad to hear you got everyone out. If you need any resources, or if the king can be of assistance…"

"Absolutely."

Rajveer cleared his throat and spoke. "It won't just be me much longer, as you know. We'll be working together. We no longer want you and your comrades to be Seclusians. After this, you're all Lumens."

"We're in agreement. If we have anyone who isn't willing to succumb to the new arrangements, can we discuss our next course of action at the first meeting?"

"I think that would be a great starting point for the agenda." Rajveer pulled at the sleeve of his jacket. "Well, might as well get this underway. It shouldn't take long?"

"Not at all." Mekari directed Hakon, who pulled at some metallic locks as they started to ascend out of the tunnels. "We have the flash crystals in place. All that's left is to secure the doors."

They stepped beyond the demarcation of where Seclus began, and of where it ended today. Hakon pulled the metal doors shut, and Mekari sealed them with his hand on a square panel. After they hissed closed, the wind trying to reach where they were protected by the rocks, Rajveer punched the panel with his metallic hand. The screen cracked to pieces beneath with a small spark.

"To a new Lume," Cora began.

"To a new Lume," the others said in unison.

Mekari tugged a button from the pocket of his trousers and pressed it. At first, they heard nothing, until a slight rumble could be felt. It was a disappointing they couldn't witness the flooding of the underground city, but the action was symbolic enough.

"Will the new city keep the name?" Rajveer asked curiously.

"We think it will."

"You think?"

"Well, we are taking direction from our new king, allowing everyone an opportunity to voice their opinion."

Rajveer smiled and glanced down at his feet. This was all Alouette's doing. She was always open to discussing his ideas for a better Lume. His life was devoted to fulfilling her dreams, bringing peace to their Lume.

"I'm sorry for your loss, my king." Mekari knelt on his knee and Hakon followed suit, then his Satelles themselves.

"Rise, my Lumens. It's a new era."

Queen

The market square was busy, busier than normal, especially given the frosty wind. Theodora walked slowly through her now citizens, holding the reins Down River. The reactions of the citizens who noticed her varied, as to be expected. Some continued to scowl, even though Rajveer explained the elaborate upheaval had been caused by Petram, sharing that the assassination plan had been formed by Maddox—only giving the truth to a small few. But most Lumens would tip a hat, or offer her a curtsy, and Theodora was mindful to acknowledge the gestures, forcing a smile on her face.

Barely a petrik ago, she'd been one of them, and she'd also been a Seclusian, too. She hadn't realized how much she would miss Maddox. Every morning since she left him on Petram, she tried to recall their last moment—before he'd realized her deception. His smirk, that defiant strand of hair. But keeping that moment—capturing it, was proving difficult.

Would it be easier to just let it go?

Theodora slowed before one of the cobblestone paths. She quickly glanced around, noting the number of Satelles around her. If she could get Down River to move further into the corner, she might be able to mount the steed. The path would take her south—again, not necessarily the weather they'd want to deal with, but it might give her the chance they needed to escape.

"Don't even think about it." Izak narrowed his eyes in her direction, his hand already on the hilt of his shinegun. She looked into his eyes, searching them to compare his resolve against her will. "We'd catch you before you even left the capital boundaries," he mocked, as if reading her mind.

"Queen Theodora." A Satelle placed a hand on the small of her back, her blonde hair cutting into Theodora's peripheral, and Theodora briefly thought of Danika, causing her to startle away. "I'm sorry to frighten you, madam, but the snow is picking up and we need to return you to the castle."

"Of course," she acknowledged, and with the help of her Satelles, sidesaddle her mare, she began her return to her new home. As Down River followed obediently, Theodora couldn't help but glance backward, in the direction of freedom she'd never meet.

Slowly

Maddox lay on his bed, staring blankly at the ceiling. His committee had spent all day overseeing the continued repairs of the high community building. His body was physically exhausted from standing. He'd needed to offer little direction. His committee members knew how to make a building; they didn't need supervision.

A chime echoed and Maddox spoke. "Accept."

"Second Committer, your presence has been requested by Chancellor Umberto immediately," the system voiced. The titles were a slap in the face.

"Acknowledged," Maddox replied, defeated. He rose and began walking out of the bedroom. His hand reached into his pocket, and when he found it empty, he panicked. *Where'd he put the pocket watch?*

Then it came back to him.

Slowly. Deliberately. Mockingly.

Klauduisz

King Rajveer Klauduisz opened and closed his metal hand, pulling a long drag from the cigarette held in his other. The castle grounds glistened from the fiedelight as it broke across the castle walls onto the newly fallen snow. The fur-lined cloak wrapped around him did little, as the metal parts of his body favored the cold air.

His human hand shook, but not from the cold. In these brief reprieves where he was left waiting, his mind wandered too far. It was one of the many reasons he refused to still, to stop moving. In the quiet moments, he couldn't keep Alouette's face from emerging and entering his thoughts—how she fit perfectly in his arms, her infectious laugh, the way her eyes lit up when she tried something new.

He let out the smoke with a sigh, watching it mix with his breath, as the horse-drawn carriage slowed outside the front gate. He made a final pull of the cigarette before dropping it and grinding it out with his new boots.

Why couldn't he drown all of this in a drink? Without his father, he'd been able to remove this ridiculous hoard in the castle, giving him plenty of reasons to just sink into oblivion—but he didn't allow himself. *Couldn't* allow it. He ignored the urge, focusing on everything else in the world, because he knew if he ever fully stopped his list of tasks, ever gave himself that break to sip on a glass, he'd crumble entirely.

"Sir?" Cora looked at him, and Rajveer nodded. She gestured, granting the Satelles stationed at the gate permission to open it. Rajveer walked forward as the carriage pulled alongside the front of the castle. He hated the politics of being king, the responsibilities and expectations he couldn't abandon, at least not yet.

The carriage door opened, and although it should've been his first wife, his true love who emerged, it was the one who'd helped to strip him of her. Theodora stepped out, her matching fur-lined cloak falling around her, and the smaller golden crown atop her braided hair only mocked him. He presented his hand for her to take as she stepped down from the carriage onto the castle grounds.

Rajveer slipped on his masked facade as king and walked through the front doors to the throne room, where they'd start implementing changes to the continent, presenting their plans to the newly established city representatives. The lords of all six major cities, plus Seclus, had been abolished. Whatever decisions Lume would make, they'd occur with Theodora beside him. Because if Maddox ever learned how to portal again, Rajveer knew he would come here first, for her.

And when he did, King Rajveer Klauduisz and Lume would be ready for him.

Epilogue

Miles' horse followed those of Rajveer, Theodora, and the other Satelles. He was too engrossed in his own grief of losing Alouette to care about distracting himself with unnecessary conversation. He swiped at his eyes again. *Fates*, he moaned internally. It had been fiedations since the last time he'd cried.

Movement in the trees caught his attention, and he lifted his head, squinting in the already failing fiedelight. A flash of her pale skin, the long black hair he remembered that was soft under his fingers.

Helena.

What was she doing here? he thought to himself, quickly looking around to see if anyone else had noticed. He dropped from the mare silently and met her along the edge of the tree lines.

"Let's run away," she whispered.

He glanced behind him, the mournful parade continuing forward, not yet realizing his absence. His gaze lingered on Rajveer. He'd be devastated…

"He'll understand," Helena answered, as if she'd been able to read his mind.

Before he could second guess himself, he spoke. "Okay."

She tugged his hand, but he pulled back. He tapped the horse on the rump, beckoning the mare to follow the others.

When she began trotting away, walking, without a breath of regret, Helena opened the portal, and they were gone.

∴ ∵ ∴

In the closet of the king's chambers, the pack on Miles' back felt heavier than it should, filled only with the klaud to his name and a handful of spare clothes.

"Ready?" she asked.

He only nodded, afraid to speak out loud.

As soon as the portal opened, a terrible storm ripped through the closet—gusts of air and a peppering of rain threatened to fill the small space. And the darkened skies? Anything but beckoning.

They stepped through, their boots hitting the sandy beach as lightning attempted to split the sky in two, thunder rumbling down his chest into his toes. They turned around, facing the electrified orb of gold. Helena handed him the pocket watch, and he dropped it inside an envelope, carefully tucked next to the note he'd written. He sealed it before slipping it inside the pocket of his incredibly old coat.

They stepped back and the portal snapped closed, abandoning them on the beach, the lights of a new city twinkling back at them in the darkness.

It would be hard, sure, but it didn't matter because they'd be together.

the end...

Author Note

trag·e·dy [ˈtrajədē] NOUN

Writing Lume's duology as a tragedy, I knew I wanted the three main characters to have to live the remainders of their lives, off page, in utter misery. I used their greatest desires as what they would ultimately lose because of one another.

Maddox's greatest desire was power and control, and he lost both, stranded on Petram with no ability to return to Lume.

Theodora's greatest desire was to escape society, to be freed from responsibilities and live alone in the woods. Now she is chained to the throne, with even more expectations falling on her shoulders.

Rajveer's greatest desire was to love. And not to love just anyone, but his Ettie. Due to his own mistake, his inability to leave her, he gambled with her life and lost, and is forced to continue his life without her.

Surrounded by all of this, in a world filled with grays, the three main characters become villains to one another, and heroes to none.

All three will continue to live, but what's the point of living now? Sometimes the worst kind of tragedy is having to live every day, constantly reminded of your mistakes.

As for the world of Lume,

Miles & Helena will return…

Glossary

Astrum: third season of the year, where leaves fall for the land mass of Lume

Aximum: rock-like material used by Petrans to manipulate time, warp space, and create portals

Conlis: the road connecting to this city on Lume is less traversed due to the need to travel through the mountains; provides stones, minerals, rocks, and gems in raw forms as well as coal and gas to other cities

Dumgun: metal pistol; typically found with filigree decorating the barrel and a wooden grip; uses single metal projectiles for firing; outdated technology

Flash Crystal: grenade; filled with explosive glass; detonates on a time delay, dispersing glass into the immediate radius, accompanied with a bright flash of light that may also case temporary blindness

Freta: a port city bringing in most of Lume's fish and other ocean resources; Satelles here continue to take scouting ships into the ocean in an attempt to determine if any other land masses exist

Fiedation: measurement of time using Fiedel; multiple petriks create a fiedation; similar to an Earth year

Fiedel: Star that is orbited by the planet containing the land mass of Lume; provides light and warmth

Fiedelight: light provided by the star, Fiedel

Heim: coldest season of the year for the land mass of Lume

Lawless: those acting against the king; *syn.* criminal, rebel

Nemaaer: northern Lumen city dedicated to serving the fates; due to its distance from other cities, it is mostly forgotten; the city produces its own resources and is self-sufficient, although Satelles are stationed here to ensure the citizens are compliant to the king

Lume: the only known land mass on the planet, containing the capital where the king's castle is located; used interchangeably to mean the capital, the continent, and the planet

Perdit: abandoned city; the late King Richard Klauduisz is attempting to remove its story from Lumen history

Petram: a natural satellite of the planet containing the land mass of Lume; reflects some light from Fiedel and is seen mostly at night

Petrik: measurement of time using Petram; multiple days create a petrik; similar to an Earth month

Remediux: medicine or treatment for a disease or injury, specifically unique to Petram

Satelle: king's guard

Satelle Cape: worn strictly by Satelles; normally worn to appear as fabric, but can absorb phaser light projectiles such as those from shineguns; cannot block flash crystal projectiles or metallic projectiles

Seclus: underground city that was recently built; home for Seclusians, who are known for their advanced technology and weaponry; most Seclusians are considered Lawless by Lumens

Shinegun: pistol; made of unknown metal found with black solar charged stonelike pieces along the top; it is charged through star light and fires a blast of hot, radiating light or phasers; weapon is fingerprint activated, with a registry held by Seclus

Solta: warmest season of the year for the land mass of Lume

Stelgladio: electrified sword; it creates a magnetic field to warp phaser light projectiles such as those from shineguns; can also be used to block metallic projectiles such as those from a dumgun

Tempat: the portal device used to transport quickly between areas; only two known in existence, both disguised as pocket watches

Vocatus: common spiced liquor with notes of cinnamon only served in Seclus; current ingredients remain unknown; origin: unknown.

Complete Works by TM Ghent

Petram Playlist

Bitter Heart	Memi, Staffan Carlén
That's What You Get	Paramore
Helena	My Chemical Romance
World So Cold	12 Stones
Hole in My Heart	Luke Friend
Joke's On You	Charlotte Lawrence
Welcome Home, Son	Radical Face
Throne	Bring Me The Horizon
Of These Chains	Red
Symmetry	JT Roach, Emily Warren
Broken	Seether, Amy Lee
Lonely	Nathan Wagner
Power Over Me	Dermot Kennedy
Remember to Remember Me	Isak Danielson
Kings and Queens	Thirty Seconds to Mars
Your Guardian Angel	The Red Jumpsuit Apparatus
What I've Done	Linkin Park
Paralyzed	NF
Say Something	A Great Big World, etc.
In Love With a Liar	Green or Blue
Lost It All	Jill Andrews
The Kill	Thirty Seconds to Mars
The Winner Takes It All	Iris Noëlle
End of Us	No Resolve
With You Til The End	Tommee Profitt, Sam Tinnesz
Drown	Boy In Space
Requiem	Dreyfuss, Park, Thompson
No Saving Me	Philmon Lee, Lindsey Stirling
Happy (In The End)	Gabbie Hanna
Ghost	Joshua Wicker
You	Keaton Henson

About the Author

TM Ghent is a fiction tragedian who loves grumpy sunshine. She likes to dance the line between morally gray hero and anti-hero characters, forcing you to question who the villain is. Refusing to adhere to standard literary tropes, her stories break the mold and defy genres, such as blending fantasy world-building with sci-fi tech or historical plots in contemporary settings.

TM Ghent lives with her husband and two children on the east coast of the United States and enjoys the early mornings with a hot cuppa.

When she isn't lost in a story, she can be found making music in her local community band, heading to the movies with her husband, or raising her own little word-lovers.

Every story doesn't end with a happily ever after.

You can follow her on Instagram at @tm_ghent

The Bear & The Rose

E.K. Larson-Burnett's *The Bear & The Rose* is a must-read!

Hypnotically ethereal, hauntingly beautiful, rich in characters, devastatingly sapphic, and wrought with an underlying sadness— it is written in a sense of timeliness in a relatable arc of how we are crafted by our pasts, in control of our presents, but all inspired by a hopeful future.

E.K. LARSON-BURNETT

E.K. LARSON-BURNETT

the BEAR & the Rose

*Springtide's reign:
death's domain.*

They once called me the Bear-Killing Maiden of Hazelfeur—a mouthful of a title, begot by little more than a penchant for stumbling upon the spawn of Artio at springtide.

In truth, I prefer Bearslayer.

I wear my accolade proudly, my neck graced with a mantle of oiled pelts and my hair knotted with dusky wraith bones, though it was by the crows' whimsy that I fell into the She-Bear's lair ten equinoxes ago. I was bare-shouldered then, and looked a maiden, even as I returned to Hazelfeur dripping ebon blood like tree sap, my imbrued scythe dangling from a frayed rope clenched so tightly in my moon-white fist that they couldn't prise it away from me, not even after I found sleep.

Now? Now I am no maiden.

I am Rhoswen, Thornfury's mistress, slayer of bears living and dead.

The púca have always made my skin crawl. They occupy a far corner of the village at its highest point and in its biggest structure, a horned stone temple encircled by flowering hazel trees and traces of the sacrifices left to invoke the sprites' benevolence—broken stalks of grain, nutshells, wraithblood stains, tufts of fur.

I drop an ichor-slick antler at the foot of the temple. It rolls to a stop in the patch of sunlight between the shadows of the horns' prongs, and, preceded by a mere tremble of wind, it is snatched up by a cloven hoof.

"Bearslayer," says the púca, its voice a rattle of gravel upon my eardrums. It towers against the woven tapestry strung from the spires of the temple, a grisly goatish beast with a greasy beard and beaded eyes of molten gold, lip curled in a greedy sneer. It turns the antler between its hooves. "An untimely share."

"The sun hasn't yet slept," I counter, grinding a nutshell beneath my heel.

The púca eyes the sky, then licks the antler's length with a warted tongue and considers briefly. "A dawn's harvest."

I don't deign to give a reply.

"Springtide draws near. You must be busy preparing, little warrior rose." Its tongue draws the antler into its mouth, down its throat. "Gratitudes."

I offer a tight-lipped smile, resisting the urge to swallow my discomfort. "Thornfury's pleasure. Until next hunting."

As I sketch a bow and turn away, the púca lets out a scraping laugh, but unwilling to be goaded or warned of Artio's spite, I march back to the village, brushing braided sprigs of bearsbane from my face. It's near sunsleep, and villagers are drawing instruments from their homes for the evening's festivities—the welcoming of spring.

I feel an unusual pulse of anxiety for the equinox, one I've not felt since before my legendary return from Artio's lair. Tonight my unease will beat in tune with the drums, and I resolve to stamp out its flame as we stamp our feet to prepare the ground for the coming season's bounty. I cannot allow it to fester, nor dwell on its meaning.

"Rhoswen!"

The call stops me before I can duck into my dwelling. The village healer—a snake-hipped woman named Onora—hurries my way, the painted glass in her hair clacking as she stops in front of me. She purses her lips as she studies my face. "Where is your brightness?" she demands, thumbing my cheek. The pad of her finger comes away smudged with deer blood and charcoal, and she holds it up for me to see.

"Up my arse," I say, shoving her hand away with a grin.

She sniffs; the wrinkling of her nose creases the swirls of saffron smeared on its gently sloped bridge. "Come. You smell."

I let her powder-soft hand take my grimy, calloused one, and she leads me to her hut, where she wrestles Thornfury from my grip.

"He's family," I protest, grabbing for the worn leather strap as she winds it around the curved blade.

"Not my family. You know he int suitable for children, Rhoswen," she rebukes me, tucking Thornfury safely inside a basket at the roundhouse's opening.

Reluctantly I leave my weapon, the weightlessness at my hip unfamiliar, and follow Onora inside, where her fair-haired children shuck dead leaves from twigs and weave them into crowns. They giggle as I enter, tiny and impish hands darting out to touch the bearskins hanging from my shoulders before Onora shoos them away.

"Sit," she commands, ignoring my quirked brow to busy herself with bowls of powder and paint. The oldest of her children—a girl, freckled and pink—joins her, grinding dried petals to dust with nervous fervor. Another of the girls, at her mother's behest, takes up a bristled rind, dips it in oil from the crushed seeds of tulsi berries, and attacks my skin with it.

"Aye!" I exclaim, surprised at her force, and she gives me an apologetic look but scrubs all the more furiously, stripping grime and blood and impurity from every pore and hair she can reach.

"D'you ever bathe, Rhoswen?" Onora asks, taking up a brush herself and coating my legs with the thick, sickly-sweet oil.

"Haven't the time, you ungrateful tuber. Too busy keeping your wee spuds uneaten." I snap my teeth at the wispy child, and she startles several steps backward. "That's enough of that rancid stuff."

With the scrubbing settled, Onora takes up a bowl of paint, dips her fingers into it, and daubs it onto my forehead as Katelia, the older girl, watches. She murmurs softly as her fingertip swirls across my brow, perhaps praying, perhaps teaching. I don't pay her words much mind.

My thoughts drift to the coming days. Springtide ushers in a season of bloom and fertility, but it also heralds the season of the bear—Artio's season, one which she rules over with relentless vengeance. I've heard old tales of the goddess, tales from when she was green to motherhood, young and tender and forgiving, but it is hard to imagine such a thing when my knowledge of her is shrouded in red. She wishes to make the people of Hazelfeur suffer, and her army of bears, material and spectral, make ever-nearer attacks on our village.

This coming spring, I fear death.

I leave when every inch of my skin is gilded with Onora's "brightness"—my cheekbones dulled by labyrinthine whorls and the harsh ridge of my nose eased by mildly swirling motifs, golden clay caked in my lashes and packed under my fingernails, my arms and legs made to look as if they were tangled in silky vines.

There's a beauty to it, but I don't think any pantheon of gods would be swayed to bring more rain or sun by pretty smears of paint.

With Thornfury returned to his proper place on my belt, I skirt the rising bustle of the village, slipping mostly unnoticed to the garden behind my hut, where bushes of bearsbane shiver in the cool breeze. I haul a heavy sack to the middle of the garden and squat to strip stalks of needles from the bushes, braiding them deftly into thick garlands, the sharp smell stinging my nostrils. I work quickly, tucking into the sack strings of varying lengths to pass out at the springtide revels—long ones to string around fences, small ones for our necks, clippings to scatter across the ground.

By the time the sun has retreated from the horizon, my

fingertips are raw and my eyes are glazed. My mind, for a while having been blessedly preoccupied, rumbles with bloated worries that reverberate in my chest and teeth.

Springtide draws near.